Blow Money Fast

BY

Charles Irving Ellis

PROLOGUE

The dark hallways were as inviting as brunch in a cemetery, James thought. But he wasn't invited. He made his way through the home using favor as his key. He climbed the familiar stairs with a new sense of purpose and his past failures behind him.

When he walked into the large bedroom, he folded his hands together and lowered his head. A young female nurse standing bedside looked in his direction and nodded then walked toward him with her eyes lowered, as they passed each other. The room was warm. He could smell the meaty bowl of soup still steaming on the dresser. When he looked down on his old friend and mentor, he tried to sound sympathetic. "This is no way to start the new year."

The old man looked up with shaky eyes. He had a quilt wrapped around his body; a pillow supported his head. He looked like he was struggling to speak.

"It's me. James. I just came to see how you are doing. I would be lying if I said you look well, so I won't. My God Roger, I am not impressed."

"What do you want?" Roger growled aggressively.

James looked at him and sighed. "You know what I want, Roger. Let's not be petty. We have come too far for that."

He followed Roger's eyes and noticed a copy of the Wall Street Journal sitting on the nightstand. "Come now, my old friend, you need not worry yourself with unimportant details." James picked up the paper.

"I am a winner," Roger leaned forward. "I have been my entire life. That's why my enemies are always behind."

James studied his face, folded the paper and placed it under his arm. "You won't last a year," he said. "Then we will see who is behind." He spun around and walked off. He was halfway across the carpet when he heard rumbling behind him.

"You will never have it!" Roger sat up.

James stopped in his tracks, turned around, and saw the weak elderly man clenching his fist with all his might. "There may be some fight left in you after all, old man," James said. "But thanks to you, we have already won."

He left the room with a smile on his face. And when he reached the top of the staircase, he slapped the railing with the newspaper. But before he could take another step, he heard Roger's coughs from the hallway. It paused him, not because he was concerned. Not necessarily. It was a

strange cough. James twisted his head to one side and realized it wasn't a

cough at all. Roger was laughing.

Chapter 1

November 24

Deep inside Decker County's regional jail in Southern West Virginia, cell block D was in an uproar. Inmates faced off and racial tensions grew. Aggressive stares were exchanged from across the room, while ethnic slurs took flight.

"Fuck'n porch monkeys," yelled a shirtless white man.

"Stupid pecker woods," an obese black man responded.

With equal numbers of men on each side, the crowds drew closer, ready for combat. Like a ring announcer at a Friday Night Fight, a tall lanky figure slid in between the intended clash.

"Gentlemen, can't we all just get along?" He stretched his arms out in both directions. "Do Y'all really want to kill each other over a TV, have the goon squad run up in here with them spray cans and bats, with them big-ass shields and start whooping black, white, and whatever ass they can reach? Then we all going to be coughing and wheezing, spiting and sneezing something nasty."

"Get out the way, Ray." A large white inmate stepped forward.

"Yeah homie, they know what time it is," shouted a black.

But Raymon didn't move. Instead, he stood there for a second, shaking his head with his arms spread, thinking, *What the hell did I get myself into?* "This is stupid," he said. "I got a real easy way to fix this mess. Your big goofy white Sports and the News come first, and on movie nights, the flick gets first option. This shit ain't that serious. There's only one TV, so we just have to compromise."

"No white guy wants to watch Black Entertainment Television," a voice proclaimed from the back of the room.

"You don't have to watch Black Entertainment Television." Raymon rolled his eyes. "Just respect the time slots."

Unsavory grins on both ends slowly turned away. And the tension in the room lowered. Then a WWE-sized white man with a bald head stepped up close to Raymon and said, "You are lucky I respect you." He smiled.

"Get your over-eating, steroid-taking ass outta here," Raymon joked. "And find a shirt!"

"Them clowns going to get what they looking for one of these days," a short chubby black inmate said.

"You right Remix. But not today," said Raymon.

"Why's that?"

"Because today my light-skin ass is out of here." Raymon gave him a pound.

"I was wondering why yo ass got in the middle of some beef on your release date. Same old Ray, looking out for yourself as usual." Remix laughed.

Some black inmates walked up. "Is that right? You 'bout to sneak out on the brothers like a cold buster."

"Call me what you want, just don't call me collect." Raymon smiled.

"Aye Ray, call my moms for me," one inmate requested.

"You know Y'all moms ain't messing with Y'all." Remix sucked his teeth.

"That's cold."

"Real talk, you better not forget about a brother," Remix said.

"I'm trying to leave all this jail shit in my rearview mirror," said Raymon.

"You something else." Remix shook his head. "That's all them business books and magazines you been reading. But you don't have to be selfish to be successful, homie."

Raymon looked his comrade in the eyes. He knew there was truth in his words, but he had to make a way for himself before he could even think about helping another, he thought. "How could I forget about your fat ass? I'm wondering who going to look out for you all when I'm gone."

"Yeah right!" A crowd of black inmates laughed.

"Raymon Platt '1'," a correctional officer opened the cellblock door and shouted.

"That's you, kid." Remix gave Raymon a brief embrace.

Raymon passed out dap to all the black inmates and made his way to the door. Suddenly, he stopped short like he just remembered something he had left behind. He turned around and shouted, "To all my CMC watchers, stay white."

The steel door slammed closed after Raymon was escorted off the block. He walked down the cold corridor with a smile on his face. Happy to soon be rid of the orange jumpsuit that covered his body for the past 13 months, he swaggered to his freedom.

The uniformed guard brought him to the front desk and passed multiple security points, where Raymon threw away his jail attire and replaced it with the same clothes he arrived in.

"Are you Raymon Platt?" an old man behind the front desk asked.

"That's me."

"Sign here."

"What's this?"

"It says we released you with your Birth Certificate, Social Security card and proper I.D."

"That's what's up, because I got places to go and people to see."

"You are broke."

"Excuse me?" Raymon's face changed.

"You did not arrive with any cash or checks on your person, and you have zero dollars on your commissary account."

"Hell nah! That's wrong. What happen to my twenty bucks? I had a twenty on me when I got here."

"We have no record of that. And you do not have a bank account or any assets, correct?"

"No, but," Raymon stammered. "Where is my twenty bucks? You stole it didn't you" Raymon gave the old man an evil stare.

"Sign here."

"I ain't never coming back to this dump."

"You will be back," the old man said. "They all come back."

"I'm not them all. I'm Raymon Platt Jr. and I got plans. But first, I need a shit, shower and shave." Raymon patted the small fro growing on his head.

The old C.O. pulled the signed paperwork back with a huff. "Yeah right."

"You will see." Raymon smiled. "Just stay tuned." Raymon stepped into a November morning. He used his finger to tap on his Timex to make sure it still worked. Then he reached inside his jeans pocket. Pulling out nothing but lint, he shook his head and looked around the parking lot for a phone. A cold breeze attacked his face. He thought about who he would call, when and if he found a phone. The Regional jail was 60 miles from town, and Raymon's short-sleeve Ed Hardy shirt reminded him what a bad idea hiking it would be. His eyes widened when he saw the black Lincoln pulling up to the curb. A Caucasian man, who looked to be in his late fifties exited from the driver's seat with a cell phone held close to his ear.

"Excuse me, my man, can I use your phone real fast?" Raymon asked.

"Are you Raymon Platt Jr.?"

Raymon straightened his back. " What the hell?"

"Raymon Platt Jr.," the man repeated.

But Raymon just stared at the man's black suit and tie, then slowly backed away. "Hey man, I'm just getting out of jail. I don't know who you are, but it's cool, I'll find my own phone."

"Mr. Platt, my name is Francias Planes and I work for a very important company that would like to speak with you."

"Would like to speak to me? Look man, I pay my taxes."

10

"Pardon me, sir."

"This company you say you work for, would it happen to be identified by three letters? You know, like FBI or ATF?"

"No sir, I work for—"

"A very important company," Raymon interrupted. "Look, I don't want no problems with the government. So, I'm a just go about my business, if that's okay with you." He attempted to put some distance between himself and the well-dressed driver. But as he walked away, he heard Planes fumbling with his cell phone.

"Yes sir, I understand sir," Planes talked into the receiver.

And like a platoon commander, he shouted, "Raymon Platt Jr.! I have direct orders to escort you to a very important meeting."

The sudden change of tone caused Raymon to stop in his tracks. He thought about making a run for it, but hesitated. He couldn't think of a real reason why the government would want to talk to him. So, he turned around slowly with his hands up. "I got nothing. What did you say your name was?" he asked.

"Francias Planes."

"Okay Fancy Pants, I can see that you are a serious character. I mean, with that British accent and that stiff suit, not to mention those shiny shoes. Where you get shoes like that? Bond? Better yet, what do you want with me?"

"My bosses sent me to collect you so that they may have a word with you. One of great importance."

"About what?" Raymon dug.

"My orders are to collect you. I just do the driving, sir. But I can assure you, it is strictly professional."

"Professional you say? This sounds like a business meeting."

"Indeed, sir it is. You are correct." Planes nodded.

"Well, I can't attend no business meeting without my home boys."

"Your home boys, sir?"

"Yeah, my crew. Mack and Chill. I ain't going nowhere without them." Raymon folded his arms across his chest and leaned his head to one side.

"I'm sure that won't be a problem," Planes agreed. "Where shall we find this Mack and Chill?"

"I'll show you the way. But first I need to hit them up, let them know I'm coming. I'm sure you can understand that. And by the way, where this meeting at?"

Planes looked at Raymon with a smirk on his face, opened the rear side door of the Lincoln Town car and said, "That would be New York City, sir."

CHAPTER 2

A day earlier, in the Big Apple, proper preparation was set in order. Behind the glass windows of a skyscraper, and inside the media lounge, reporters pounced at the chance to ask questions.

"Ms. Gains, is Welloff software going under?"

"Hardly so. That is just fake news, my dear. We are as strong as we have always been."

"But with the passing of Roger Bennet, the founder and majority shareholder, the stocks in the company are reportedly taking a nosedive," one reporter persisted.

Lisa Gains took a long look at the young female reporter, as a dozen others readied their recorders, and lifted their pens. "How old are you?" Lisa asked.

"I'm 25 years old." The reporter pushed her glasses up on the bridge of her nose.

"So young, petite, and beautiful you are. My dear, before you were born, Roger Bennet started a small software company that grew into the billion-dollar empire that it is today. And he didn't do that by studying the stock value. He did it with hard work and determination. Now I can assure you, that hard work mantra is alive and well. And so is Welloff software."

"Ms. Gains, Ms. Gains!" multiple voices called out and raised their hands.

"I'm sorry, but that will be all for now." A company representative took to the podium.

Cameras flashed as Lisa walked off. She could still hear her name being called out behind her. When she reached her floor, she stepped off the elevator, flew passed her receptionist, and ordered, "Hold all calls." She entered a secured boardroom and locked the door behind her.

"I don't care what the old man said, we simply cannot," James was heard saying as she walked in.

"The will is legally binding. We don't have a choice in the matter." Michael sat across from him.

Hearing the debate had already started, Lisa took a seat at the table. "Stop your bickering. There has to be another way."

A knock on the door paused all three of them. "What is it?" James shouted.

"I have your requested paperwork," a male voice claimed from the other side of the door.

James rose to his feet and made his way to the door. He swung it open, snatched a folder from the young man and slammed the door in his face.

"You asked for another way, and here it is." James held up the folder and reclaimed his seat.

"Well then, let us have it." Lisa leaned forward.

"What do we know of this Raymon Platt Jr.? Nothing! But here I hold a file on the boy so detailed, Roger took great precautions to see that we could not read it until after his death."

"What are we up against?" Michael asked.

"Let's see," James began. "He is 29 years old, lives in West Virginia for God's sake, has no kids and no stable financial plan. My lord!"

"What is it?" Lisa sat up straight.

"It seems that this Raymon Platt has a criminal history. According to this, he is currently serving time on a possession charge." James looked up and shook his head.

"A common criminal," said Michael.

"How can we possibly proceed, knowing all this just now?" Lisa asked.

"Hold on a second. It says here that he will be released on November 24th."

"That is tomorrow."

"Yes, it is." James smiled.

"So, what of this plan of yours?" Michael threw his hands up.

Silence fell over the poorly lit room while James explained. Expensive portraits of former CEOs looked down and bore witness to the sinister plot.

"We cannot allow some thug to come in here and take all that we have worked for." James clenched his fist.

"We must see to it that he doesn't," Lisa said.

"Roger has set out many rules for this Raymon character," Michael added while viewing the folder. "If he breaks even one, the contract is void."

"With that being said, we have some work to do." James stirred up his associates.

Lisa looked at the contents of the folder and chuckled. "He doesn't seem to follow rules very well."

"Then it is settled. We will play this game and see that this Raymon Platt returns to his rightful place in society. Have a car meet him upon his release. We need to play this close to our chest. Clock his movements and act accordingly."

"And so, we shall," Michael agreed.

"From the looks of him, we can't lose," Lisa assumed.

Chapter 3

The black Lincoln cruised up Interstate 95. Raymon sat in the backseat of the luxurious vehicle with Bigmack on one side and Chill Will on the other.

"Damn, dog, how long is this ride?" asked Bigmack.

"Yeah, I'm hungry. And what this all about?" said Chill Will. "You ain't been out a hot second, and you already got us on some crazy ride."

"Sit back. Y'all act like you had something better to do. You should be thanking me." Raymon frowned.

"Thanking you for what?"

"For not kicking both Y'all backs in for not picking me up."

"I forgot." Chill Will dropped his head.

"You know baby moms ain't trying to let me use her car no more." Bigmack tried to lie.

"Yeah right! You bum ain't send me one dime. The least you could have did was pick me up. Hey Fancy Pants, how much longer?" Raymon asked.

"We shall be arriving at our destination shortly, sir," Planes answered from the driver's seat.

Snowbank after snowbank flew past the tinted windows while Planes navigated the busy highway.

"You ain't got no beats?" Chill Will sat up.

"Beats sir?"

"Yeah beats. Music. Some tunes."

"Why yes sir." Planes reached for the radio.

"Hold up Fancy Pants", Raymon leaned forward. "That's not necessary. We don't need no extra noise. You two need to sit still and keep quiet. I'm trying to think over here. Plus, old Fancy Pants don't know nothing about no real slap. You about to have us in here listening to some library music. Just relax."

"Fresh out and he already giving orders." Chill Will laughed. "I thought you would at least grown a mustache in there."

"Libraries play music?" Bigmack looked lost.

"Fresh out, and I got you bums headed to the Big Apple in style." Raymon smiled.

"Let me find out you went soft in jail," said Bigmack.

"The only thing soft on me is these leather seats. Y'all must have forgot who be making things happen for us."

"We pose to be in the studio Ray. Making music happen," said Chill Will.

"Studio time cost money. Money that none of us have right now." Raymon sat back in his seat. "Over a year and you two haven't done nothing but sit on your backs. If you want to win, you have to make moves. But as always, I got to do it. So, chill out. Let's see what Fancy Pants got for us in the big City."

Bigmack looked at Chill Will and said, "He got a point."

"He just thinks he know it all." Chill Will turned his head and swatted the air with his hand, like there was a fly near his face.

"That's because I'm the brains and you two are the talent." Raymon spread out his arms and patted his friends on the back.

"I'm the talent." Bigmack rubbed his gold tee.

"So, what that make me?" Chill Will felt offended.

"You like that bad liver nobody wants, but you can't cut it off cause it's a part of you," Bigmack joked, and the car lit up in laughter.

Planes drove passed the final toll booth entering the City, and heavy traffic sounds came alive. The smell of smoke crept threw a cracked window. One tall building after another increased in size as they passed by.

Amazed by each structure Raymon's eyes widened. He looked to his left, his right, and then front to back, admiring the on-going action around him. Traffic lessened and the town car maneuvered in and out of lanes like a trained boxer.

Bigmack rolled down his window, and shouted at an unsuspecting lady standing on a sidewalk, "Ooh girl, you fine."

Chill Will was frozen in the moment. He pinched himself to make sure it was real. "Them country boys is here now."

"Calm down, play it cool," Raymon told him. "Don't get weird on me."

"I ain't never been to New York City," Chill Will confessed.

Bigmack shook his head. "None of us have, fool."

When the car came to a halt, Raymon sat forward. "What's happening?"

Planes exited quickly, stepped onto the curb, and opened the rear side door. "This way sir." he extended his arm.

Stepping out of the vehicle and into the cold weather, it felt like a movie to Raymon and his pals. Chill Will looked up at the building in front of them, it looked to be made out of glass. It seemed to never end. The large structure shot straight up to the clouds headed for heaven.

Raymon stepped forward and used his hand as a visor while attempting to climb the skyscraper with his eyes.

"That's a big ass building." Bigmack stepped onto the sidewalk.

"I hope they got some food and drinks," said Chill Will.

Planes played chaperone. They entered the building, passed by security, and got on an elevator. Bigmack constricted his wide body frame into the lift, and Chill Will couldn't resist. "I hope we don't fall," he joked.

"Shut up. We in a classy spot, dog," Bigmack responded.

"I don't like it. Something is off." Chill Will rubbed his chin.

"What you mean?" asked Raymon.

"It doesn't' t make sense. New York City. What are we doing here?"

"Well, we bout to find out."

"I hate to say it, but I agree with Chill," said Bigmack. "This is some weird shit, dog. You just got out and some fancy driver tell you some half-ass story about some meeting. And you jump right on it."

"Both Y'all sound stupid right now," Raymon said. "You really think I haven't did the math on this. Fancy Pants don't move like no Fed, and he came looking for me. That means he clearly knew I was getting out today. So, what that tell you?"

Bigmack and Chill Will shrugged their shoulders at the same time.

"It could only be one thing. The majors got a listen of that mix tape we put together before I went in, and now they want to talk numbers." Raymon rubbed his palms together. "Just let

me do all the talking."

Seconds later they reached their floor. They stepped off the elevator and approached a desk in the dim-lit lobby. A young Asian woman greeted them with a smile. She wore a headset on her head and held a pen in her hand. "Sign in please."

Chill Will nudged past his friends to be the first to make a connection with the attractive woman. "Don't mind if I do."

"Hold up, dog." Bigmack grabbed Chill Will by his fleece collar. "She was talking to me."

"No, she wasn't," Chill Will argued. "She was looking right at me."

"You in the way, dog."

"Your big-ass belly in that tight-ass thermal is in the way."

"A fine woman like this don't want no short, short man in a pair of Vans," Bigmack shot back.

"She definitely doesn't want no fat guy in a little coat." Chill Will countered.

"Man, you got on them old jeans and that tight do-rag. Them braids ain't even fresh, boy bye. Plus, you too short to even see over the counter. Watch out!"

"Chill out," Raymon interrupted. "At least act like you got some class."

Bigmack shook his head. While Chill Will mumbled under his breath. "My style on fleek."

"Besides, she was talking to me any ways." Raymon winked.

Then Planes placed his palms flat on the desk top and said, " Mr. Raymon Platt Jr. to see Mr. James Preacher."

A minute after the call was made a young white man appeared in the lobby wearing a pin-striped shirt and tie. "Which one of you gentlemen is Mr. Platt?" he asked.

"That would be me," Raymon stepped forward.

"This way please, if you will."

"What about us?" Chill Will held up his arms.

"The request is only for Mr. Platt."

"We good." Raymon turned around and held up his hand. "I know how to deal with these industry type. I got this. Just try not to break nothing while I'm gone."

Chill Will gave Bigmack an unsure look. Then Raymon disappeared behind a doorway. He was led into a boardroom and met by three blank faces staring at him from behind a

long table. The room was bright. He could see city billboards far off through the large windows. Nice view. The fresh smell of carpet cleaner rose up and filled the warm air. He noticed a small brown table in the corner with a coffee pot on top of it.

"Would you like a cup?" Lisa asked.

"Sure. Why not?" Raymon helped himself to an empty seat at the end of the table.

"Benjamin, be useful and get our guest a cup of coffee," James ordered.

"I'm a straight-up type of guy." Raymon leaned back in his chair. "So, let me say this right at the start. We are not interested in a 360 deal."

"A what kind of deal?" Michael sat up in his seat.

"You see, Raymon Records is an independent label. All we need is for you to cut them checks. You feel me?"

"Mr. Platt, I believe we may have a misunderstanding," James tried to explain.

"We came a long way. If you think I'm going to give up the rights to my Masters, then you right, we do have a misunderstanding." Raymon raised his eyebrows and puffed out his chest.

When Benjamin returned with cup in hand, he placed it on the table in front of Raymon.

"That will be all." James raised his voice. "Leave us!"

Raymon watched Benjamin lower his head and walk out of the boardroom. When the door was shut behind him, Raymon refocused his attention on the poker faces before him.

"We haven't been clear as to why you were requested to be here," said Lisa. "And we apologize for that."

Raymon crossed his arms and waited for the punchline.

"My name is Lisa Gains. This is James Preacher, and to my left is Mr. Michael R. Willard. We are the CEO's of Welloff software."

"Welloff what?"

"Clearly you have heard of us. We are one of the largest and most successful software companies in the world."

"Sorry lady, I'm more of a hardware guy, if you catch my drift." Raymon grinned. "But still, what does this have to do with our music?"

"Is your father Raymon Platt senior?" Michael sounded annoyed.

The question caught Raymon off guard. He sat up in his chair and looked Michael in the eyes.

"And your mother. What do you know about her?"

"I know this is creepy as hell," said Raymon. "What yall want with me? What is this?"

"Mr. Platt, your mother's name was Sarah Platt correct?"

"Yeah, I guess but, none of that matters right here right now." Raymon felt his blood start to boil. "I never met my parents. Never knew them."

"Yes, we are aware of the tragic accident."

"If you know so much, why you asking me all these weird questions? And you still haven't told me what this is about."

"Mr. Platt," Lisa interjected. "Your mother's maiden name was Sarah Rene Bennet. Her father's name and your grandfather's name were Roger Welloff Bennet. Mr. Welloff Bennet is the founder of this company and its largest shareholder."

The room appeared to have grown in size. Raymon pondered the magnitude of what he was told. A grandfather he never knew. What did it all mean? An inheritance maybe. But from whom? His parents had passed when he was a baby. Maybe this grandfather was looking for him this whole time, scraping through files and paperwork while his grandchild was lost in the public system. Could it be? Then Raymon realized the truth; he was gone also. "Is this about some bread?"

"Bread," said Lisa.

"Yeah! Money, moola, paper, scrilla. Some dinero. The bag!"

"It is about an inheritance," said James finally.

"Well let's have it. Where it at?" Raymon held out his hand.

"Mr. Platt, I'm afraid it is not that simple."

"What's the problem? Check, cash, credit, I take them all. But no debit cards, them things easy to fake."

"Let's just play him the DVD." Michael picked up a remote control with a clear attitude.

"What DVD?" Raymon looked confused.

Without explanation, Michael aimed his controller at the back wall. The lights in the room lowered to a dark shade. The curtains closed slowly, and a large screen dropped from the ceiling. Raymon spun around in his chair just in time to see the old wrinkled face come alive on the projector.

"If you are watching this, it could only mean two things. You are alive, and I'm dead. My name is Roger Welloff Bennet. And I'm your grandfather."

Raymon stared at the elderly white man claiming to be his kin. He checked for some kind of resemblance and listened to his words.

"Your mother was stubborn! She never listened. When I was your age, I went out into the world to make a way for myself. Nobody will do that for you! I scratched the ground

with my fingernails and made a living. I was hungry! I was married numerous times, but I only had one true love. Your grandmother. She gave me my only child, your mother. Then she took her own life. Your mother blamed me of course. She said I only cared about money and my work. She said that is what pushed my love to suicide. She had to grow up without her mother. Let her tell it, she had to grow up without a father also. So, when she ran off with that black boy. I shut her out completely! We never spoke again. I traveled all over the world. Twice! I started a small company and built it up like a child, watched it turn into a juggernaut, and got my tip wet more than a few times. I made associates and lost friends. Above all, I made a lot of money! I succeeded in life, but I failed as a father. Now you are the only heir I have left on this greedy earth. So, it is to you, I leave all that I have."

Raymon sat in silence, leaned forward in his seat and anticipated.

"But you have to first show yourself worthy," the old man paused in between a violent cough. "You must learn to respect it, before you can collect it."

Raymon pushed back in his seat with a confused look on his face. "What gives?"

"You will receive a percentage of your true inheritance, which you must spend in 30 days. If you succeed, you will receive the remainder. But if you fail, you get nothing! And there are rules to the game. Your mother wasn't so good at rules. Let's see how you do. Because sonny boy, if you break just one rule, you get nothing! My associate will explain these bylaws as they are written in my will. This counsel of sorts shall watch over you to see that you act accordingly. With power comes ruthlessness, and without it, you deserve nothing at all. And sonny boy, don't spend it all in one place." He laughed and coughed uncontrollably until the screen went completely blank.

Raymon spun around in his chair and took another look at the counsel. Lisa's red hair was pulled back and pinned up. She wore too much makeup, but he could still see the freckles on her cheeks. Her hands betrayed her youthful look. She was old, yet attractive in a way. Her smile had bad intentions and Raymon knew she couldn't be trusted. Michael was an old grumpy-looking man. His rough voice and tough face rubbed Raymon the wrong way the second he spoke. Even though he remained seated, he seemed to be a tall man. Raymon didn't like him, nor the faulty hairpiece sitting on his head.

"What say you?" James interrupted his concentration with an English accent.

He has to be the leader of the bunch, Raymon thought.

His blue eyes were staring a hole into Raymon's face. Gray hair surrounded the open crown on his head. He kept a serious tone of voice. All business.

Raymon attempted to match his demeanor. "Is this some kind of joke?"

"I'm afraid not."

"So, you want me to spend some money in order to make some money?"

"Exactly," Lisa joined in. "More importantly, you have to follow the rules. It is a contract." She held up a brown folder. "Once you sign these forms, it is legally binding."

"And I have 30 days to spend it all?"

"Correct again," Michael growled.

" You white people are crazy." Raymon leaned back in his chair and giggled. "So, what's these rules?"

Lisa pushed back in her chair and stood. She pulled at the end of her suit dress with one hand, and held the folder in the other. "Your grandfather has set the rules as follows." She made her way toward Raymon. "You must not obtain any assets with the percentage amount received. You cannot engage in any illegal activity with the percentage amount received. You cannot give away any of the percentage amount you receive. You must not tell anyone about this contract, your task at hand, or the stipulations set forth here today. You cannot spend the percentage amount received in one place or venture. And after 30 days, you must return here by 12 noon, penniless and completely broke." Lisa placed the folder on the table in front of him. She then pulled out a pen from her lapel, and handed it to him.

Raymon looked at the open folder and said, "A lot of rules, aye." He scribbled his name across the documents with half a smile on his face. "Old fool wants me to spend his bread, I can do that. He wasn't no grandfather to me anyways. How much we talking, fifty thousand, sixty maybe?"

"M. Platt, your grandfather was a very wealthy man." James cleared his throat.

"Okay. What, a hundred thousand then? The old fart must a been really moving them packs, aye?"

Lisa returned to her seat with the signed forms and passed them to James.

"You will be given 500 million dollars," James announced. "If you are successful and you fulfill the contract as set forth here today, you will receive your true inheritance of 2.5 billion dollars."

The muscles in Raymon's legs stiffened. He could feel his heart rate increase. His jaw loosened, and his eyes grew in size, performing back flips off of tables and moon walking on the ceiling, shouting "Wo!" and screaming "Yes!"

"Mr. Platt, are you all right?" Lisa snapped her fingers.

"500 million dollars." Raymon tried to focus. "You want to give me 500 million dollars?"

Michael grew irritated. "For God's sake, do you understand the rules?"

"500 million dollars," Raymon repeated.

"Yes, Lisa spoke softly. "500 million dollars that you must spend in 30 days in order to claim the 2.5 billion. Your true inheritance."

"500 million dollars." Raymon ran his hands threw his poorly kept hairdo.

"As soon as you leave this office, the clock will start." James pointed to his wristwatch. "So, I hope you understand what is at stake. You have 30 days, Mr. Platt, and by my calculations, that means you should arrive here on the 25th of December, before 12 noon, completely broke, or you will have forfeited your inheritance. As the overseers of this ridiculous game, we have provided some added insurance to protect our interest in this matter. I'm sure you can understand. To see that the contract is honored properly, we will have one of our own shadowing you. The young man who escorted you in here, his name is Benjamin, and he is a fine accountant. He will keep records of your spending. Although he is in the blind to our agreement, he is a trusted worker. And he happens to be my son. Mr. Planes is at your disposal. He is one of our finest chauffeurs. He will see to it that you get to your destination of choice. A trusted man, who also knows nothing of our agreement." James attempted to give his best efforts at forming a smile, but fell short of a grin.

"All that sounds nice, but where's the cash?" Raymon stood to his feet and rubbed his palms together.

"Mr. Platt, this is New York City," Lisa warned. "It wouldn't' t be wise to move around with that amount of cash on your person. We have provided an open account in which you, and

only you, can draw from at your leisure. Here is the card. The pin number is your date of birth." She walked over to him.

Raymon looked at the black plastic in his hand for a few seconds. Then he lifted his head and said, " It's on now. "

Back in the lobby, Bigmack and Chill Will took turns flirting with the receptionist.

"What's your name cuteness?" Chill Will asked.

"It's right there on her shirt genius." Bigmack slapped the back of his head.

Then the doors to the boardroom flew open. Out shot Raymon, with Benjamin close behind him. He had a new glow in his eyes, and a walk fresh off the lot. Bigmack watched as he floated his way toward them.

"What's up dog?" Bigmack was alert.

"It's all good," Raymon shouted. "Let's get out of here, we have a lot to do."

"Who the white boy attached to yo ass like cancer?" asked Chill Will.

"This is Benjamin, and he with us. Fancy Pants too. Let's go!"

"Ray, what happened?" Chill Will had to know.

"Like I said, it's all good." Raymon led his new entourage to the elevator. He pressed the down buttons repeatedly until the steel doors finally closed.

Chill Will gave Bigmack a side eye. Bigmack shrugged his shoulders and pointed to Raymon.

"What's up Ray?" Chill Will couldn't resist any longer. "What's going on? You acting like you just robbed a bank."

Raymon rocked back and forth like he needed to find a bathroom, and fast. He tapped his foot on the floor and couldn't stop his hands from fidgeting.

"What they give you, an energy drink or something?" Bigmack looked worried.

"I'm rich," Raymon whispered so nonchalant.

"You say something Ray?"

"I am rich," he raised his voice. But he could see that his friends were stuck on stupid. So, he placed a hand on each of their shoulders and said, "No more worries, my friends. I tell you no lies, I am rich."

The elevator doors opened, and before Raymon could fully explain, camera lights flashed in his face in flurries. The press wasted no time. "Mr.

Platt, how does it feel to become a billionaire overnight?" One reporter

shoved his microphone.

Finally realizing the weight of Raymon's words, Bigmack and Chill Will

pushed their way to the front of the elevator and shouted, "We rich."

The two grown men embraced each other, then pulled Raymon in for a

group hug.

"Mr. Raymon Platt Jr, you were reported to have inherited billions, how

do you feel?" Every mic was aimed at Raymon' s mouth.

With the bright lights beaming down on his caramel complexion, and all

eyes squarely on him, Raymon took a step forward, stared into one of a

dozen camera lenses focused on him, and said, "My name is Raymon Platt

Jr, and today I just went from do-rags to riches."

Reporters scurried about. Some swiped at their phones, while others

scribbled on their notepads. "Are you the sole heir to the Welloff empire?"

They pushed for more information. Camera crews and story seekers

followed Raymon's every move. They ended up outside the building. The

cold breeze reminded Raymon to buy a coat with his new wealth. No

assets, he thought-checked himself.

Bigmack decided to take control of the media frenzy. "Ladies and gentlemen, as best friend and chief of operations, I have to ask that you give Mr. Platt some room."

"And as his other best friend," Chill Will chimed in, "I ask that you hold any further questions until a more proper time."

Raymon smiled. His pals were already taking positions and titles. The wheels in his head started to spin. And with only 30 days to squander a fortune, he had no time to waste.

"That's right people," he shouted. "These are my best friends and top employees. This short, brown-skinned tattooed fellow right is Mr. William Jeffers. Better known as Chill Will. He is my chief advisor. And for $10,000 a day, he better be the best adviser of all times."

Hearing the news, Chill Will grabbed his chest. "Hello!"

"And this tall chubby handsome, blacker-than-me fellow right here." Raymon continued, "his name is Kevin Mack, but we call him the Bigmack. He is indeed my chief of operations, and you can direct your questions to him. I'm paying him over $70,000 a week to handle my business, so trust that he is more than qualified."

"What type of business do you do?" a voice climbed over the crowd?

"Who said that?" Raymon looked around.

A petite dark-skinned woman with eyeglasses raised her hand and fought her way through the sea of journalist. "I did."

"And what is your name, pretty lady?"

"Natasha King, from Channel 6 news." She readjusted her specs.

"And what is it you do for them exactly?" Raymon asked.

"I follow hot topics and report the news."

"And what do they pay you for being so hot yourself?"

"Excuse me?" Natasha leaned backwards.

"I will give you $200,000 a month to be my personal assistant." Raymon stared into her green eyes. "What do you say?"

Natasha looked around for a second, then she tossed her notepad and recorder in the air. "Hell yeah!"

"And you!" Raymon pointed his finger.

"Who me?" a young man taking photos said.

"Yeah you. I need copies of all the photos you took here today. This is a big moment and we need to live in it. I will pay you $2,000. for each photo."

"You got it Mr.!" He nodded wildly.

"Let's get away from all these vultures," Bigmack whispered in Raymon's ear.

Raymon strutted down the salty walkway like a peacock. "I'm going to show you city folk how to really ball. There is a new show in town and poppa got that bag." He turned to face the thirsty cameras. He walked backwards and waved his hands at onlookers, but before he could utter another word, he felt himself crashing to the floor.

With his back flat on the frigid concrete, he looked up at the light gray eyes staring down on him. Her black curly hair was pulled back into a bun, and her golden complexion matched her nose ring. Raymon managed to stand up, but he found it hard to take his eyes off her. His mind told him to say something, but his lips wouldn't move.

"You really should watch where you are walking." She pulled the headphones from her ears.

"I could ask the same of you." Raymon dusted himself off. He noticed numerous CD cases spread out on the floor. When he reached down and read the art work, he said, "Honey Drop English. Is that you?"

"Yeah, it is. Real name, no gimmicks," Honey announced.

"So, you an artist?"

"What's it to you?"

"I'm just saying, you out here pushing CDs on Thanksgiving eve. You must be really serious about getting on."

"This New York City, the grind never stops." She snatched the case from Raymon's grip.

"I can understand that."

"Can you? I mean, you don't look like you are from around here."

"Why you say that?" Raymon asked.

"Look at you. Nobody wears Reeboks around here. Your whole swag is off, kind of whack."

Raymon looked himself over and laughed. " Okay, you got that. But why you out here with these CDs? I'm just saying, CDs is played out. They ancient, ma."

Raymon's use of the tag name got Honey to crack a smile. He watched her carefully and checked her out from head to toe. Her quarter waist-length coat helped him see her small waist. Her black leggings hugged her thighs. She wore some brown Ugg's on her feet and a gray shirt with a portrait of Richard Pryor painted on the front of it. Her thick eyebrows had a perfect arch. And the beauty mark on her right cheek seemed to be in the proper place.

Bigmack showed up. "Ray, you good?"

"I'm great." Raymon smiled, then bent over and started to pick up the CD cases on the floor.

Bigmack helped. But when he looked up, he saw Honey watching them closely and said, "Can I help you?"

"I would like the rest of my stuff so I can be on my way," she said.

"I'll tell you what." Raymon stood straight. "Let me buy all these for $100 apiece, right here and now."

"What about my pain and suffering?" Honey held out her hand.

"Pain and what?" Bigmack stood up.

"Yeah, I think my neck's starting to hurt right now."

"Oh, you trying to hustle a brother," Raymon said.

"Hey, you the one talking big."

"Okay, okay, I see what it is. I will give you $2,500 flat for an out-of-court settlement right now. But I get to keep the CDs."

Honey leaned back and checked his eyes to see if he was joking. "Deal," she said a little too fast.

"Hold up. I got one more condition. I get to drive you home." Raymon tilted his head and waited for her response.

Honey put her hands in her coat pockets. She looked at the media circus a few feet away from them and rolled her eyes. "I guess."

Bigmack had a bad look on his face. "You got hustled."

Then Raymon waved the rest of his crew over.

"Fancy Pants, we need to give this nice lady a lift," he said. "Mack, I want you to take Chill and my new assistant, find the dopest, most fliest, freshest hotel in this town and get us some rooms. I'm talking top notch, none of that save a buck mess you be on. Benji, you with me, but you riding in the front."

With the news cameras and reporters in his rearview, Raymon looked to his right and caught Honey staring out the closed window with a blank look on her face.

"Where to Ms. Honey Drop?" asked Raymon.

Chapter 4

Harlem seemed to have a life of its own. People of different hues marched along the pavement providing a pulse. Long streets lined up side by side for miles out. Kids shot hoops from a dry spot on an open court surrounded by melted snow. Shadowy figures bundled up on street corners with homemade shelters nearby. Light from an early moon shined down on a broken housing complex, connected to a shabby liquor store.

The wheels on the top car stopped rolling on the corner of 142nd street. Honey looked to her left and found Raymon smiling back at her.

"So, this is your neighborhood," he said.

"Not fancy enough for you," Honey replied.

"It's cool. Beats the hell out of them woods I grew up in."

Honey held out her hand once again. "Well then."

"Easy, lil mama, I told you I got you."

"Business is business. Don't got me, get me!"

"This the thing," Raymon tried to explain. "I got the money. Trust me, I got the money. But I have to hit the bank real fast to get some pocket change."

"What you take me for?"

"Pretty hot and tempting." Raymon winked. "Naw, but for real, I don't have no cash on me. I ain't trying to play you. I know where you stay at now, let me bring it to you later tonight."

"No! My number is on the back of the cases. It's for business only. Text me and we will set up a meet. Don't show up here, and don't play no games." Honey opened the car door and put one foot on the side walk. "Business only"

Raymon said. " Business only!"

Planes attempted to help Honey to her feet, but she waved him off.

Raymon watched in amusement. *How could someone so dreamy be so hard?* he thought. As soon as the door slammed closed, Raymon rolled down the window and stuck his head out. "I'll call you."

"Text me! And, you better bring my money." Honey looked toward the three hooded men walking her way. "It might be a good thing you don't got no cash on you."

Raymon sank back to his seat. Planes quickly found the cockpit and locked the doors. Benjamin looked over his shoulder and asked, " Where to now, Mr. Platt?"

The shiny automobile was drawing attention in the worst way. Raymon rolled up the window and left pedestrians no choice but to stare at their own reflections in the tints. Raymon leaned forward and said, "To the bank of course. I need to make a withdrawal."

The Grand Dora Palace was located in Manhattan. The five-diamond rated hotel, with advanced design concepts and the highest quality furnishing, had surplus attention to its guest's expectations. As one of the most famous hotels the city had ever known, A-list celebrities preferred to rest their heads in one of Grand Dora's luxurious rooms. Royals raved on social media about fabulous stays at the long-standing establishment.

Bigmack pressed his tummy against the front desk. His fitted cap was cocked to the side. He held the counter with both hands and leaned forward. "We need one of your fliest joints."

The receptionist took one look at him and lowered his gaze.

"Yo dogg, you don't hear me talking," Bigmack reiterated.

"There are no dogs or joints here. Please leave," said the man behind the desk.

Chill Will tried his hand, "We just trying to book a room, dude."

But the reception didn't bother. He just stared into a large white book without giving the new aggressive voice addressing him a glance.

"This fool crazy." Chill Will threw up his hands.

"The app didn't say nothing about rude service here." Bigmack turned his back.

"Maybe I should try." Natasha eased her way in between the guys. "Hello, my name is Natasha King, formally of Channel 6 news. I am now the head assistant to Raymon Platt Jr. He recently found out that he is the sole heir to Roger Welloff Bennet's fortune and would like to rent space here at your wonderful hotel while attending to business in New York."

The receptionist's face lit up like he had a light bulb hidden in his mouth. "Roger Bennet is family here at The Grand Dora. How may I help you?"

"Ain't that some horn cow drop," Bigmack slapped Chill Will on the arm.

"You gotta tell a sucker your whole life story to get a room around here." Chill Will leaned on the counter. "It's cause I'm black, ain't it?"

"She black too." Bigmack pointed.

"Yeah but, she ain't that black, if you know what I mean."

"Blacker than you."

"But ain't nobody blacker than you," Chill Will joked.

"Can you two please keep it together?" Natasha said. "This is a classy place."

"What you trying to say? We ain't got class?" Bigmack turned his hat around.

Natasha looked them over, one at a time. Bigmack's sneakers were leaning to one side. Chill Will's braids were sloppy and unkept. She noticed the Playboy bunny tattoo on his neck and shook her head. "You'll get special ed class." She laughed.

"Are you using cash or credit?" the receptionist asked.

"That will be cash," Raymon shouted from a distance with a briefcase in each hand.

A dozen glass chandeliers hung from the ceiling over his head. "I think I'm going to like this." He smiled and nodded his head. The open area had loveseats and long couches, wall-to-wall carpets, shiny wood tables, and baggage carts spread out. The lights shined bright and illuminated the paintings hung on the walls. Sounds from a piano played softly in the background. "This will work." Raymon greeted his friends.

"Where you been?" Bigmack made a face of disapproval.

"Handling my business. How about Y'all?"

"We checked out all the dope hotels. This one had the highest approval rate." Chill Will looked to be exhausted.

The Grand Dora had a 24-hour barbershop and beauty salon, a boutique mall, movie theaters, and massage parlor. The staff wore blue tuxedos with white shirts and ties.

"Well, what floor am I on?" Raymon slammed his briefcases on the counter.

"We're getting the room number right now," said Bigmack.

"Room number. Don't you mean room numbers?"

"These rooms are like $5,000 a night," Chill Will confirmed.

"I ain't sharing a room with nobody," Raymon declared.

"Ray, these rooms are like apartments, with six rooms and multiple bathrooms."

"I'm Raymon Platt and everybody down with get they own room, they own space."

"How long will you be staying here at The Grand Dora?" The receptionist smiled big.

"I was thinking about 30 days."

"That will be very expensive, sir."

Raymon looked at Natasha and sucked his teeth. *This fool doesn't know.* Then he popped open one of his cases and slammed down a handful of money stacks. "Use this to dry your palms, son."

Before the cash could completely vanish behind the desk, the receptionist waved for a service worker and additional clerks. "Show these gentlemen to their rooms," he ordered.

Raymon and crew rode the elevator to their respective floors. Odd stares from other guests seemed to follow them throughout the building. When Raymon finally reached the top floor, he stepped off the lift and approached the nine-foot double doors of the Royal Suite like a great adventure awaited him.

"Your suite, sir." A young bellhop led the way, slid a card across the wall and motioned for Raymon to place his hand on a scanner to unlock the doors.

Raymon stepped inside and marveled at the marble floors beneath his feet. He had enough open space in front of him to run a basketball team practice. He saw a swirling glass staircase was on his lift. The all-white decoration scheme gave him a feeling of holiness. He had to force his jaw closed as he took it all in. The Royal Suite included two Jacuzzis the size of some swimming pools, six bedrooms, five bathrooms, a private office, plush furniture and a balcony the size of an inner-city backyard, complete with a helicopter pad.

Raymon ran to every room like a little kid. He checked the stock behind the bar, patted every cushion, and said, "I want to die here. It's perfect. Now I just need the entire floor."

"The entire floor?" the bell hop looked confused. "But sir, there are no other rooms on this floor."

"You are right, I mean the other floors. What your name?"

"I am Si-mon from Yemen."

"From Yemen. What you doing in the big city?"

"My family is very poor. I come here to learn, but now cannot afford to return home."

"So, you are working your way back?"

"Yes! I need to return home soon so that I can take care of goat."

"Goat!"

"Yes! My goat."

"Well Si-mon, I like my own space. And my team gotta have their own space. So, I think it's best that I pay for the entire floors they are own also," said Raymon.

"It is the holiday, sir."

51

"So what?"

"That will be very expensive for you to do," said Si-mon.

Raymon placed a hand on Si-mon. "I'm just getting started. I would also like to open a spending account for me and my crew. Bill everything to my suite. Si-mon, my friend, I'm going to need your services quite a bit, so try not to sleep too much. And one more thing, call me Mr. Raymon." He stuffed a few thousand dollars in the front of Si-mon's uniform pocket.

"Thank you!" Si-mon nodded his head.

Raymon felt bad for the immigrant. He reached in his pocket for more cash to give him, but he paused. *You can't give it away,* he thought about the rules.

In walked Benjamin, "is everything all right?"

"Everything is great," Raymon lied.

An hour later, Bigmack busted through the entrance with the new doorman on his heels. "Yo dogg, this spot is dope. You gotta see my room."

Before the doorman could get a word out, in ran Chill Will with Natasha close behind him. "Your room, my room is the shizznit."

"It's fine." Raymon waved at the doorman. "Y'all can't just rush up in here like that. This is the Royal Suite. Plus, you got your own space to explore."

Chill Will looked at Raymon reclined in a leather loveseat. "Our own space, that's putting it lightly. They gave us our own floors. It's just me up and down that whole joint," Chill Will said.

"Yeah Ray, I don't know how you got them to do that. Looks like you living good your damn self." Bigmack looked around the huge room.

"Must be the money." Raymon smiled.

"Speaking of that, I been meaning to talk with you." Bigmack eased closer. "I mean, I googled a little information from the built-in laptops in the rooms, but how good are you?"

"Trust me, I'm good." Raymon knew what Bigmack was insinuating.

"We talking M's or we talking B's?"

"Put it like this,"—Raymon lifted his feet—"Bill Gates is my new neighbor."

"Mr. Platt," Natasha interrupted.

"Call me Ray, or Mr. Raymon please."

"Well okay. Mr. Raymon, I purchased some suits for you, as you requested. These are Tom Ford." She held up two bags.

"Tom Ford," Raymon shouted. "I ain't wearing no Tom Ford. I'm Raymon Platt Jr. I ain't wearing nobody but me from here out."

"But Mr. Raymon, you told me to get some nice suits, and spare no expense."

"But nothing! I know what I said, and I changed my mind. Can I do that? Now get me a personal tailor, and call up a personal jeweler."

"What about these?" Natasha held up the bags

"Throw them away."

"They are thousand-dollar clothes."

"Hey Ray," Chill Will stepped forward. "You might want a slow down a little."

Raymon stood to his feet, "I ain't no cheap pusher. I want all my clothes made from scratch. Spare no expense. And lose them glasses." He pointed at Natasha. "And dye your hair, too."

Natasha grabbed the end of her shoulder-length hair. It was black with light-brown streaks. She looked at Raymon and waited, as if he was going to say, just joking. Instead, he forged the look of a world-series poker player.

"You the boss." Natasha stormed out of the suite.

"Damn right I am." Raymon sank back to his seat. "Now where is my man Si-mon?"

"Who?" Bigmack's face twisted.

"My man with the goat."

"Somebody got a goat up in here?" Chill Will had a lost look on his face.

"The damn bellhop," said Raymon.

"That reminds me," Bigmack sat on the couch in a rush. "I gotta show you this."

"Let me show them." Chill Will jumped.

"Somebody needs to show me already," Raymon snarled.

"It's the coolest thing ever." Chill Will grinned like a kid with a new video game. "You don't need to call or ring no bell or nothing. If you trying to get at your bellhop, or a

service worker, or if you just want a pizza, all you got a do is call ya girl."

"What?" Raymon was losing his stern!

"Check it out," said Bigmack. "Victoria! Call the front desk."

"Calling front desk," a woman's voice replied.

The sound of a phone ringing echoed throughout the apartment. After two rings a man's voice answered, "Hello, front desk."

"Yeah, this Raymon Platt Jr," Bigmack impersonated. "Send my bellhop to the Royal Suite ASAP. The one with the goat. Semen or semi, something like that."

They laughed out loud when the call ended. Raymon stood up and said, "That's some cool work right there."

Chill Will gave Bigmack a handshake. "We done came up."

"And she in every room." Bigmack celebrated. "It's like some auto Google next-level-assistance-type hook up. Check this out. Victoria! What is the population of West Virginia?"

"The total population of West Virginia is 1,844,128 people."

"That's crazy." Raymon shook his head in disbelief.

" Victoria, who is the richest man in the world?" asked Chill Will.

"The richest man in the world is William Gates."

"Victoria, how long is my shaft?" Bigmack joked.

"Answer unknown."

"She been talking to my baby moms."

"I got one," Raymon said. "Victoria, who is goofier, Mack or Chill?"

"Mack and Chill is an urban diner."

"She must be a white girl." Raymon laughed harder.

"Whatever she is, she sound sexy." Chill Will licked his lips.

A knock at the door interposed the fun. In walked Si-mon with his hands locked together in front of his chest. "You requested me sir?"

"Si-mon! I need you to call up the best tailors," said Raymon. "Get in touch with the finest jewelers. Tell them Raymon Platt Jr is in town. I don't care what time it is. I need them here yesterday."

Si-mon pulled a pen and notepad from his pocket. " Will that be all, sir?"

"No! After the bling bling, I want five exotic whips out front, along with three limousines and a chopper on call ready to land at my request. I want a private jet fueled and available around the clock. Now Si-mon, make it clear to all parties that I am looking to rent only. I do not want to purchase these things, just pay to use them."

"Hold up Ray." Bigmack hopped to his feet. "Renting is going to cost you a lot more money in the end. It would be smarter to purchase the toys you like."

"I got this, homie." Raymon stretched his arm out. "Trust me, time is money and every second counts. Back to you. You got all that Si-mon?"

Si-mon looked confused, but he kept scribbling on his notepad. Then he looked up at Raymon and Bigmack. "Yes sir, I have. it. Bling Bling and jets. Wait! Where shall I find whips and choppers?"

"My friend HEFE will explain that," Raymon said.

When Bigmack walked off with Si-mon under his arm, Chill Will saw a chance to talk sense with Raymon. "I hope you know what you doing," he said quietly.

"What you mean by that?" Raymon pulled away.

"I know you balling now, and that, but keep a little for the homies."

"For the homies, aye? It's cool. I got this, Chill. And I'm paying you by the hour to do your part. And let me do mines."

"And what exactly am I pose to do again?"

Raymon looked around with his hands on his head, like he was seeking out the answer. Then it hit him. " I want you to play the net, spread the word, let New York City know that Raymon Platt Jr is having a party tonight. Invite the best of the best, and let them know we celebrating up in here."

Chill Will formed a sneaky look on his face like the Grinch that stole Christmas. He thought about all the sexy women falling out of their stilettos trying to get in a party of this magnitude. He could taste the fun to come and envision all the liquor being poured. He forgot all about his previous concerns and focused on the night's possibilities. "You got it, Ray." He smiled.

CHAPTER 5

Latin music played in the background while Honey scurried around the kitchen. Her three siblings danced in circles around her as she prepared plates. The smell of baked chicken excited the young children. Heat from the open stove helped to warm the small apartment. Honey carried a plate in each hand, placed them on the dinner table, returned to the kitchen, picked up two more and repeat. Then she grabbed a large jug full of Kool-Aid. "Vamos! " She yelled to grab everyone's attention.

Her two younger brothers, one nine years old the other ten, raced their five-year-old sister to the dinner table and chose seats.

Honey's mother walked in and smiled. "Gracias mi nina, this is wonderful."

The table had a box of bread, a pot of white rice, two pans of beans and a bowl of salad. Honey took her seat at the end of the table.

Her mother sat across from her. "What are you wearing?"

Honey looked down at her torn sweater and her black-boy shorts and said, "It's nothing, Ma."

"Nothing is right. You need to put some clothes on." Honey's mother spoke English with a Spanish accent. Her pronouncements caused the children to giggle a little and pieces of chicken escaped their mouths.

"Chew your food," Honey demanded.

"Mi nina pobre, look at your hair."

Honey's hair was wet and without curls. It hung over her shoulders and covered her breast. She looked like she just stepped out of the shower. She shook her head in silence and tried not to answer her mother's taunts. But as she poked at her meal, her mother continued.

"When you going to find a man? You don't look happy. You need to stop all this music talk. It is no good for you. You need a man to help take good care of you."

With her chin touching her chest, Honey lifted her eyes only. Her mother was so caught up in her own rants, she couldn't see the stream of emotions building up across the table. "Enough, Ma!" Honey slammed down her fork. "Dios mio, let me live my own life."

"What kind of life is this?" Her mother looked shocked. "You go outside, you come back inside. You go out, you come back in. Nothing changes. You need a real job."

"I have plans, Ma. I have dreams too. I do all I can for you and mi hermanos, and yet you still complain."

"Dreams, what dreams? Dreams no pay bills."

The room went silent like everyone was frozen in time. Honey looked at her brothers and sister. Their innocent faces stopped her from lashing out in a verbal rage against her ungrateful mother.

Honey stood to her feet and said, " Te amo mi madre, but just because you never chased your dreams, doesn't mean I won't catch mine. Enjoy your chicken that I paid for." She left the room, placed her unfinished plate on the stove, and turned around. "Dishes is on you little monsters tonight."

Honey made it to her room and closed the door behind her. She sat on her mattress, opened her laptop, and connected the Internet service. Her mind was racing so fast, she could have gotten a ticket for thinking. Why couldn't her mother just believe in her? She pressed her face in a pillow. Through clouded vision, she tried to focus. Not fully aware of her intentions - she typed in Raymon Platt Jr and hit search.

The words that came across her screen forced her to lean back a little. Heir to a billion-dollar throne. Honey clicked on another page and found a caption that read: Streaming live, billionaire bash. Her eyes widened at the sight of half-naked women in a lofty apartment waving bottles of wine in the air. She struggled to identify a familiar face, until she spotted a dark figure with a top hat on his head. Honey stared at the man and convinced herself that she was looking at the same guy who ran to Raymon's aid earlier in the day.

Big money having a hoedown. She frowned. She tried not to anger herself anymore than she already was. But Raymon owed her money and she planned on collecting, one way or the other. Her bad angel wanted her to close her computer, find the address to the blowout, and get her cash in her hand. But before she could obey, her ears were pulled in by audio coming from the speakers. The sound was thick. She listened attentively. Her eyebrows sank when she clearly recognized her own voice. Suddenly she spun her head around at the sound of her smart phone blinging. She jumped to her feet and snatched it off the dresser. "Hello!"

"Even your speaking voice sounds good," said Raymon.

"Who is this?"

"You forget everyone that gives you a ride home?"

"Big Money," Honey sighed, "you lucky I answered. I don't do the unlisted call thing, and I told you to text me."

"Lucky me. I'll take that."

"Where is my money?"

"Easy tiger. I told you, I got it. Imma have someone pick you up so we can meet. If that cool?"

Honey smiled. Seconds ago, she was planning to go out hunting for her cash. Now she was being offered a ride straight to it. "Tomorrow, is good."

"Then tomorrow it is. And I would like to pull your ear about some other business if you're interested."

"First things first Big Money. Just make sure you do what you say. I don't want to have to come looking for you," Honey said.

"Damn, I'm okay, I got you." Raymon slurred. "See you tomorrow. Sweet dreams Ms. Honey Drop." Raymon tried to sound attractive.

Honey pulled her phone away from her ear and gave it an aggravated look. "Boy bye." But after the call was disconnected, she allowed her thoughts to roam. What other business did Raymon have in mind? Sitting on her bed in her scrubby room, Honey closed her eyes and fancied a better life.

Chapter 6

Hip hop music shook the walls of the expensive suite, while party goers

danced on the shiny floors. Intoxicating smoke rose to the ceiling like spirits

freed from their tormented bodies. Champagne bottles were waved in the

air as folks swayed their hips to the rhythm.

Bigmack weaved his way through the crowd, with a female companion on

each arm. Feeling mighty. Chill Will face-timed on his new phone with a

half-empty bottle in his other hand.

Benjamin sat on a couch in the corner, typing numbers into his laptop,

while Planes stood close to the entrance with his arms crossed and his

head on a swivel. Meanwhile, Natasha rested her backside on a barstool

and swiped at her phone in between sips from a small glass.

The DJ changed the track, and the crowd threw their hands up in

approval of the new tempo. Woo!

Then the master bedroom doors swung open. Raymon gavotted out in

white boxers, red socks, black house slippers, and a long furry robe. "I'm

rich bitches," he shouted. "This

the milli rock." He waved his hands over his body one after the other.

His guests shouted, "Yeah!" And the shirtless host staggered off. Raymon gave out high fives, hugs, and daps to complete strangers. A foxy gal wearing a Coogi dress handed him two edibles, and he quickly popped them in his mouth. He then pressed his lips to hers and shouted, " We made it!"

Chill Will stumbled into the DJ booth and snatched up the microphone. "Listen up, listen up." The music came to a screeching halt. "I want to give a shoutout to the man of the hour. This dude is like my brother. Ray, we go back like recliners and vaginas. I love you, man. Now we can finally put our music out for the whole world to hear! Y'all get ready for Mack and Chill the album. The album coming to take over the game. It's Raymon Records for life. The double R! It's going down."

Bigmack had to calmly take the microphone from Chill Will and escort him away. "Sorry people, enjoy the party," he said.

Raymon laughed so hard his stomach began to hurt. But with all the action going on before him, he couldn't stop his mind from drifting off. He knew his friends very well. He wanted to tell them about his task and what he had to do. *We ain't made it yet.* But he knew the rules wouldn't allow him to do that. Chill Will was obnoxious, almost by nature. He couldn't control what came out his mouth no more then he could fix his stupor.

Bigmack was loyal to a fault, but very dogmatic. He thought he had all the answers, but never took a single test. Raymon had to play his cards right. But how could he spend 500 million in 30 days without anyone knowing his true intentions?

He focused his eyes on a small table by his office door. He recognizes the CD cases from across the room and made his way over to the table, side stepping wild dancers like a drunken karate master. Then he picked up a case and rushed it to the DJ. "Play this," he ordered.

The musical transition paused the movement, but only for a second. What Raymon heard was Alicia Keys, Aaliyah, and Jhene Aiko all rolled into one voice. Honey's vocals produced a beat of their own. The background noise did nothing to appreciate her talents, yet everyone grooved to the track like Timberland produced it.

Raymon listened with his eyes wide open. He watched men and women nod their heads. "Who that?" one man asked.

Clarity formed in his mind. He mentally replayed Chill Will' s shoutout and knew what had to be done. A buffet with enough food to feed a small country was set up near the balcony doors. Raymon ripped off a chicken leg and helped himself to a slice of apple pie. Then he journeyed outside into the high-altitude winds. His legs found the naked bench that sat in the middle of the balcony courtyard. His entire life, Raymon had to get his from the bottom. And there he was in the greatest city, with enough money to buy a regime. He sat back, pulled his phone out of his robe pocket, and checked the number before he dialed.

Twenty minutes later, he awoke in the blitzing cold, with a vague memory of his brief conversation. *I must have passed out*, he thought. He attempted to stand up, but a gentle hand pushed him back to his seat. When he looked up, he saw a sexy figure standing over him. Her white blouse was halfway unbuttoned, showing off her immaculate bust. She wore white pants that fit tightly around her long legs. Her blonde hair blew in the wind like a flag. "Am I in heaven?" Raymon asked.

She took him by the hand, pulled him to his feet close to her warm body. "Not yet," she answered.

Raymon was last seen, being accompanied to his bedroom by the Amazon angel. And when the doors shut behind them the first round had already begun. Ding!

CHAPTER 7

November 25th - Dec 4th

Mr. Planes sat behind the wheel of a black sedan, parked by the curb, in front of the Grand Dora. He looked in his rearview mirror and noticed his passenger sitting motionless. She stared out the side window in a daze of sorts. A podium was set up in front of the hotel. Raymon stood behind it, wearing a white mink coat with matching hat while directing people's movements like an orchestra conductor.

A thousand New Yorkers trekked in the cold weather on Thanksgiving morning to break bread with the seemingly opulent one. Twelve tables were set up, six on each side of him. The tables were covered in food. Whole turkeys and different flavored pies were stacked four-feet high. And with more than enough birds to fly south for the winter, Raymon promised each person their own.

Hotel personnel was awarded extra tips for their helping hands. Bigmack shook hands with strangers and offered them a happy holiday. Natasha passed out warm desserts. Benjamin stood aside texting on his phone, while Chill Will shook his head at the turnout of hungry people.

"Is there a problem Ms.?" Planes asked.

Honey pulled at the door handle, but it would not yield.

"Let me." Planes hurried into the snappy wind, opened the door, and extended his hand.

Honey waved him off at the same time the heel on her boots met the sidewalk. She moved at a moderate pace. He attempted to shield her from the drove as they marched forward.

When they reached the lobby, Chill Will was hot on their heels. "What is she doing here?" He snatched off his designer sunglasses.

"A requested guest of Mr. Raymon's of course," said Planes.

"Let me guess, she looking for a handout like the rest of these bums."

Honey pulled her hands from her coat pocket and locked her palms together. "All I'm looking for is what's owed to me."

Chill Will looked her up and down like he was searching for something. Her cocky bow-legged stance appeared aggressive. She wore a winter hat pulled down to her eyes, and tight blue jeans.

"I know who you are." Chill Will stepped back. "You that clumsy chick with the CDs."

"Excuse you." Honey tilted her head to one side.

"You tricked my man into giving you a ride. But if you think we bout to give you some bread, you crazier then Brittney Spears with an umbrella."

Before Honey could clap back, Raymon walked up behind her. "Nice outfit," he said.

Honey turned around with a mean facial expression. "My money please."

"Straight to the point." Raymon laughed. "I like that about you."

"They call them gold diggers," said Chill Will.

" You better get your boy," Honey said.

"I rather get you." Raymon smiled and walked off. "Please escort Ms. Honey Drop to my suite. Show her to my office. I will be there shortly. If she needs anything, please assist her."

Planes nodded his head without looking up.

But Honey didn't budge. "I came to get my cash. That's it. I don't need to see nothing else. Not no suite or no office. You walk in talking all fancy, got your midget sidekick over here talking fly. Where is my money?" She stomped.

Raymon could see the fire in her eyes, and he liked that. He stepped onto the elevator with a smirk. The rich smell of hot food invaded his nostrils. He saw Chill Will staring at Honey with an alarmed look on his face. He knew his friend had a bad hangover and a greedy nature. "It's Thanksgiving, he said. You going to get your chicken. Just come on up."

The elevator doors closed and broke Honey's stare-down challenge. She shook her head and gave Planes an evil look. "Come on."

An hour later, Honey sat on a black leather couch in Raymon's office space. She shifted in her seat, checked the time on her watch, then stood up. She was ready to storm out of the room when Planes appeared. "Mr. Raymon will see you now," he said.

Honey was led through a massive hallway, up the swirling staircase, past a movie theater, down another passage, and into a wet room, where Raymon was relaxing in a Jacuzzi. He had a cigar in his hand and a bottle of wine by his side. When he noticed his guest arrive, he stuck out his bare chest a little more. A solid gold chain hung from his neck, with diamonds encased in each crevasse. His earrings looked like shiny rocks hanging from his lobes. "Look who made it." He searched for a cool pose.

"Look dude, I don't know what games you trying to play, but I want my money." Honey was losing patience.

"It really is all business with you, aye. Do you ever just chill out? Smile a little maybe? I know what you need, you need some down time. Hop in, the waters great."

"Naw, I'm straight. Plus, I don't got a bathing suit."

"Your birthday suit is just fine." Raymon smiled.

But Honey didn't. She looked around, squinting her eyes at the naked sculptures against the walls and huffing at the bowls of fruit on small tables around the room. "You bought all this nonsense?"

"Who me? Naw, I'm just renting the place for a while. All this stuff is rented. It's the new thing." Raymon lifted up his chain.

"Looks like a waste of money if you ask me."

"What does that mean?"

"It means, if I was the heir to a billion-dollar fortune, I would invest mines, not spend it on dumb shit."

"Well, I'm kind of new to this whole money thing," Raymon said.

"Duh! it's all over the net."

"That thing went viral." Raymon laughed and lit his cigar. He watched Honey's movements closely. Her hoop earrings brought more attention to her flawless face. She had on a brown sweater under her coat, yet he could still see the model shape figure

she tried to hide so well. "I listened to your work," he said.

Honey swung her head in his direction. "Good! Now listen to this. I

want my 2 Gs and I mean now."

"You said strictly business, right! Well, I got some business strictly for

you."

"What are you talking about?"

"Music! I'm talking about some music business."

"And what Big Money know about music?" Honey put her hands on her

hips.

"I know you got skills. I know you got fire inside you. And with the right

touch, you could blow. Pun intended. No offense ..."

Honey shook her head and started to spit out a few curse words before

Raymon interrupted.

"I'll give you a million-dollar signing bonus," Raymon cut her off. "And a

record deal."

"A record deal?"

"Did I stutter? I want to make you a star, girl."

Honey folded her arms across her chest and looked for the truth in

Raymon's eyes. What were his intentions? she wondered. Was it really about the music, or was it a lame scheme to get her in bed? Honey pondered for a few seconds, then she remembered hearing her song being played in the background at Raymon's billion-dollar bash, and the reaction from the crowd of people. Could it really be about the music, and if so, was that what she really wanted? Honey weighed her options and realized she had more to gain than lose. After all, it wasn't like she had industry execs kicking down her doors.

"Why me?" she asked.

"It's the fourth quarter, and we need to score." Raymon exhaled smoke. "I need a real artist to relaunch my label. And if we going to get them records spinning, then we will need the right English." Wink, wink.

"I got my own thing going on right now." Honey played hard to get.

"I can see that."

"What is that supposed to mean?"

"Well, you said my business was all over the net. So, I'm guessing you are computer savvy."

"So, what!"

"So, what I don't understand is, why you out pushing CDs. Why not just post your music and build up your following, create a fan base? Don't you have an IG page?"

Honey rolled her eyes and put her hands in her pockets. "I ain't with all that fake shit. Trying to be known, but not really know anybody. That's whack!"

"I can feel that, I guess. But why the eds? That stuff is ancient."

"My music is personal. I need to connect with my listeners," she said.

"And that's why I need you." Raymon pointed his finger like an old Uncle Sam poster.

"All right, I'm in. But I need a say so in everything that has to do with my music," Honey demanded.

Raymon looked her in the eyes, then sank underneath the warm bubbles. When he emerged, he shouted. "It's a deal then!"

Natasha walked in the room, fumbling multiple cell phones in her hands. Her hair was cut low and dyed a dark red with gold streaks.

"Who are you, how did you get in here?" Raymon joked.

"You said, for me to get my hair done." Natasha smiled.

"Yeah, but not red."

"What's the matter, you don't like?" Natasha struck a pose.

Raymon took an exaggerated gulp from his bottle of wine. "Hell no. Get that thing fixed. We running a business over here, not some kind of clown show. And make sure they put it on my bill," he yelled.

Natasha's face dropped. Maybe he was playing, she thought. But his body language said otherwise. She rolled her eyes, and turned around so fast, she almost crashed into Chill Will. "Watch out," she snarled.

"What's her problem?" Chill Will asked. "Hey Ray, some bougee Bespoke Tailors are here to see you."

"It's about time." Raymon raised his arms. "Tell them I will be right out. And can you please show Ms. Honey Drop to her room?"

"Her what?" Chill Will snatched the hat off his own head, then looked Honey up and down. "She staying here? This mess gotta stop, Ray. You got these freeloaders downstairs with their hands out like we owe them something, and now you talking about moving one in."

"She is no free loader." Raymon laughed. "This is my new artist. We going to put her album out first as the relaunch to Raymon Records. The new and improved. "

"Slow down, Ray. What you doing, man?" Chill Will tried to reason. "This is about us. The Mack and Chill album. More Fish, remember?"

Honey held the palm of her hand over her mouth and tried to seal in her laughs. "I'm sorry."

"You think this funny." Chill Will gave her a mean look.

"No, I'm just saying, Mack and Chill sounds more like a BBQ joint then an album."

Raymon couldn't help but to laugh out loud. But Chill Will kept his poker face. He tightened up his chest muscles looked to Raymon and said, "So this what we doing now."

"Nice chain," said Raymon. "What's that, a Patek on your wrist? You got all kinds of new bling. Is that white gold?"

"Naw, this platinum." Chill Will admired his own accessories. "That's what I'm trying to tell you, homie, the money is in houses and assets..."

"Relax homie." Raymon stopped his wisdom. "Ms. Honey Drop English is the one who will take my label where it needs to go. All them ideas you got can wait. Right now, this is what it is."

"This fake Rihanna meets Jenny from the block," Chill Will exploded.

"You clown suit wearing fake Money-Mike-looking fool." Honey had about enough.

Raymon jumped to his feet. With water splashing in every direction, he tried to control the narrative. "Chill out, calm down! We going with Honey's album first and that's it. Chill, I got you and Mack, just like I always have. You just going to have to trust me on this one," he said.

Chill Will gritted his teeth and made a slow exit, leaving the slippery scene behind him.

Honey watched him closely. She stared a hole into his back while thinking, *What's his real problem?*

"Sorry about that," said Raymon. "He gets like that when he doesn't get his way. Plus, you taller than him. And I know that pisses him off. You okay?"

"I'm good," Honey whooped. "Now where's my money?"

Raymon stood there in his swimming trunks shaking his head. "You just don't stop."

Chapter 8

Bigmack was busy making calls, checking boxes, and giving out orders. His job was to create a studio of the highest quality inside Raymon's Royal suite. A lounge area was quickly transformed. Extra walls were constructed and reinforced with soundproof installation. A staff was hired to manage sound checks and the recording process. Raymon's slogan, Spare No Expense, was honored. Bigmack purchased the most expensive equipment available to assist in crafting a contemporary sound.

Elite voice coaches were summoned. Artist and Repertoire agents were called, flown in, and readied at Raymon's disposal.

Social media raved about the new billionaire playboy attempting to make an overnight success out of some unknown girl from Harlem. Reporters were camped out in front of the hotel waiting to see who would be next to usher their services to the extraordinary paying hands of Raymon Platt Jr.

The sounds of quickened feet whistled across the floor. Coffee, liquor, and bottles of water were carried back and forth by maids and butlers trying to avoid collisions.

The muffled sound of helicopter blades shook the glass balcony doors. Raymon watched from an elevated position. He stood on top of a brown box stool with his arms spread. With his ear jack connected, he held position while a tailor corrected his dress shirt. "Where is Si-mon?" he asked. "Has anyone seen Si-mon?"

Planes waited patiently for the helicopter to land, then slid open the balcony doors and assisted the safe extraction of its passengers.

When he returned inside, Chill Will closed the doors behind them and attempted to make formal introductions. "Ray, this is Planet Pluto production," said Chill Will.

Raymon ignored him. "I'm Raymon mother#*cking Platt Jr. You tell P. Diddy, Puffy, Brother Love, or whatever he calling himself these days, that there's a new show in town, and if he wants to stay relevant, he better get with it."

Chill Will lowered his head and waited for Raymon to end his phone call.

"All right, all right that's good. That's what I'm talking about, real players linking up. Okay, later then. Phone off! Where is Si-mon?" Raymon asked.

Chill Will took a deep breath. "Planet Pluto productions, this is Raymon Platt Jr."

Two Asian faces looked at Raymon and smiled. They looked like they were pulled out of high school. They both had a set of headphones around their necks, book bags on their backs, and laptops under their armpits.

"My sources tell me that you two are the next Neptunes," Raymon said.

"They dope." Chill Will was hyper. "They IG is popping and the net going crazy over the beats these two put out. Check it out. The short one, that's Mark. And this young Jet Lee looking cat, his name is Play."

"They both short Chill."

"I know. Ain't that crazy?" Chill Will smiled like a proud father.

"Which one is Mark, and who is Play again?" asked Raymon.

"I think, this Mark. And ... I'm not really sure."

"Well, I know one thing," Raymon stopped his friend's buffoonery, "I just flew they ass across the world, so they better be good."

The babyface beat makers just stared at Raymon and smiled.

81

"Show them around," Raymon ordered. "Are we done yet?" He looked down at the eccentric garment crafter.

"I just need to hem these pants," the tailor said.

"How much is this all going to cost me?"

"The Brothers of Bespoke suits are made to measure and flatter a man's body. These suits will fit you to your exact measurements and taste. You are receiving the Bespoke experience as we speak. All your clothes will be made by hand, Mr. Platt."

"How much money we talking here?"

"Well, this suit alone is worth $1000." The tailor batted his eyelids.

"That's great," Raymon said. "I want 365 of them. One for every day of the year. Make it 366, just in case it's a leap year. I never keep track of these things."

The tailor's jaw hit the floor.

"How fast can you have them made?" Raymon asked.

"In, I believe, two to three months," the tailor stuttered.

"I was thinking two to three weeks."

"Mr. Platt, that would take—"

"I will give you half the cost now, and the other half on full delivery," Raymon insisted. "But I do not want to buy or own them."

"Excuse me?" The tailor had a confused look.

"I just want to rent these fine suits that flatter a man's body. You can have them back after I'm finished."

"I don't understand, sir. We have never—"

" I understand," Raymon interrupted. "I am a man of different taste. I do things my own way, and I'm willing to pay for it. And I really like your suits,"—he smiled—"but I don't want to buy them. I want to pay you for your service and for the material needed to create a closet full of clothes that fit me perfectly. But they will belong to you. We will call it the Raymon collection." He looked to the heavens.

The tailor forced a smile to form on his face, then he frowned. He shook his head then began to nod. Raymon's request was wacky at best. The Brothers of Bespoke had dealt with exotic clientele before, but nothing like Raymon Platt Jr. In the end, it was business and Raymon was a sure thing, so he thought. "I think we have a deal sir."

Si-mon entered the suite with a notebook in his hand. "Mr. Raymon, you requested me?"

"Si-mon, where you been?" Raymon lit up. "I need you to tell me more about Yemen. But not right now. Right now, I would love one of those expensive ice liquor drinks we talked about. They are expensive right?"

"Yes Mr. Raymon, very expensive."

"In that case, get me ten of them."

When Si-mon exited, Natasha walked in wearing black sunglasses. Her hair was jet black and shoulder length. She avoided eye contact with Raymon. Then Chill Will popped up beside him, nodding his head wildly.

Bigmack strolled in and lowered his cell phone. "Look at you," he said.

Natasha smiled. "You like," she flipped her new hair.

"You looking like a real mob boss now," Bigmack talked past her.

Raymon checked his reflection in the mirror a worker held up for him. "Yeah, I am looking fly." He admired his fresh haircut and new clothes.

"Everything is ready," Natasha mumbled.

"Thank you." Raymon stared at himself. "Chill, you need to get some of these suits. They are great."

"Naw, I'm a stick to this polo and Gucci glow I got going on right now. You feel me?" Chill Will dabbed.

"What about you Mack? You can't do the 50-cent look all day. We got money now."

"I'm feeling the suits," Bigmack admitted. "But ain't nothing like this Louis I got going on right now. Look, I got the matching socks too."

Right on cue, Honey stepped into the room with Planes right behind her. She had on some black tights and a gray hoody. Her hair rolled down her back as she released it from a hair pin. She froze the room.

"Hey Ray," Chill Will broke the ice, "you need to get your new artist a tailor."

"You ready to work?" Raymon's eyes were locked on Honey.

"I never recorded like this before," Honey confessed.

"Like what?"

"Like this. All these people running around. The fancy equipment and stuff."

"You just bring the heat, let me handle the rest. It's simple," Raymon said.

Honey shook her head. "I like simple. I can do simple. But you got Planet Pluto up in here. You really trying to flex on me. This is too much. Ain 't they from China?"

"I don't know." Raymon shrugged. "Victoria! Where is Planet Pluto Productions from?"

"Planet Pluto Productions, Mark and Play are from Tokyo Japan."

Honey tilted her head to one side, and crossed her arms. " Yeah, that's really simple."

Time traversed, and the sun fell from the sky. A winter breeze blew in through a crack in the balcony door. At night the city lights looked like a million stars far off in the distance. Inside the studio, no one could hear the honking car horns on the streets, nor see the floating steam from a rooftop of a nearby restaurant. Everyone's attention was given to the rhythm pushing out the speakers. The bass thumped inside the recording lab. It made the walls rattle. In came the snare; it increased the tempo. Piano keys played in the background as the drums connected.

Then a soft falsetto grew like an incoming wave. It collided with the beat and became one. A dozen occupants sat in the twilight and viewed the artist from the other side of a soundproof glass. The smell of marijuana danced in the air, while ice cubes soaked in Hennessy spun in circles. Engineers adjusted their equipment; producers pressed headphones to their ears; and technicians pushed the proper buttons on the sound board.

A large computer screen gave off just enough light to find Raymon seated in the back of the room on a leather couch. He nodded his head with the hypnotic tunes.

"Fresh air from my mouth spreads," Honey's voice rose.

"Stop! Bring it back," an engineer interrupted.

86

"Fresh air from my mouth spreads," Honey tried again.

"Stop! From the top."

The childish game of Red-Light Green-Light popped into Raymon's head. The engineer continued to reset the live recording at the slightest vocal flaw, and Raymon lost his vibe. After ten tries, he noticed Honey sounding frustrated and annoyed.

"I'm doing it like you said," she shouted into the booth microphone when the track restarted yet again.

Bigmack looked unimpressed. A wave of headshakes traveled around the room.

"She just ain't got it." Chill Will looked at Raymon.

Honey was ordered to try again, but Raymon had heard enough. He jumped to his feet, walked over to the controls and leaned forward. "Let's take a breather," he spoke into the intercom.

Huffs sounded off around him. Some of his staff leaned back in their chairs, while others began to rub their hands.

"Take five", said Raymon. "The poor girl has only been in there for eight hours straight, giving her all, track after track. I would love to see one of you try that." He gave Chill Will a sharp look.

Then he entered the recording booth and closed the door behind him.

"I told you it would be simple," he joked.

"I just need a minute." Honey breathed.

"If time is money, I think I can spare a minute."

"It's this atmosphere. I can't feel the music."

"I feel you. You have been doing a great job. This is the last song for today. Do you think you can handle it?"

Honey took a sip of water and leaned her back against the wall. Sweat formed on her forehead and nose. She looked at Raymon with uncertain eyes.

"What seems to be the problem?" he asked.

"Everything. All of this. It's just not me."

"It's just not you are. Okay, let's go with that. Who are you then?"

"Not this. All the high-tech flashy bullshit. I'm from Harlem. This isn't even my sound. Maybe I shouldn't even be here right now." Honey lowered her head.

"Maybe you shouldn't. Maybe I shouldn't either. But we both here, right now. Life is funny like that. Sometimes great things happen to people that don't deserve it. But what they do with it, that's all that really matters. So, I'm a ask you again, who are you?"

"I'm the product of a poor Spanish mother and a Black British bastard that I never knew." She pushed off the wall. "I never had nice things unless I busted my ass to go get it. I'm a realist, a woman and a fighter. And I don't take no shit."

Raymon could see her nose flaring as she stared him down. "That sounds about right." He laughed to relieve the tension building. "Now take this track, put the real you all up in it, and make it your bitch."

As Raymon walked away, he could feel his heart beating faster. He had more in common with his new artist then she knew. But Raymon was on a mission to riches. He didn't know if Honey would reach her ultimate goals, albeit one thing was clear to him at that moment. Honey was a fantastic problem.

Raymon opened the door and paused in mid step. He looked over his shoulder and said, "A realist, a woman and a fighter. I like that. Now let's get this money."

When he reappeared, all eyes were on him. He looked around and clapped his hands.

"Let's get to work people."

"Fresh air from my mouth spreads, I long for now who I be." Honey nailed the delivery.

Surprised looks formed on almost everyone's face. And Raymon just smiled.

Honey sang the chorus like she was possessed. " I've Arrived, I've Arrived! I belong, I'm claiming my seat." Honey found herself in that booth with no real idea of what was to come next.

The song titled "Arrived" hit the net like a tidal wave. Pictures of Honey in the recording booth were posted on social media and linked to live chats. A Facebook account was created. Honey Drop English received 200,000 views and 150,000 shares before the sun came up. Tweets came pouring in. Where she come from? "Rich guys get all the diamonds," read one. Someone cracked the seal on a champagne bottle and a celebration began. Through high fives and glasses being waved around, Raymon saw Honey taking off her headphones, still inside the booth. *Perfectionist*, he thought.

When she looked up, she tried her best to withhold an overdue smile. She failed. Their eyes connected, and Raymon raised his thumb. "Good job."

It was 30 minutes before sunrise. Raymon had not slept. Instead, he sat behind his office desk in deep thought. He held his smart phone in front of him and swiped at different scenes of poverty around the world. Benjamin sat across from him on a couch seat with his laptop open.

Silence was their only company. Finally, Raymon sat up and placed his hands on the desk.

"Did you run those numbers again for me?" he asked. "And what about those cars? You been gone half the day."

"The numbers are correct." Benjamin smiled. "I will run them again if need be. Let me find the receipts." He scrambled through some paperwork. "And the car company does not have all of the vehicles you wrote down in stock. We will have to contact multiple companies at once."

"Tell me about Roger Welloff," Raymon switched gears.

"Your grandfather. Well, Mr. Bennet was the founder of Welloff Software. He started the company in the early 60's, I believe."

"I know all that. Google knows all that, but it doesn't say much else about him. What type of man was he?"

"I don't know. I mean I didn't spend much time around him," Benjamin fumbled. "But my father, Mr. James Preacher, the tall man with the gray hair, he pulled me into the company after I finished law school, and he knew your grandfather very well. I am not allowed in board meetings, and shortly after I started to work, Mr. Bennet grew terribly ill."

"What was wrong with him?"

"I'm not sure. My father said he was being eaten alive with guilt. Whatever that meant."

"No girlfriends running around?"

"Who me?"

Raymon gave Benjamin a loaded look.

"Of course, not." Benjamin laughed at himself. "Excuse me. Not that I know of."

"Was he a generous man?" Raymon asked.

"Heavens no! That is one fact everyone in the corporation would agree on. They would joke, behind his back of course, that Roger Welloff Bennet was so tight, if he ate a piece of coal, he would shit out diamonds." Benjamin chuckled.

When he noticed the serious look on Raymon's face, he stiffened up and said, "Forgive me sir."

"It's cool. Laugh it up. I never knew the bastard. And you can call me Ray, or Mr. Raymon. I was just trying to get some understanding. Why would a rich stingy old fool, who never gave nothing to no one, now give his all to a grandson he never knew?"

"Mr. Bennet was against charity. He never gave a single donation. He called Bill Gates an idiot. My father told me over and over what Mr. Bennet told him: Business is for Family, and Family is the business. I never truly understood, but my father sure does say it a lot. That along with, how much he is not impressed with me. I didn't know that you two never met."

"Met who?"

"Your grandfather. I am sorry for your loss. It must be some kind of emotional ride. To find out that you lost a family you never had and gained a fortune all at once. I can't imagine."

Raymon stared at the little naked men painted on the ceiling. The warmth of the room caressed his skin. His Hublot reminded him that he was on the clock. Raymon thought about the last few days and his next move. Although he never knew what true family was, he was all about is business. "Where we at?" Raymon suppressed his emotions.

"According to my math, you have four hundred and seventy-five million dollars available in your spending accounts and 2.5 billion in a frozen savings account."

"$475 million! I know I spent more than that." Raymon pushed back in his chair. "Your math must be wrong."

"Mr. Raymon, I assure you that my mathematics are correct and on point, down to the cent. This is what I do."

"I thought you went to law school."

"I did. But that was after eight years of accountant work."

"So, you telling me that I have only spent $25 million dollars on all this shit?"

"Mr. Raymon, $25 million is a lot of money. This is no joke. And in a matter of days, that is not good. If you don't slow down, you may be broke in a year."

"I was thinking in 20 some odd days," Raymon spoke lightly.

"Excuse me sir?"

Raymon looked at Benjamin like he had something strange on his face. For a moment he had forgotten that Benjamin was in the blind. Then it felt like someone had turned on the lights in his skull. Tell no one. The kooky council had left one of their own outside the loop, Raymon replayed the rules in his head. Okay let's play, he thought. Twenty-five million in two days wasn't close to what he would need to waste in order to get his true inheritance. He had to find a way to spend more in a rapid pace. He disregarded Benjamin's existence for a moment and thought about an article he once read about a shining city. Then he straightened his back. He felt like someone had slipped him an energy drink. His eyes opened wide. He looked at Benjamin and asked, " Have you ever been to Vegas? "

It was a Friday night inside Welloff Software headquarters and the building appeared to be abandoned. Dark office rooms kept silent, while heat hummed threw the ventilation vents. A man in a brown uniform materialized, bobbing his head and pushing a buffer back and forth down the hallway. He quickly removed his headphone from his ears when he noticed the six-foot figure stomping his way.

"Back to work." James barely noticed the janitor's existence. When he reached the end of the hall, James pushed open a cracked office door. He entered the room and saw Lisa's silhouette below a dim desk lamp. She looked up and saw James staring at her.

"Working late again I see." James helped himself to a chair.

"Someone has to save this company," said Lisa.

"Well, I just got off the phone with the Bloomberg's. They want to call a shareholders meeting stat."

"That's great news." Lisa frowned.

"Yes, it is, my dear."

"I was being tongue-in-cheek, James. For Christ sakes."

"What are you doing here, in the dark, all covertly?" James stood up and walked toward her.

Lisa slammed a folder closed and leaned back in her chair. "This Raymon character is very bothersome to me."

"Oh, come now," James placed his hands on her shoulders. "You can't believe for a second that this boy will succeed."

"I am not so sure. And that is what bothers me. I don't think sending the media after him was a good idea."

"He is a hoodlum, Lisa. He and his homeboys. Surely, more attention will throw him off and corrupt his task at hand."

"Have you read this?" Lisa pointed to the folder.

"I read enough."

"Well maybe you should read it through. This hoodlum was an orphan. He bounced from home to home, never remaining with a foster family for more than a year. Yet somehow, he gained credits at a local college for business and survived on his own. "

"The boy was in jail when we found him." James spun her chair around and looked Lisa in the eyes.

"Oh yes, he was. The only charge on his record. For almost 30 years, not a single arrest. I believe there is more to this hoodlum, as you called him. And I won't make the mistake of underestimating him. You shouldn't either."

James slowly leaned forward. He stared into Lisa's green eyes and began passionately kissing her. "A boy like this has never seen the amount of money that we threw at him. He is out throwing parties and carrying on." He pulled her head back by her hair. "With the rules in place and his level of actual intelligence, he doesn't have a chance." He kissed on her neck.

"Do you think Roger knew that we were preparing to vote him out of his own company?" Lisa asked.

James stopped. His facial expression changed. He stood up straight and his eyebrows sank low. "Listen here, and you listen good. This company is our family. Roger forgot that. He let the loss of his daughter change him. It made him weak and indecisive. And for what, a daughter that already left him. I was not going to sit back and watch this family be destroyed, not then and not now. That money belongs to the company, to the family, to us. And this degenerate, this Raymon Platt Jr, he is clearly a screw up. All we need is for him to screw up one more time."

"And if he doesn't?" Lisa grabbed his belt buckle.

"Oh, he will, my dear."

"The stakes are still too high. We need a backup plan."

A pregnant pause caused James to ponder. He put his hands on Lisa's face and said, "All right, my dear. I have just the thing. You want insurance, you got it. Now tell me again about your tongue-in-cheek methods. "

CHAPTER 9

"Tell the people how you feel right now," said Raymon, holding his smart phone pointed at Chill Will.

"This is stupid," Chill Will shouted. "I'm not going through with this."

"This is light work," Bigmack yelled.

"You want me to hold your hand?" Honey teased.

"After this, lunch is on me," Raymon proclaimed.

" That's if we can still eat," Natasha responded.

"This ain't going to work." Chill Will closed his eyes and shook his head.

"You got this," Raymon said. "Look at Mack, he tough and ready."

Chill Will opened one eye and saw Bigmack smiling in his direction. Then a voice announced, "Ten second till drop point."

Raymon checked his straps, fixed his head gear, and looked at his comrades. "Let's do this."

A door slid open and a powerful wind shook the aircraft. A skydiving instructor yelled out orders and proper procedures, then asked, "Who's first?"

Honey moved forward with a smile. She approached the open door and the instructor placed his hand on the small of her back, and guided her to jump.

"One. Two. Three." He pushed.

Honey's body vanished and Bigmack was bound to be next. Natasha followed behind him. Then Raymon grabbed Chill Will's hand and attempted to pull him to his feet. But he wouldn't budge.

"This ain't for me," Chill Will resisted.

One instructor dived out of the plane like he saw gold in the sky. Another reached for Raymon. "Your turn."

Raymon pulled at Chill Will, but he seemed to be glued to his seat. "Come on," Raymon shouted.

Chill Will just shook his head. Raymon shared a stare of understanding with the second instructor. Then he remembered an article he read about the fight or flight reflex. It said: everyone has a natural instinct for self-preservation. When faced with a life-threatening encounter, the body will make a choice for survival.

With no time left to think, Raymon look at Chill Will and shouted, "The plane is going down. We going to crash!"

It was like a fire alarm was set off inside Chill Will's head. He hopped to his feet, pushed Raymon to the side, waved his arms and made the plunge into the open air.

I can't believe that worked. Raymon leaped out of the plane with the instructor behind him. A small camera was strapped to the front of his helmet. He wore a parachute pack on his back and nose-dived above some clouds in the distance. He saw Chill Will becoming a part of the sky below him. Then he spread his arms and began to soar like a bird over the open desert.

Honey performed front flips in the air, then she steadied her fall with the forceful wind beneath her. Bigmack lay flat and tried to scream, but when he opened his mouth, his cheeks couldn't stop their flapping. Natasha's body twirled in the air, traveling at a high speed with her knees bent. Raymon flew in closer, cut through some low clouds and gave them a thumbs up.

Their heart rates increased as their bodies descended closer to the ground. Chill Will reached for his pin and pulled. Natasha's wristband was beeping and blinking green. She released her hemispherical canopy, followed by Honey and Bigmack. A large blue blanket shot out from their packs.

Raymon quickly followed suit, and seven bodies floated above the Nevada sands.

Chill Will peddled his feet like an airman track star, glad to be so close to the land. " You are all crazy." He crashed to the ground.

"Now that's how you make an entrance." Bigmack pumped his fist.

When Raymon landed, he threw off each strap from his shoulders. Then he noticed a stretched Hummer truck approaching them. "There's our ride," he said.

Chill Will heeled over and lost his breakfast. "I told y'all this wasn't for me," he spat.

"That's just nasty." Honey lifted her parachute and stepped past him.

The joy seekers jumped in the vehicle and left the momentous event behind in search of a new one.

Benjamin sat in the passenger seat with his laptop open. He looked behind him and saw the excited faces. "You guys are insane."

Raymon popped a bottle of champagne that was chilling in a bucket of ice. He filled glass after glass, then looked to Planes behind the wheel. "Fancy pants! Take us to the casino. We just getting started."

Two hours later, Raymon stood in the casino lobby, ready for the world. He wore a tailored suit with tuxedo shoes that shined brighter than the city lights. He was adjusting his million-dollar cufflinks when Bigmack and Chill Will approached him from behind. All three men stared at their own reflections in a mirror next to the elevators. Chill Will had on a Maison Michel top hat, an Armani suit, Stacy Adams shoes, and a Hermes scarf around his neck. Bigmack wore a green baggy suit and crocodile shoes. He complimented his outfit with an obsessive amount of bling.

Raymon brushed his low fade with his palm. "You think you got enough jewels on?"

"You can't ever have enough shine," said Bigmack.

"Especially when you as ugly as you," Chill Will joked. "Looking like a big fake-ass Bishop Don Juan."

Raymon couldn't hold back his laughter. "He got you on that one, Mack. Do you even know what year it is?"

"Forget y'all," said Bigmack. "I look good."

"This fool ain't never had no money." Chill Will laughed.

"Y'all chill out." Raymon put a hand on each of their shoulders. "Tonight, we own this town."

As sudden as an unexpected rainfall, the elevator doors dinged open. Honey stepped out wearing a pair of red Valentino heels and a cream Dulce and Gabbana backless dress that could stop trafficking at the border. Her hair hung down her back so gracefully, it seemed as if an angel had a hand on it. Her legs had a glow that made it easy to notice the definition in her calf muscles.

Raymon helped Bigmack close his mouth. Chill Will snatched off his sunglasses. They stared at Honey like they saw in her a fountain of treasure. "Drinks please."

"You still think she needs a makeover?" Raymon said.

"You look nice," Chill Will stuttered.

"I feel weird," Honey said. "I never had any reason to dress up before. I didn't even pick these shoes out."

"But they fit you perfectly." Natasha walked up next to her.

Raymon couldn't find the words he was looking for. He looked at Honey hard and refused to blink.

Natasha twisted in her Fendi dress, cleared her throat, and said, "She looks great, right fellas?"

"Yeah! She looks wonderful," Bigmack confirmed.

Raymon kept his stare. "Let's spend some money." The casino game floor inside Las Vegas Nevada's Emerald City Hotel was compressed with players. Bells rang out at the same time Raymon and his entourage passed a row of slot machines. The aroma of freshly baked cakes filled their noses;

the sound of poker chips clashing together excited their minds and widened their eyes. Bigmack's stomach growled. Raymon's phone blinked. People from all over the world dressed to impress had come to risk it all on their game of choice.

Raymon checked his surroundings for particulars. He was anxious, but not confused. He remained enthusiastic, but not hasty. He thought about all those nights of jail poker with Remix, how to spot a tell and identify the mark at the table. Then his senses kicked in. "Tasha, take my phone. Take down messages if need be, I'm a be busy all night. And tell Benji we are on the casino floor. It's time to gamble."

"I will see y'all a little later." Bigmack headed for the bakery shop.

"Y'all tripping. The real money right here." Chill Will took a seat at the nearest slot machine.

Raymon weaved through the crowd with Natasha on one side and Honey on his other.

"Is this seat taken?" Raymon stopped at a table of Omaha.

The card dealer extended his arm and Raymon pulled back the chair and guided Honey to take a seat. He took a seat across from her with a smile on his face.

"Fifteen million for the lady," said Raymon. "You do know how to play?" He looked at Honey.

"I can call my own hand." Honey trembled. " Don't be nervous, that's good enough."

"And for you Mr..."

"Platt, Raymon Platt Jr.," he said matter-of-factly. "This is a high risk no limit table, correct?"

"Yes sir, Mr. Platt."

"Then I will start with fifteen million myself."

The dealer whispered doubts in the ear of his assistant standing behind him. Then Benjamin arrived with a black briefcase handcuffed to his wrist. He stood behind Raymon and nodded his head at spectators.

Word spread fast throughout the gambling ring, and the sharks quickly found the right pool to dive in. The table was full of players faster than the dealer could say check or bet. Raymon sized up his competitors while Natasha stood over his shoulder texting and taking calls.

"The bet is to the lady," said the dealer.

Honey looked up. Her eyes circled the table. She was the only female at the event and wanted nothing more than to play her cards right. "I bet 10,000." She tossed her chips into the middle of the table.

"I raise 50,000," said the man to her left.

He had on a black baseball cap that read GAMBLER on the front of it; he wore it so low it was hard to see his eyes. The man on his left folded his cards in a hurry. Raymon took a glance at the big bettor then planted his eyes on Honey and admired her glow.

"Mr. Raymon," said the dealer.

"I'm all in." Raymon pushed his stack of chips into the pot.

The man on his left folded. Honey chuckled and straightened her back.

The board was showing: the three of clubs, the six of diamonds, and the deuce of diamonds. Honey leaned forward and bent the tip of her cards just enough to take another peek.

The king of diamonds and the ten of diamonds gave her hope. She looked at Raymon, he showed no facial emotions and no fear. She placed her elbows on the table and rested her chin in her palms. Raymon's eyes dropped to the floor and she thought, he wouldn't bluff with that much money. "I fold," Honey decided.

The black baseball cap rose up slowly. His eyes were right below the brim and pointed right at Raymon. He was younger than the full beard on his face proclaimed. He held his chips in one hand, stacking and reorganizing them over and over.

"What's your name?" he asked.

"Who me?" Raymon looked up.

"Yeah you."

"I'm Ray. And you are?"

" Rob."

"Well Rob it's on you to call or fold." Raymon leaned back in his chair.

"I'm aware of that," said Rob. "What I'm wondering is, what makes a guy who just got some real money want to lose it all so fast."

"It will only cost you about fifteen million to find out." Raymon stared back at him.

"I'm a gambler."

"Yeah, we all see the hat." Raymon got jokes.

"But some bets are just dumb. I fold." Rob flipped over his cards and revealed the ace of diamonds and the four of diamonds.

Spectators around the table exhaled ohs and awes. Raymon tossed in his cards face down to the dealer and pulled in his winnings. Natasha stood behind him like a statue. She had to tell herself it was all right to breath. She knew Raymon wanted to gamble, but with two off-suited nines in his hand, she worried about his strategies to win.

"He had pocket aces," Rob announced.

The crowd grew larger. Men and women stood around the table with a mix of facial emotions. Hand after hand the game got more intense.

"Drinks for everyone," Raymon shouted after winning another large pot.

His gracious gesture received no applause, just odd stares and silent laughs. Natasha had to remind him that all drinks in the casino were already free. Honey lost a big portion of her chips on a second-best hand. When she looked at Raymon, he smiled back at her. "Nice try."

Chill Will came stumbling over broke after one too many drinks. He wanted to see what all the commotion was about. Rob played his cards close to his chest. He did his homework on Raymon and knew all about his new-found riches. He felt it was only a matter of time before he caught the reckless spender in a huge pot.

Raymon bet big on every flop. He pushed all in on his weakest hands and yet his aggressive style caused the other players to become cautious and thrown off on every turn. They folded rather than go pound for pound with the heavyweight at the table. Over two hours passed and it looked like Raymon couldn't lose. His fifteen million turned into twenty-eight million. And he was livid.

Onlookers were open-mouthed at what appeared to be his calm demeanor and relentless intuition. Natasha wondered how long he could continue to get away with his unorthodox play. He bet millions on lackluster hands and threw away high pairs. She scratched her head. And when she nudged him to call it a night, he waved her off.

Bigmack showed up with cake crumbs around his facial hairs. He stood behind Natasha and Benjamin right as the next hand was being dealt out. "What's going on?" he looked over their shoulders.

"Ray is up, Honey is down," said Benjamin.

Another hour crept past. Observers had come and left Raymon remained in his chair with Honey still seated across from him, hanging on to her last few chips. Five players turned into three. Raymon had already doubled his buy-in. He squirmed in his seat with frustration.

Honey's eyes widened when the flop revealed the ace of spades, the ace of hearts and the ten of diamonds. Worried about the hot-handed aggressive bettor, Rob checked to Raymon.

Raymon covered his cards with one hand and took a peek. He saw two clubs hidden beneath. The three of clubs and the five of clubs.

He looked around the table; his opponents showed signs of fatigue, then checked his watch and said, "It's getting late, so I guess I'll bet one million dollars."

"The bet is at one million," said the dealer.

Honey was aware of the pocket pair of tens sitting face down in front of her. Now or never, she convinced herself then threw her hair to one side and pushed for an all-in raise.

"The raise is two million dollars," the dealer confirmed.

Rob didn't hesitate to call the three-million-dollar bet. He was determined to send Raymon home busted or suffer the same fate.

I raise," said Raymon. "Twenty million more."

"Trying to protect your little lady friend I see." Rob laughed. "If you want to keep her safe, keep her in the house. I call!" He pushed in his chips.

The dealer reached for the turn card and flipped over the ten of spades. Silence fell over the table and all eyes and ears awaited the next move.

Rob had a serious look on his face. He had already lost millions chasing Raymon down to the river. He sat with no motions thinking his luck may have just changed. "I'm all in." He made his move.

The tension instantly increased. Bigmack crossed his arms and watched carefully. Honey leaned back in her chair. Chill Will had a frown on his face, while members of the audience covered their mouths and tightened their cheeks. Rob tugged at his cap with a confident look. He had thirty million, total, in the pot. The hush that consumed the arena made it hard to tell if anyone was breathing at all. Rob knew he made a gutsy play and while others held their breath, he was holding his nuts.

"This must be one of those dumb bets you spoke about." Raymon smiled. He could feel the eye beams cooking a hole in his back. He knew it was a bad call, and yet he felt relieved. "I call!"

The dealer turned the river card and all those watching exhaled so hard the table seemed to rattle. With all the chips on the table, Rob snatched off his head gear and stood to his feet. Honey stared at the table and saw the king of spades looking back at her.

The dealer looked to his left and Honey revealed her cards with a slight sigh. Then Rob slammed down a royal flush and shouted, "Yeah!" He gave out high fives to spectators and kissed an unprepared woman on the mouth. Cheers erupted around the table. "This is my house," Rob screamed.

It was the biggest pot of the night. Honey looked at Raymon with questions in her eyes. Natasha shook her head. Raymon stood up and removed his suit jacket from around his chair. He felt a pain in his stomach and looked for the exit. But before he could escape the judgmental glares, Rob reached over and flipped his cards.

With Raymon's hand exposed for all to see Rob pointed his finger and said, "Now that's a dumb bet."

Laughter ensued. Bigmack balled up his fist and leaned forward. Chill Will turned over his empty wine bottle and took a step back.

"Now you know that's not table etiquette." Raymon gave Rob an evil stare.

"Sorry man, I'm just having some fun." Rob laughed.

Raymon told himself to remain calm; he had to remind himself of the mission. He knew what he had to do, but he didn't like the thought of losing to an annoying creep like Rob.

Natasha hooked her arm around his and guided him away from the mocking faces and signifying tones, and the crew followed.

They reached the elevators and noticed strangers passing by holding their mouths and pointing. Honey lowered her eyebrows and sucked her teeth. "Bout to slap a fool."

Bigmack patted Raymon on the back, " Don't sweat them clowns."

"You should have punched that jerk in the face," said Chill Will.

"Then he would be in jail," Natasha responded.

"After losing all that money, somebody needs to be in jail." Chill Will took a sip from his cup.

Raymon thought about the night in reverse. He seemed to be the butt of the joke. He wanted to clarify his motives, but he knew the cost of that was too high. So he kept his

mouth shut and let the criticism fly. When he finally reached his deluxe presidential suite, he looked himself in the mirror attached to the wall and said, "Now that sucked."

A knock at the door pulled Honey's attention away from her computer screen. She walked barefoot across the marble floor, pressed her body against the door, and looked through the peephole. " Big money."

She opened the door and found Raymon leaning against the entrance. He stuck his head in, "Got company."

Honey tilted her head with a look of sarcasm on her face. Her silk gray teddy sparkled in the dim lighten. Her hair was in cornrows. Raymon looked down and admired her pedicured toes.

"What time is it?" Honey asked.

"About 4 a.m." Raymon smiled. "You going to let me in?"

Honey exhaled, then yielded by stepping to the side and allowing Raymon to enter her hotel room. "What's up?" she closed the door behind him.

"Just checking for intruders, mice, and other pesky vermin."

"Don't think just because I let you in that I'm a let you in."

"What! That never crossed my mind," Raymon lied. "I see you all cozy in here. Got your Facebook jumping."

Honey rushed back to her laptop. Her room had a white leather couch with a furry brown rug underneath it. Her artificial fireplace brought warmth to the front room area, and the smell of a Caribbean incense floated around the open space. She had a half-empty bottle of wine sitting on the rug next to her computer. She sat on the rug Indian style and placed her laptop on her lap. She noticed Raymon crash down on the sofa in front of her and questioned his intentions.

"Yeah, I'm still trying to get the hang of this social media thing," she said. "But for real, what you want?"

"Damn! I can't check on my artist."

Raymon rested his six-foot frame on the soft cushions. His dress shirt was halfway unbuttoned; it exposed his chest a bit. His diamond earrings looked like small stars in the poorly lit setting. Raymon pulled out his cell

115

phone and started swiping at the screen. "What you doing up this late anyways?" he asked.

"I'm updating my Instagram account. You the one who said I need to engage the fans more."

"Oh, okay. I thought you was Googling me again."

"What makes you think I haven't already?"

"Well, if you have, don't believe everything you read." Raymon laid his head back.

"So you wasn't given a fortune overnight?"

"You already knew that."

"So what are you saying?" Honey dug.

"I'm saying, you too fine to be so tough. That's what I'm saying."

His sudden show of fondness caught Honey off guard. She looked up and took note of the brown eyes staring back at her. The overly sized watch and expensive suit pants were too much, Honey thought. She shook her head and realized that his charm was liquor influenced.

" You gotta be tough in my world." She lowered her gaze.

"I get it. You think you the only one that had to put up walls to protect yourself. I didn't ask for all of this. I didn't ask for shit. Some old bastard had me dragged all the way to New York. He said he was my grandfather.

And surprise! He is dead. Just like my parents. Dude talked to me on a screen in post-mortem. With all his connections, he could have at least spoke to me when he was alive. I guess I was some kind of an embarrassment. The half-black grandson of a rich white tycoon. Shit, a few weeks ago, I was in a jail cell breaking up some Ramen noodles. And look where I'm at now. So trust me, I know all about walls."

"Why was you in jail?" Honey's interest grew.

"It was some bullshit. They gave me time for possession of some weed. That shit wasn't even mine."

"What do you mean?"

"I have known Bigmack since we were eleven. Mack was one hell of a football star until he blew out his knee. We met Chill Will in high school. He was hustling back then. He always had some tree on him. We were just kids, but we stuck together. Chill was always missing a few marbles, if you know what I mean. He would spend his money before he even got it. As we grew into adults, I would always look out for them. That's what good homies do. One day, Chill dropped off a black bag at the apartment I was staying at. We used to record music there so everyone had a key. But the spot was in my name. I didn't even know what was in the bag, well I kind of did, but not really, you know. Anyways, a few days passed, and one day I wake up to a police revolver in my face. I don't know what made them come there on that morning, but I was arrested. And snitching ain't an option when it comes to family. So I did the time."

"But you didn't do the crime."

"Of course not. But they going to find a way to put a black man in jail no matter what. Innocent or guilty." Raymon sat up.

"I didn't see that on Google." Honey smiled. Feeling like she may have been too quick to judge, Honey placed her computer on the floor and leaned back with her hands holding her up.

"My mother is big on helping other people," she said. "Every Sunday she volunteers at a shelter. She often says, you can't help everyone, but you can help someone. It's funny because, she doesn't believe in my music career. She won't lift a finger to help me achieve my goals, but she enjoys helping strangers." Honey stared into the air, not focused on any particular object, but fully present in her thoughts.

Raymon looked at her with new perspective. He could hear the hurt in her tone, feel passion in her heart, and see the desire in her eyes. *Can I trust her?* he thought.

"So how does it feel?" Honey asked.

"How does what feel?"

"How does it feel to have the power to change lives?"

"We all have the power to change lives." Raymon leaned back. "But first, we have to change ourselves."

"Okay Raymon Douglass." Honey laughed. "So you going to nut up and tell me the real reason you came knocking on my door at four in the morning?"

Raymon's face changed suddenly. He squinted his eyes, and his nose flared like he smelled a foul odor. "I still can't believe I let that homemade-hat wearing lame get my money." he admitted.

"Why did you call the bet?" Honey asked.

"I gotta play the game."

"You just threw all that money away."

"More risk, better the gain."

"What were you thinking?"

Raymon realized that he was about to break one of the many rules that would have left him broke and without a dime. He slapped himself on the cheek and stood up.

Honey closed her mouth, but in her head, she couldn't understand why someone would throw away all that money without a conscious.

"We had fun out here," Raymon changed the narrative. "But tomorrow it's back to work."

He made his way to the door with Honey hot on his heels. He fought the urge to say more. He wanted to tell her how beautiful she was, how warm he got when around her, but he knew it would only complicate things more than they already were.

Inches from the door, Raymon stopped and turned around. It was so sudden, Honey almost smashed into him. They stood in silence, almost face to face, only for a moment Raymon looked into her eyes and lost himself.

"I almost forgot," he managed to say while reaching into his pocket.

Honey looked down at the diamond flooded collar chain in his hand, and when Raymon tried to extend his arm, she pushed it back with her hand. "I can't."

"You earned it. Consider this a welcome-to-Raymon Records gift."

Honey tried not to laugh as Raymon placed the chain around her neck and sealed it closed.

"You throw money away, and buy expensive jewelry for others, but rent custom made clothes. I just don't get it," she said.

"What? All the ballers doing it. That's how the rich stay rich."

"I can't figure you out." Honey rubbed her new chain.

"Get some sleep."

"I'll sleep when I'm dead."

"You see, that's how I know you will make it with or without me."

"What does that mean?" Honey reached for the door handle.

Raymon took another look at her backside, then quickly straightened his eyes. He was growing feelings unexpected. He felt like a dog chasing a cat. Even if he caught her, he didn't know what would happen next. He was fully aware of the fallacy that claimed, business and

pleasure would not work. It formed in his brain. But he shook his head like a kindergartner who just got busted by his teacher. *I didn't do nothing.*

"Well thank you for the lovely visit." Honey gave her best British accent a try and opened the door.

"You know what, maybe I should stay the night just in case something happens," Raymon tried.

Honey gave him a light push in the back." Trust me, ain't nothing going to happen." She closed the door with a smirk on her face then pressed her back against it, feeling blandished.

That's cold, Raymon thought. But he was just warming up.

CHAPTER 10

Dec 5th-10th

Inside James Preacher's private office, Benjamin's face appeared on a sixty-inch flat screen. Michael Willard and Lisa Gains sat silently on a sofa, while James questioned his son.

"Are you telling me that over ten days this character has spent over one hundred million dollars. How could this have happened?"

"Well, he spent over fifty million in Vegas alone," Benjamin tried to explain.

"Has he purchased any assets?" Lisa asked.

"Not to my knowledge. He insists on renting almost everything. It's unheard of."

"I am looking over your numbers you sent us," Michael spoke up. "How does one spend twenty-five million on a skiing trip?"

"That skiing trip was in Andorra, sir." Benjamin cleared his throat.

"That is just ridiculous," said James. "How could you allow this to happen?"

"Mr. Raymon wants to do things his way. After all, it's his money."

Lisa gave James a stern look. The freckles on her face crashed into her nose as she fought to hold her tongue. James was aware of her stare. He paced back and forth over his expensive rug. When he looked at Lisa, she gave him a nod and he knew what needed to be done.

"Son, I'm going to tell you something of the utmost importance. This is completely confidential. You cannot utter a word of this to a single soul. Can I trust you son?"

"Yes, of course, Father."

"Welloff software is going under. All that we have built will no longer exist if and when this Raymon Platt goes broke."

"I don't understand." Benjamin shook his head.

"I know, son. So let me explain it to you. You cannot allow him to go broke. If he does, so do we. All the privileges you have been spoiled with will cease. You will be like a bum on the streets, without Daddy's connections to correct your screwups. Do you understand that? Can you see that cardboard box you will be forced to live in? Can you imagine having to see me and you mother ripped from our home and pushed onto welfare? Is that what you want?"

"No sir. But—"

"Then we must do all we can save our own lives, son."

"But how can we stop Mr. Raymon from spending his own money?" Benjamin asked.

"Well, my son, that's the billion-dollar question. These African black Americans waste millions on the dumbest of things. We are only trying to save him from himself," James lied. "But you cannot mention this to him or anyone of his home boys. There are stipulations in play that you need not know all about. But son, we cannot allow him to go broke. That money belongs to the Welloff family, and we cannot allow this outsider to destroy our lives."

Benjamin was pulled in. "What can I do to help?"

Michael sat up in his seat. He could see that James chose his words wisely. Benjamin was motivated and ready to please. "According to your numbers, Mr. Platt is spending a lot of resources on music equipment," said Michael.

"Yes! Mr. Raymon had built a massive recording studio in his suite at the Grand Dora Hotel. He's creating an album for his new artist Honey Drop English: music, videos, magazines spreads, interviews, you name it. Raymon Records is all in on this project. Not to mention the outrageous salaries he is handing out."

Benjamin sounded so excited, it vexed Lisa. She raised her voice. "Do you realize what is at stake here?"

Benjamin leaned back from the screen. He looked confused. He suddenly felt uncomfortable like a goldfish with a nosebleed in a tank with three sharks. A second passed, just enough time for him to gather his thoughts. He took a deep breath and said, "I understand."

"I truly hope you do, son. I am not impressed with your action thus far. I want you to continue to text me about this person's actions. I want to know what he is doing and who he

is doing it with. We cannot allow him to throw away our future. I need you to use your accountant skills and figure out a way to help this man save money, instead of losing it

at a foolish rate. Now make me proud." James hit a button and disconnected his skype.

The future of Welloff software depended on Raymon's inheritance falling into the right hands. Roger Bennet created a game that put all company employees at risk. And behind closed doors in a meeting only known of by four, the rules were just changed. A new piece was added to the chess board, strategic in nature. But there was only one problem. No one told Raymon.

Back in New York City, Raymon held a press conference outside of the Grand Dora. Honey stood on his right, wearing a mink full-length coat and icy jewelry.

Bigmack was behind the podium, addressing the crowd of reporters and the sea of microphones. "Her name is Ms. Honey Drop English, real name no gimmicks. And she is the first lady of Raymon Records, now known as the Double R."

"Where is she from?" a reporter asked.

"Is this a joke?" shouted another.

The questions came in rapid fire. Bigmack started to worry for his own safety. He thought he might be hit with tomatoes while he bobbed and weaved with his answers. Honey lowered her head. Her muscles tightened with anger while being called a fake Jo Lo by one reporter and a wanna be Rihanna by another.

Chill Will chuckled. "I told you."

The onslaught by the media was too much for Bigmack to handle. He stumbled over his own words and fell short of convincing even himself. When he looked over his shoulder at Raymon, he shrugged with panic in his eyes.

"Why should we even take this stunt serious?" asked one reporter.

"Because she is one serious artist." Raymon stepped onto the platform and grabbed the microphone. He put a hand on Bigmack's shoulder and relieved his sweating friend from further duty. Raymon's black three-piece suit matched his wrap-around shades. He held the microphone to his mouth and adjusted his blazer. "Is this thing on?"

"Mr. Platt, do you really think, just because you got rich overnight, that you can now create an overnight success?"

"Ms. Honey Drop English is no overnight success. She has been succeeding in this tough city her whole life," Raymon said.

"But you can't just put hot producers with some unknown artist and expect her to sell records," a reporter claimed.

"I'm not! What I'm doing is putting top talent with great producers to make great music. We already have DJ Khaled, Mike Will Made It, and the legendary Planet Pluto on the album. We have collabos with Bruno Mars, Drake, and The Weekend. Also, we have guest verses from the Migos, Big Sean, and Cardi B. The remix to our second single, "Taste of My Love", featuring Rihanna is tearing up the air waves as we speak. Honey Drop English is no fake. She is the real deal."

"Sounds like one expensive album," a voice shouted out.

Raymon looked behind him and saw Honey staring right at him. "Ladies and gentlemen," he faced the crowd, "is this not the big city of dreams? This young lady has something to say. And I feel blessed to be able to help her relay her message through the music. Our promotions may be over the top, but our goal is to see that she is heard. As for me supposedly throwing money around in order to sell records. You don't have to worry about that because I'm releasing the album for free. "

Question erupted simultaneously. They drowned out the honking car horns and charity bells ringing across the street. Raymon rubbed his palms together and took in the surprised reaction of all those in attendance.

"What is the album titled?"

"It's call 'Naughty or Nice'."

"When will it be released?"

"It will drop on Christmas morning."

"What genre of music is it?"

"We have created a Jazz and R and B soul sound mixed with Hip Hop and Pop."

"How did you meet her?"

"I guess you can say, we kind of bumped into each other." Raymon smiled. "We have a lot to do, so thank you for coming. Please follow the

Double R on social media sites and witness the making of a star!" Raymon dropped the mic and hustled off the podium with cameras flashing behind him. He walked over to Honey, put his arm around her shoulders, and smiled for the photos.

As he waved, Honey gave him a side eye. She was taken aback by Raymon's announcement. She never saw it coming and questioned his actions. She was confused. If Raymon planned on releasing her debut album for free, why wouldn't he have mentioned that to her, she wondered. Honey played the role and continued to smile. But behind her pearly whites was a breathing fire of uncertainties.

Chill Will made no effort to hide his frustrations. He tossed his champagne bottle to the side after hearing Raymon's plans. There were reporters everywhere. The news had caused such an uproar that no one noticed the grown man stomping his feet and cussing in the corner. Chill Will tried to gather himself. Ray must have a bigger plan, he thought.

Then he broke out in a light jog to catch up with them. He had to hear about this new plan, and now. They retreated inside the hotel lobby, where Benjamin appeared with a briefcase in hand. "I have taken the pleasure of preparing your transportation for the day, sir," he said.

"That's all right Benji, we got a ride ready." Raymon shot passed him and onto the elevator.

"But Mr. Raymon, it is much cheaper this way," Benjamin tried.

"Hey Ray," we need to talk." Chill Will caught up. "You gotta slow down with this spending. We came from nothing, now you wasting big faces like you forgot that. Why the hell would you put all this time and money into an album you talking about giving away for free? We gotta make money, brah, not waste it! Listen, let me talk to a few people. A album like this, we can sell the rights to it for a flat fee and get paid. I heard of this public relations attorney that we can hire to clean this mess up. We will get our money back and more. What you say?"

Honey looked at Raymon in suspense as they all road up the crane.

"Ain't nothing cheap about Raymon Platt Jr." Raymon stepped through the open doors and onto his floor. That's the problem, you all thinking small. This is big business and there's only one way to do big business. So get with it, or get out of the way. I got Kanye West meeting us at the video shoot in New Jersey. Then we headed to Connecticut to do First Take with Steven A. Smith. Tell Natasha to book us some reservations, we going out to eat tonight. And forget about that attorney selling the rights to the album nonsense. We doing just fine. Get your head in the game, Chill. I know what 'm doing."

Raymon was ranting on the move. They entered his suite and followed him to the balcony doors. Before Chill Will could rebut, he slid back the door and a gust of wind poured in.

A helicopter awaited. They ran towards its open side door with their backs bent forward like they were creeping out of town. Honey had to hold her oversized hat to her head, just to prevent from losing it to the sky. Raymon lifted her aboard, then pulled himself up. Benjamin followed behind him. But when he tried to reach for Chill Will's hand, Raymon stopped him.

"I need you to stay here, and hold it down," Raymon shouted.

Chill Will's eyes grew and his shoulders dropped. He had no choice but to watch Raymon slide the helicopter doors closed. Benjamin shook his head in silent disapproval. Then Chill Will took a dozen steps backwards as the aircraft lifted off the roof. He reached for his cell phone, quickly dialed a number, and held the phone out in front of him. "We got a big problem," he said. "Yeah, he is getting out of control. We have to do something."

The helicopter flew high above the city at a swift speed. Raymon had on an oversized pair of headphones. He looked at Honey wearing a similar pair and gave her a thumbs up. Twenty minutes later, they landed in an open airfield. When the red bottoms of Honey's shoes hit the ground, she saw the fleet of luxurious vehicles lined up on the runway.

"Can you drive?" Raymon stepped up beside her.

Benjamin couldn't believe his eyes. He jumped down from the aircraft and stood in amazement. "You did it," he managed to say. "You found every last one of them."

The all white Koenigsegg Regera looked like a spaceship on wheels. A tall red Ferrari LaFerrari Aperta was parked next to it. A tall man with an Italian accent stood beside a Bugatti Chiron worth 2.9 million, smiling and hugging his full-length peacoat to his body. He explained the difficulties he had transporting the McLaren pl LM from Paris and the Pagani Huayna BC from France.

Honey ran her hand over the hood of the black Aston Martin Valkyrie. When she asked how much it cost, the Italian dealer pulled out a tablet, punched in a few keys and said, "Three million American dollars."

Benjamin was impressed, but he told himself to act natural. He was supposed to help Raymon spend less, not encourage his reckless squandering. He watched Raymon seated in the cockpit of the three-million-dollar Lamborghini Veneto, like he belonged there. And he lost himself. Benjamin ran to the Lykan Hyper sport with his mouth wide open and his heart racing. When he hit the ignition, the engine purred like a curious lion.

Raymon rolled down his windows and motioned Honey to do the same. When he saw the whites in her eyes he said, "Follow me. And try to keep up."

The Lamborghini handled the city terrain like roller skates on a fresh waxed marble. Honey played with the powerful Aston Martin. She swung in and out of lanes like Danica Patrick.

Benjamin remained careful behind the wheel of the 3.4-million-dollar Hyper sport. He tried to stay close, while watching Raymon and Honey race across the GWB bridge. "This is great." He smiled.

They reached Newark, New Jersey in record-setting time. The three cars pulled into a large warehouse. When they parked their rides, they slid out with sounds of laughter and joy. The warehouse was full of workers. Light equipment was being carried by a group of men. A camera crew was setting up tripods and opening boxes. Security personal hustled left and right with flashlights on their hips. A young woman greeted Raymon with a hug, then handed him a clipboard. The video for Arrive was filmed, with exotic animals, birds, and fruits. A street scene constructed using a green screen with skyscrapers in the background. Honey had to go through numerous wardrobe changes for eight different scenes and four different videos. The backgrounds were changed over and over throughout a course of hours. Special guests came and went, and when everyone was ordered to take a thirty-minute break, no one was more thankful than Honey.

After hours of shootings, she had to rub her feet to relieve the strain. When an assistant offered to help, she respectfully denied her services. Honey watched men and women hovering over Raymon from afar. She noticed Benjamin texting in a corner; he seemed more focused on his phone than being surrounded by half-naked women and workers aimed to please. She thought about how much all this most have cost. Then realized she couldn't even fathom. Honey watched animal trainers secure cages and waitresses pass out drinks. Who was Benjamin texting all this time? She stared. Then like a sign on a wall, she was reminded of her mother and siblings. She wondered what they were doing. She hadn't called or texted them all day. Her mother was equally happy and surprised to hear Honey's voice on the radios. She told Honey to be smart. And Honey measured her mother's worries about a corrupt industry, one that destroys lives and hurts families. She tried to shake off the feeling, but it sat on her chest. There she was, surrounded by a cortege while her family remained in a crammed apartment in Harlem. At that moment, a young man wearing a tight short-sleeved shirt approached her and offered her some grapes. "I'm

fine." Honey waved him off.

But that wasn't truth. Honey felt guilt growing in her stomach. She was

being overwhelmed with what she saw as unnecessary favor. It hit her like

a hundred pounds of pleasure to the head. She looked toward Raymon, but

he was taking numbers and signing autographs. So she stood to her feet,

wrapped her silk robe around the sexy get-up she wore underneath, and

walked off the set. She sat in front of a vanity, staring at herself in the

mirror. She could barely recognize the face looking back at her. *What am I*

doing here? She looked away. *What's wrong with you?* she thought. The

self-questions continued to pour in. But the true answers she would have

to wait for.

Chapter 11

CRYSTALS was New York City's finest restaurant. Available tables were auctioned off online, rather than offered at the door. Crowds stood out front, looking in the large windows just to steal a peek at the privileged.

When Raymon rejoined his entourage seated around their combined tables, draped with white covers, he said, "They got baby wipes in the stole."

Bright lights shined down on them. Crystal chandeliers chimed. A small orchestra played a symphony over the sounds of champagne glasses crashing and silverware bumping. The smell of cooked vegetables, streamed rice, baked fish, and warm loaves traveled across the room. Raymon took his seat and a waiter quickly tucked a handkerchief around his collar. "Thank you very much." He smiled, then picked up his fork and knife and sliced through a T-bone steak.

The table was covered with a variety of meals: Lobster tails, mashed potatoes, macaroni and cheese, chicken and shrimp soups, steamed broccoli, spaghetti, cheesecakes, pies, exotic salads, and seafood dished. A dozen bottles of wine were situated around the table for easy access.

Honey sat at the tail of the table. She wore an expensive dress with peek-a-boo shoulders. She leaned her head back and bit into a gigantic burger, then wiped the side of her mouth with her hand. Bigmack wasted no time. He was on his third dish already, tearing through crab legs and chasing the cold meat with hot French fries. Natasha was baby-sitting her glass of liquor. She picked at the cooked eel on her plate like she didn't know how to eat it. Chill Will and Benjamin enjoyed their deserts. They took turns tasting the varieties of flavors laid out for them.

"Waiter!" Raymon raised his hand. "Waiter, I need a portion of each one of these meals, including the sweets. Pack em in doggy bags and bring them to the black party van parked out front."

"What are you doing Ray?" asked Chill Will.

"Fancy pants got a try this food. It's great!"

"Now this is real eating," Bigmack said with his mouth full.

Natasha cringed. "You all are going to eat yourselves sick."

The men shared a laugh, then Raymon asked, "What's your story Tasha?"

"Who me?" She looked up with her chinky eyes and cleared her throat. "My story, I don't really have one. I'm just on my journey like everyone here, just trying to become the best version of myself. Seeing that I have had my hair dyed almost every color in the rainbow in a matter of weeks," she cut her eyes at Raymon, "I think I'm getting there one step at a time."

"How you get into writing?" Raymon asked.

"I graduated from Hampton University with a degree in journalism, moved back home and became a beat writer before getting a gig at Channel 6. So, I guess I have always been some kind of a writer."

"And home is New York," Chill Will said.

"Yeah, I'm from Yonkers."

"How did you get a job at a news station so fast?"

"Let's just say I was hungry."

"With that little frame, girl, you still look hungry," Chill Will joked.

"Shut up! All you do is drink," Natasha fired back. "Don't worry about my eating habits."

"I'm just saying. You wavy and all that. But I need my lady to have a fat olé ass and some meat on her bones." Chill Will enjoyed his own humor.

"Fall back," Raymon said. "Stop being so rude and show some class, homie. By the way Tasha, your hair looks great."

Natasha felt on her bangs hanging right above her eyebrows. Her hair was even cut in a blondish brown hue.

"What do you know about the Welloff Corporation?" Raymon pulled off his handkerchief.

"I know they are going under," Natasha said.

"That's not true," Benjamin lied and choked on is beverage.

"Yes, it is. I have been working on this story for over a year and their monthly reports keep dropping. Sometimes they just come up missing, all together."

"Where did you get this nonsense?" Benjamin took another drink.

"I told you. My reports over the last year," Natasha defended her work.

"That's dumb. I mean, that's not accurate. Those reports are too young to show a real return on investments. I can assure you, Welloff software is doing just fine."

"Then explain the losses in finances and the shareholders backing out." Natasha sat back in her chair and folded her arms.

"What losses? What you call losses, we call risk gain. Anyone in business knows the more risk the bigger the reward."

"Now I can relate to that," Raymon jumped in.

It was like the elephant in the room shouted, "Hey look at me." Raymon had ten eager eyes staring right at him, ready to pounce. Seeing his mistake, he lifted his glass in an attempt to make a toast. But the door was already open, leading to a conversation he would have rather avoided.

Chill Will attacked first. "Real talk, homie, you doing the most. You getting crazy with the spending habits. We got to make investments, use money to make money. Not waste it!"

"Honestly speaking," Natasha said. "I have never witnessed anyone spending dough the way you do."

"There are some better moves we could be making," Bigmack added.

Honey was stingy with her words all night, like she had something else on her mind. "I have to agree, you are doing too much," she said.

"Okay, I get it." Raymon leaned back. "You all don't think I know what I'm doing."

"Look at it like this," Benjamin used his Harvard twang. "You could invest a nice sum of money in a bank, for instance, gain interest, and still live the kind of lifestyle you choose."

"This is what I'm saying," Chill Will raised his voice. "You renting shit when buying it is cheaper. You wasting money on flights to places we can drive to, parties we don't need to have, and a damn album you talking about giving away for free. Come on, homie! I'm your partner. We need to do right, invest some real money into condos and buildings. I mean, look how far we have come. I can't just sit back and watch you fuck it all up."

"That's funny." Raymon smiled. "Me fuck it all up. Don't forget who is the real fuck up at this table, brah. Thirteen months for your stupidity, you remember that?"

Raymon and Chill Will shared a long silent aggressive stare.

"Y'all chill out." Bigmack waved a drumstick. "Let's just do the math. Hey Benjamin buttons over there, as to wins and losses, what is my homie's financial state?"

"Financially, Mr. Raymon is losing money at a rapid speed," said Benjamin.

Chill Will threw up a hand. "You see."

"If you don't start to see some quality returns on your investments, and I mean soon, you will have lost over a quarter of your total inheritance in a few weeks. And believe me when I say, that's not good." Benjamin shook his head.

"Maybe we could do a listening party, and charge at the door." Honey spoke up.

"She does have a brain." Chill Will smiled.

Honey shot him a look but decided not to entertain his foolishness. Then she focused her eyes on Raymon. "I just don't want you to lose no more money over me."

"Y'all too much." Raymon laughed and tried to hide the truth. "We are good. I know what I'm doing. Just sit back and enjoy the ride. We got this. The world is ours and all that good stuff."

"You know what they say, never go MC Hammer," Chill Will said.

"MC Hammer," Bigmack scratched his head. "Don 't you mean Eric Benet?"

"What's the difference? They both got screwed." Chill Will lifted his glass.

Raymon felt a tap on his shoulder and turned around.

"Excuse me, are you the Raymon Platt?" the stranger asked.

"Well, yes I am." Raymon picked up his cloth to wipe his mouth.

"I'm sorry to bother you like this. I'm in the shipping business and I was wondering if I could have a word with you."

"Can't you see we are trying to enjoy our meal," Chill Will snarled at the man.

"Yeah man. beat it," Bigmack said.

The middle-aged man straightened his back, lowered his head, and started to turn away when Raymon pulled his arm. "Hold on now, my colleagues can be a little rude at times, but they are harmless. What would you like to talk about?"

"Import, export," the man answered vigorously. "All I need is a small investment. I have a few hundred animal vending machines ready to be shipped in from China right now."

"Animal what?" Chill Will shouted.

"Animal vending machines. They are the next big thing. I just know it."

The table shook with laughter. Raymon looked at his crew, raised his eyebrows, and said, "You all said I should invest more."

"Come on dog, not in this." Bigmack straightened his face. "This fool trying to play you."

"This is crazy." Chill Will slammed his palms on the table. "Animal vending machines, really! The damn animals going to be dead before they even get here. It's a waste of money, Ray. And a waste of our time."

Raymon ignored his naysayers and listened carefully as the man explained their future partnership. He took the stranger's business card and agreed to a verbal contract worth eight figures. Word traveled fast, throughout the restaurant. Raymon Platt Jr. was sweeter than a honey-melted-ice-tea Sunday. As soon as the animal vendor walked away, another scamster parked his chair next to his.

The late-night feast turned into an open invitation for would-be entrepreneurs and enthusiasts to shake hands with the copious billionaire. Raymon had Natasha take down names and contact information, while Chill Will balled his face up at the crowd of strangers forming around the table. Bigmack couldn't figure out what was going on inside Raymon's head. To even entertain the zany ideas and foolish proposals filling up his ears was insane.

Raymon stood to his feet surrounded by men and women, all speaking at once like they were at a stock exchange on Wall Street. He made his way to the exit, smiling and shaking hands.

Someone called out, "Raymon Platt for mayor!"

Raymon laughed and held up his hand in the middle of the melee. Then he stopped and waved for his team to catch up. Honey slid passed him, put on her mink coat, and watched carefully. Raymon stepped onto the sidewalk with a smile on his face. Cheers followed him, mostly due to the fact that he offered to pay for every meal ordered on the night.

As he soaked himself in the admiration of others, Benjamin paid the bill with a heavy head.

Raymon pumped his fist in the air and said good night. But before he could make it inside the warm vehicle parked by the curb, he felt a strong pull on his arm. "Help me," a sickly man wearing a worn-down sweater and dirty hoody said.

Raymon could see the desperation in the man's eyes. His coat looked like he had found it in an oil field, his face was filthy, and when he spoke, his teeth looked like a block of cheese. When Raymon removed the man's hand, he could feel it shaking from the cold air.

"Help me," he repeated.

Raymon reached into his pocket. He could feel a fist full of money. He noticed Benjamin walking up behind, staring at him with those blue eyes. Then he heard his grandfather's voice in his head, with power comes ruthlessness, and he paused. He looked at the beggar and turned his back.

Honey stood frozen. Her eyes followed Raymon into the van. She looked to the beggar with sadness in her heart and reached inside her leather purse to pulled out a hundred-dollar bill. A minute later she sat inside the party van, positioned on its heated seats, feeling upset and confused. She did not utter a single word. And when they arrived back at the Grand Dora, Honey felt she was altogether in the wrong place.

Chapter 12

The four Cs of a quality diamond were explained to Raymon, reclined in his office chair. The Cut is based on how it looks to the eye. The table cut is an ideal cut; light shoots down and back up through the precious jewel. Clarity determines the number of inclusions and blemishes that can or cannot be detected. From flawless to eye visible inclusions, the value of a stone is set extremely high or affordably low. The Color is given a class from A-Z; clear colorless diamonds are normally the most expensive, but S Class yellow rocks have an eccentric following. The Carat is the measurement of how much a diamond weighs. Needless to say, the bigger the better.

Raymon closed one eye and looked through a magnifying glass at the flawless 15-carat diamond in his hand. He placed it on a black cloth covering his desk and chose another from the extensive collection. The medallion hanging from his platinum chain crashed onto the desk when he leaned forward.

Chill Will sat on a sofa in the corner of the office with one leg hanging over the arm of the couch. He thought about ways to stop Raymon from spending so unconsciously. He knew he wouldn't listen to reason. Tried that. Every attempt was for naught. He sat pondering a new angle.

Then Natasha hurried across the gray carpet, placed some forms in front of Raymon and handed him a pen.

"What is this?" Raymon snatched the pen.

"It's the insurance forms for the diamonds."

"Why do you have two forms?"

"You still haven't chosen which set of diamonds you want. This one is for the H-class diamonds with the table cuts, and this one is for the more expensive A-class flawless ones. I stress more expensive, but I have a feeling that doesn't move you," Natasha said.

"And you would be right." Raymon laughed. "We do everything big here. Give Benji a copy of the signed form and tell him to shred the other one."

"Anything else?"

"Yeah! What's up with your nails?"

"My nails," Natasha pulled her hand back.

"We have to look professional at all times, Tasha. That means, look our best. So, hit up the nail shop downstairs and have them bill me."

Natasha snatched up the forms, looked at her nails, and stormed out of the office with a huff.

"We need more promotion," Raymon shouted.

"The Internet is giving us all the promotion we need," said Chill Will. "What you need, is to be easy with all this over-the-top. We do everything big bullshit."

"We got fifteen days until the album drops."

"You talking about the album we giving away for free? That album?"

"I know you can't understand my moves right now, but trust that I'm the same dude I have always been."

"I hear you." Chill Will sat up. "But that silk dress shirt you got on is really loud. You feel me? Tell me this, what is the point of coming up, and you can't even impact other people's lives?"

Raymon gave a fake laugh and leaned back in his chair. "You really don't understand."

"Understand what? Help me understand because I just don't get it."

Natasha returned with her phone pressed up against her ear. Raymon felt relieved and used the distraction to escape Chill Will's snare.

"What's up?" said Raymon.

"Someone has been calling all day from a correction institution," Natasha explained. "I ignored them the first twenty times, then I recalled you telling me to accept all collect calls."

Raymon took the phone and smiled. When he put it to his ear, he saw Chill Will pouring himself a glass of liquor, out the side of his eye.

"Who dis?" Raymon asked. "What up, Remix! You get them magazines I ordered you and the fellas? Good good."

Raymon laughed and shouted into his phone. He pretended not to notice when Chill Will left the room mumbling something about knowing how to get money. Remix told Raymon about his bond hearing. He said $50,000 would make him a free man. Raymon asked about the other inmates and explained the lavish lifestyle he was now living. Remix was excited. He didn't believe a word about Victoria and asked to speak to her himself. When Raymon put him on speaker phone, Remix asked question after question and listened carefully as the voice gave him the proper responses.

"With that type of money, you could bond the whole jail out," said Remix.

But Raymon had to play by the rules. He listened to his incarcerated friend with one ear and heard negative talk about his actions in the other room. He wanted to help, but it wouldn't be possible until he completed his task.

"I got you," Raymon repeated over and over as the phone call was reaching its end. He stared at the wall thinking about Remix's fate. He suddenly felt a heavy burden collapse on his back. And with no one to counsel him, Raymon thought the only thing he could do was finish the game.

He jumped up with the phone still in his hand, rushed out of his office and into the front room. "Listen up," he yelled. "We have two weeks to complete this damn album. No more play play. This is serious business. I want more promotion! I don't care if we have to drop a bag off at every radio station in this city, I want promotion, promotion and more promotion."

"Arrived is getting crazy spins on power 105 right now," said an unfamiliar face.

"Who are you?"

"Lily. You hired me a week ago for the album artwork."

" And how much am I paying you for that?"

She smiled. "You said you would give me $1,000 an hour."

"And are you finished yet?"

"No. But I will be in a day or two."

"You see. This is what I'm talking about. You lack motivation. You should have been finished. You up in my spot drinking my drink and eating what you want. I gave everyone that works for me their own rooms, their own space, and this is what I get. I am now paying you $5,000 an hour to get the job done."

"Yes sir." She smiled and walked off.

Bigmack showed up. "Slow down, dogg. Paying these creeps more money will just make them work slower than they already are."

"Where you been? Just worry about your own job," Raymon snapped. "And where is Honey? We got work to do. I need two videos for each song on the album. Si-mon! Get Honey Drop. Tell her she is needed asap. Tasha! Where is Natasha?"

"Ray, calm down, dogg. What's gotten into you?"

"I don't need to calm down. What I need is some loyal, competent men and woman around, so that we can get the bag. You want that bag? How about you, you want that bag?" Raymon pointed at random engineers. "Who trying to get money? I'm giving you a raise. Everybody gets a raise! Now I want them twitter fingers moving, recording gear shining, masters printed up, drinks flowing, and them songs ready to knock. I want the best work, from the best people for the best price. And I want it now. I'm talking, over the top promotions and the Double R smoking. Can you handle that?"

He looked around the room, and all eyes were staring at him. No one said a word, then heads began to nod slowly in agreement. Raymon clapped his hands, and workers scattered in different directions. Bigmack stood there with his hands on his waist and his head low, tossing it side to side.

"What I tell you?" Chill Will stepped up beside him.

"What's up with him?" said Bigmack.

"I don't know, but we have to do something, brah."

"You sure this is legit?"

"My guy is the best. We got a handle this business. Stop being so scary." Chill Will nudged him.

Bigmack watched Raymon head back to his office and thought, *Maybe Chill Will is right for once.*

Si-mon flew right past them as they were leaving the suite. He rushed through the living room and right into Raymon's office." She is gone." He took deep breaths.

"What do you mean she's gone?" Raymon questioned.

" I cannot find her. I am very sorry."

"She must be somewhere. Did you ask her door man?"

"Yes sir. I asked her door man, maid services, and I even had security check the cameras to see if she was in the building, the shopping mall or lounge."

"She couldn't have just disappeared." Raymon leaned against his desk. "Victoria! Dial Ms. Honey Drop English."

"Dialing ..."

But there was no answer.

"Victoria! Dial Fancy Pants," Raymon tried.

"Dialing ..."

"Hello sir," Planes answered.

"What's up Fancy Pants? We having a little problem up here. We can't seem to find our lovely artist, Ms. Honey Drop. I'm calling to see if you can help us out," said Raymon.

"Why of course sir. Ms. English asked me to give her a lift first thing this morning."

"A lift to where?"

"I do believe that I do not know sir."

"Come on Fancy Pants, we don't have time for this. Are you telling me you don't know where you took her?"

"No sir, that is not what I am telling you."

Raymon looked at Si-mon with a long face. "Seriously! Then what are you saying?" Raymon asked.

"I'm saying that Ms. English asked me to drop her off at a location unfamiliar to myself, and I did as she asked."

"Do you think you could take me to this location?"

"I believe so, sir."

"NO. Better yet," Raymon hesitated. "Which car did you drive her in?"

"I made use of the Rolls Royce, sir."

"That's perfect. No worries, I will use the GPS and locate the spot. Enjoy your room Fancy Pants. I'll take care of this."

Raymon could hear the water splashes in the background. He disconnected the call, grabbed his jacket, handed Si-mon a roll of money, and headed for the elevator.

Thirty minutes later his chrome wheels slid through Brooklyn like a fancy sled. Snowfall covered the streets and began to stick. He paused at a red light and marveled over the corners full of culture: concrete walls painted with urban arts, homemade drum sets, a young boy dribbling a basketball trying to control its awkward bounce, street lights struggling to reach full power, a Bodega with flyers and food ads covering its windows, a small crew of men maneuvering past the sidewalk with their eyes locked on their cell phones, and a group of girls standing at a hot dog stand, biting into their smoking buns. *This is living.* Raymon smiled behind the tinted-glass windows.

When he reached the mapped location, he parallel parked and stepped out the ride. He pulled his Navy-blue coat closer, wrapping himself in it like a burrito. The leather shoes on his feet found the sidewalk and he looked up. The building in front of him had a sign above the door that read: Food, clothing, and shelter.

When he entered, the sounds of an infant crying leaked out the door. The weak lights made it seem like there were a thousand shadows moving about in the open space. Raymon teetered. He felt like he might have entered the wrong place. The smell of fried chicken pulled him in for a closer look. He saw an old man bunched in a corner, holding a Styrofoam plate. A woman sat on top of a cafeteria table breast feeding a baby in her lap. Raymon looked at the quarter-million-dollar watch on his wrist and exhaled. There was a line of people formed in the back of the room. He walked over and noticed multiple tables joined together, with people wearing white aprons standing on the other side serving foods.

He shifted his head - and tried to get a clear view. At first he thought his eyes were deceiving him. Then he felt relieved and hurried his step.

"I'll take a double burger with cheese." He bumped into the middle table.

No one laughed. Instead, Raymon had a few dozen eyeballs looking at him like he was lost.

Honey looked up and found him smiling like a big kid. "What are you doing here?" She continued to place chicken sticks on each plate that passed.

"I was going to ask you the same."

"My mother needs my help. Do you even know what that is?"

"What is that supposed to mean?" Raymon lost his smile.

"Nothing," Honey shook her head. "Just leave."

"Well, we have a deadline and appointments with some powerful people in the industry. Not to mention some more video shoots."

"Everything ain't about you. Why can't you understand that? And I ain't doing no more video shoots."

Raymon felt the room go silent. It seemed like all ears were tuned in, waiting for his response. "Did I miss something?" he asked. "Trust me, I get it. But what you don't seem to understand is that your music helps people, Honey."

"You mean your music," Honey said. "I never asked for this."

"Que pasa?" Honey's mother put her hand on her daughter's shoulder.

"Nada mami," said Honey.

"Quien es?"

"Mi hefe."

"El hefe," Honey's mother shouted, and blew kisses.

Honey shook her head, pulled off her apron and gloves, and made her way around the table. She grabbed Raymon by the arm. "Come on."

As she pulled him away, Raymon looked over his shoulder and waved at the smiling ladies. When they reach outside, Raymon asked, "Who was that?"

"That was my mother," Honey said with her hands on her head. "What do you want?"

"I want you. I mean, I came to get you." Raymon stumbled with his words. "Your ride is here," he pointed to the Phantom.

Honey look around, took a deep breath and said, "Look Ray, I don't think this whole superstar make-over thing is for me. You come down here, in the slums where people are struggling to eat, in a half-a-million-dollar car. I get it! You came up, but there are still a lot of people who are not that fortunate, and they need real help, in real time."

"You wanna see real time," Raymon pulled up his sleeve.

Honey turned her head with a disgusted look on her face.

"Okay, that wasn't funny," Raymon said. "I see you being real and that's why I chose you. You from the struggle, but so am I. I can see the hurt in your eyes when you see others struggling, and that's deep. That's what makes you special. I want to help people. I want to help you. Don't tell me you don't want this. I can see the hunger in your eyes. You that same girl out on Thanksgiving Eve, pushing CDs. But if you really want to help others in this world, the first thing you have to do is help yourself."

"I got a family to feed, two brothers one sister. You just don't get it." Honey lowered her head.

"You got me out here in the cold, telling me I don't get it. No, you don't get it. You the one with the talent. You got the skills to make a difference, and all I'm trying to do is record that gift, make hits so the whole world can feel it. Yeah, I got lucky, left me some bread. But I gotta follow the rules just to get paid. I would rather have my parents. But ain't no amount of money going to bring them back. I see people starving, you think I don't want to throw them a bone? I do! But there's rules to the game and I..."

Raymon caught himself. He put his hands on his face and turned away. He paced back in forth like an angry boxer. When he looked up, Honey was staring at him with her heart.

Her lips looked softer than grapes. She looked him in the eyes and waited for him to continue, but he didn't. Raymon felt a fire in his chest. He imagined himself screaming into the streets, melting the icy tips and warming the hearts of the poor. But instead, he bit his tongue and remembered the cost.

Honey straightened her head and allowed her eyes to meet his. She knew that she had a passion for music and a thirst for success. Raymon's arrogant spending made her irate, but she wanted to believe there was more to him. She found truth in his words and felt connected to him in a way. He looked lost in a new world, unfamiliar with his surroundings. In that moment she thought, maybe they could help each other. "What do you want from me?" she asked.

" I just want to see you become, the best version of yourself." Raymon stepped closer.

"We still have a lot of work to do inside."

"I understand completely."

"So, when I'm done then."

"That's cool. Take your time. I'll tell all them famous over-charging producers who are waiting to hold up, Y'all gotta wait. My girl Honey Drop is passing out plates right now, and she say everybody going to eat!" Raymon put some bass in his voice to add effect.

"You do that. It ain't like you can't afford it." Honey smiled and walked away. Her blue jeans looked like they were painted on her legs. She peeked over her shoulder and caught Raymon with his eyes down.

"Nice jay's," he lied.

"I gotta go." Honey reached for the door. Her smile was so bright, it could have melted all the snow on the corner. She had her hair pulled back in a ponytail.

Raymon wanted another look at her tantalizing eyes. "Don't forget this," he tossed his car key in the air. "Bring Moms, the two brothers, and sister you mentioned to the hotel. I think we got room for them." He smiled. "And tell Moms I said nice seeing her."

Honey looked at the electronic triangle and said, "What about you?"

"I think I will go for a stroll. See you tonight, Ms. Honey Drop."

"A stroll. Okay, but this is Brooklyn. You might want a hide that watch," Honey yelled as Raymon headed down the block.

An hour later, Raymon stopped and looked behind himself in amazement. How far had he walked? He'd lost track of time. He was so deep in thought he forgot his true destination. Surrounded in doubt, he thought of new ways to waste his wealth without breaking one of the rules set on his mission to blow 500 million and gain 2.5 billion. *How stupid,* he thought. He shook his head at the sight of hungry faces living on the streets. He felt the weight of his burdens lay on his conscious. In a flash, he saw his parents' faces staring at him. They smiled. Raymon blinked hard and threw his head side to side. He couldn't understand where the image came from. He never saw his parents as an adult. He was told they died in a plane crash. A lightbulb formed and he remembered the photograph he was given as a child in foster care. They were surrounded by trees in the photo. His mother pressed her cheek up against his dark-skinned father's. They looked happy and proud. Raymon wondered why the memory was so clear to him after being so long forgotten. When he looked up from his woolgathering, he saw TV screens inside a local pawn shop looking back at him. He focused on the words running across the screens: Gangster Rapper faces life sentence for felony charges.

Raymon stepped up closer to the plexiglass and saw the image of a young black man being escorted from court by police officers on both sides. The subtitles seemed to jump off the screen: When you a real Nigga, they never trying to see you come up. Now get that fu#%&$# camera out my face.

The man spit saliva all over the camera lens. Then a reporter stepped in front of it. "Rapper Manhood, known for his gangster lyrics and political views, will now have to serve real time in prison for racketeering charges and possession of illegal weapons. An appeal bond has been set today at ten million dollars. Seems like this rapper isn't going anywhere anytime soon."

Raymon put his hand on his chin, turned to face the street, and hailed a cab. He sat in the back seat with new direction and ambition. He pulled out his phone, hit speed dial, and said, "Benji, meet me at the police station." Shit just got real.

Chapter 13

At the Grand Dora, inside the open bar area, little attention was given to the well-dressed man seated alone. He took sips from his glass and scanned his surroundings. The Patek Philip on his wrist read 2 p.m. He tapped his foot on the floor in a steady pace while turning his head every which way. Finally, he spotted Chill Will and Bigmack standing at the entrance. When their eyes met, he waved them over to the bar. They claimed a stool on each side of him and shook hands. Chill Will introduced the Caucasian man to Bigmack as Brad from downtown.

Brad got straight down to business. "You can't steal second base and keep one foot on first."

Bigmack listened carefully, while a hotel guest played the piano in the background. The aroma of honey barbecue wings roasting over the counter seemed too much for him to ignore. He interrupted Brad's pitch to order a plate.

"This is serious business," Brad explained, then recited his occupation and qualifications. The diamonds in his pinkie ring lit up like fireflies. He talked, using his hands to illustrate each sentence.

Chill Will nodded his head in agreement like a member of the church listening to a Sunday service sermon.

Bigmack shoved food in his mouth, licked his fingers and asked, "What is it going to cost us?"

"That depends. You want a big win, or you want to win small?" Brad said with an accent.

Bigmack looked at Chill Will. He wondered where the two of them could have met, was it legal, and if so, should he trust Brad from downtown? He wanted to speculate deeper, but Chill Will jumped to an agreement so fast it left him stuck. Brad stood to his feet, snatched an envelope from Chill Will's hand, nodded his head, and disappeared just as mysteriously as he arrived.

Chill Will ordered two drinks, feeling good about himself.

Bigmack sat with a blank look on his face. Ice cubes rattled in the glass after Chill Will drowned himself with liquor. A moment of silence passed, then Bigmack stood up and looked around. He had his eyes focused on the entrance way. He looked at Chill Will with concern on his face. "What the hell you got us into now?"

Benjamin scratched his head in a confused state while James stacked questions on top of questions. "Has he purchased any properties, or taken ownership of any assets? Has he spoken to anyone about the conditions of his inheritance? Has he given any funds away in exchange for nothing in return, work favor or otherwise?"

"No, I do not believe so." Benjamin spoke into his phone.

His hesitation frustrated James immensely. He sat up in his office chair, stared at the screen on his phone, and shouted, "Do you understand what is at stake here, son?"

"I have been asked this same question numerous times and I guess the true answer is, no I do not understand all that is going on." Benjamin was becoming irritated. "This whole thing doesn't make sense. You asked me to see to it that Ray doesn't go broke. To help him save more and spend less. Then you tell me that he cannot have any assets, which doesn't make sense at all. Something isn't adding up, and you keeping me in the dark hurts my chances of helping. How can I when I don't know the whole situation?"

James sat in silence for several seconds. He looked at the framed picture of him and Roger on the golf course and cursed the memory. It was Roger who put him and his colleagues in this predicament, he reminded himself. And with shareholders jumping ship by the hour, the pressure was mounting. He had to do whatever it took to secure the billion-dollar inheritance, for the future of the Welloff company and his own. James took a deep breath, dropped his eyes, and watched Lisa's red hair bob north to south in his lap.

"Father, are you still there?" Benjamin asked.

"Benjamin James Preacher, my dear son. Forgive me for treating you like a child. You are a grown man now, and I must trust you with the truth. This is confidential, son," James lowered his voice. "You cannot tell anyone."

Benjamin sat up in his bed. He was alone in his room, yet he felt like he was being watched. He held his phone close to his face with both hands. His eyes widened as if he were about to find out who really shot JFK.

"Are you listening son?"

"Yes, Father."

"Good. Raymon Platt Jr is the sole heir to the Welloff fortune," James cleared his throat. "But he is a criminal. My dear friend Roger Bennett wrote in his will, if Mr. Platt even attempts to do anything illegal with his inheritance, then it will be stripped from him and the remaining amount will be given to the Welloff Corporation."

"A criminal!" Benjamin gasped. "I don't understand. Why then, give him that amount of money in the first place?"

"Roger was a sympathetic man. I knew him better than most. Behind that iron mug was a man missing his daughter. He thought by giving this hoodlum of a grandson a chance at a real life, it would somehow bring him peace in the afterlife, peace he never found amongst the living, of course."

"But Father, I have spent a lot of time around Mr. Raymon. He isn't a bad person, he's kind of cool."

"Believe me, son, that's what he wants you to think. The boy has a rap sheet a mile long. Whatever you think of him, think again!"

"But I'm around him all day. If he—"

"Oh really," James interrupted. "Where is he now?"

"I believe—"

"My point exactly. Unless you are sleeping with the guy, you couldn't possibly know what he keeps under the covers. You need to stop believing this and that and start finding out the truth of things, son."

"If all this is true and Ray is some career crook, why would you ask me to see to it that he doesn't go broke?"

"You are so much like your mother," James laughed, "trying to read in between lines that don't exist. It is clear, son. I asked you to look after him, help him save more, spend less, see that he is responsible, because sooner or later he is going to break the rules of his inheritance and the money will return to its proper place at Welloff software. And the more, the better. The company needs that money for real reasons. Jobs and lives depend on this company's continued success. Better us than some ex con bling blinging with his hoes and posse all around town."

"Can't we just explain that to him, make him see reason?" Benjamin said.

"No! Under no circumstances are you to say a single word about this to anyone. I thought I could trust you, damn it!"

"You can." Benjamin searched for his father's approval.

"Just make sure this Raymon hasn't engaged in any illegal activity, with his inheritance or otherwise, can you do that? I know you don't have the gall to do what needs to be done. So, I have to do it for us all. This criminal could ruin the Welloff name and the lives of our family. I won't let that happen, and neither will you."

Benjamin listened to his father give out orders and instructions. He allowed his mind to drifted off to a place where Raymon could possibly be this crime boss James spoke about. But he didn't know that version. He clearly wasn't the adventurous music mogul he raced along the highway with. Yet and still, James made it clear, he felt Raymon was headed for the wrong side of the tracks and would soon show himself unworthy of the Welloff name.

Seconds after Benjamin ended his Facetime conversation, his phone blinked. The flashing lights pulled him from his stupor. He saw the caller's name across the screen and rushed to answer, "Hello! Ray, where are you? What! wait a second. The police station?"

Chapter 14

Dec 11th - 20th

News vans lined up and down the narrow street, crammed the limousine waiting by the curb. The half-shoveled walkway led to the front of the New York police station. When the double doors flew open, the sounds of dry salt crunching and camera flashes commenced.

Raymon stepped into the night with his arms raised and tried to block the sharp lights aimed at his eyes. A group of police officers walked in front of him and shielded him from the information mob.

Benjamin rushed to keep up. He trailed behind with a briefcase held tightly in his arms. Questions came in from all sides, as they made way to the open car door.

"Are you purposely endangering the public?" a reporter said. "Do you really believe this to be a smart course of action? Why are you helping a convicted felon?"

Raymon stopped, stood beside the limousine door, and turned to face the waving microphones with one hand on the roof of his ride. "Is this still America, land of the free and home of the brave?" he asked. "Isn't a man presumed innocent until proven guilty? Well then, in the words of Doctor

Eddie Murphy, give a nigga a chance."

At that very moment, two uniformed officers pushed their way out of

the station doors. They shouted at media workers clogging the walkway. A

dark-skinned man with a bald head appeared behind them.

"Manhood!" someone screamed, while he was led to the limousine.

"Are you going to clap back at the authorities?" asked a reporter.

"Are you going to flee the county?" asked another.

"How do you know Mr. Raymon Platt?"

But Manhood remained mum. He ducked his head and vanished inside

the luxury ride.

"Mr. Platt, Mr. Platt," an eager voice called out. "Will he be on Honey

Drop's album? Why pay a ten-million-dollar appeal bond for a guilty man?"

The question grabbed the attention of the entire block. Silence arrived

and itchy recorders awaited a scratch of relief.

Raymon looked around like he lost his keys, then stretched his arms out

wide and said, "Merry Christmas to all!" He sat down, closed the door, and

waved to the cameras behind the tinted window. When Planes drove off,

Raymon slapped his hands together. "Now that's how you get sprung from

jail."

"Yo son, good looking out." Manhood rubbed his wrist.

"It's cool. I know all about the struggle," said Raymon.

"Word! The po po tried to kill you too?"

"No, but I know people look at you all crazy, just because you did a little time."

"So, you been locked up before?"

"Hell yeah! I mean, it was county jail time. But the food was terrible." Raymon shook his head.

He could see Manhood scoping out his new surroundings. He looked at Raymon with a smirk, like he knew something Raymon didn't. When he gazed out the window, Raymon asked, "So where can we drop you off?"

"Drop me off?" Manhood laughed. "You just picked me up. Naw son, I'm feeling your vibe. I think I'll stick around for a while. Plus, I feel like I owe you god."

"You don't owe me nothing."

"Naw son. I feel like I do. Them crackers was trying to bury me in the system. They don't want to see the people rise, but the end of the new Jim Crow era is almost over. You bust a stupid move getting me out, and for that I rocks with you."

Raymon looked lost. He was trying his best to keep up with Manhood's use of the urban dictionary.

"I know who you are. You that cat that got all them tickets a few weeks back. A real-life Richie Rich. Naw son, I rock with you hard body."

Raymon saw the letters M.O.B tattooed on his hands. He had on a fitted Bubble coat and some Timberland boots. Big gold chains swayed with the car's movements throughout the ride.

When Raymon tried to read the cryptic tattoo on his neck, Manhood caught him staring.

"What's up with your record deal?" Raymon tried to act innocent.

"Them hoes dropped me from the label the second the verdict dropped. They ain't ready for real life. They just trying to control the masses. You three me?"

"Come again..."

"You understand. Come on god, do the math."

Raymon nodded, looked off into the passing traffic, and wondered what real-life issues Manhood had circling him. He started to second guess his latest move. He thought a man facing life in prison would want to find the quickest way out the country. The ten million would be lost when he skipped town. But the rapper seated across from him seemed to have more layers to him than expected. Raymon scratched his head, then thought, *Just stick to the plan.* "I think we could do some business," Raymon said.

The front glass slid down and Benjamin turned around from the passenger seat. "Excuse me. Where shall we drop off the gentleman?" He grasped his briefcase close to his chest.

"He's staying with us, at the Grand Dora."

"I don't think that's a good idea," said Benjamin.

"Why not Benji. You a lil scared?" Raymon laughed. "Don't worry, he's just another artist. Don't let the news trick you, that's just an image. This is a good man, trust me. So, Manhood, where you from?"

"Brooklyn!"

The second Raymon stepped foot inside his royal suite he was bombarded with questions.

"Really brah. This is crazy." Chill Will threw up his hands.

"I thought we were businessmen. What were you thinking?" added Bigmack.

"You asking for trouble. What's wrong with you? You do know this dude is going to run?"

Raymon allowed his team to pry uninterrupted. He sat on the couch, extended his legs, and rested them on an armless chair. He pulled out his phone and started pushing buttons. "Where's Natasha?"

"Where's your brain," Chill Will said.

Right on time, Natasha pushed through the entrance and passed the doormen. She had on a gray suit dress and green pumps. She held her phone up in the air. "Ray, your home boy from the county keeps calling collect."

"Good, that's what's up. What he talking about?"

"Something about bond money. A few other requests, but mostly money related," said Natasha.

"Tell them I'm working on it. Keep calling collect, I got them. And make sure you accept every call. I'm talking the whole fifteen minutes. Show some love."

"The whole fifteen minutes?" Natasha questioned.

"The whole fifteen minutes. Guys in jail like to talk."

Bigmack looked at Chill Will and shook his head.

"Oh, and Tasha, I really like your nails." Raymon smiled.

Natasha walked off cursing under her breath. When she was gone, Chill Will took a seat in front of Raymon. "Hey Ray," he looked him in the eyes.

175

"My man, my partner, this is nuts. We got all these expenses for the album, real unnecessary stuff," he spoke in a moderate tone. "You wasting money left and right and now you go bond out a guilty man for ten million. He going to skip town. You do know that. And when he does, the state going to keep that money. Not a smart move brah, not at all."

Raymon sat back. "Who says he's guilty?"

"He went to trial, he lost. The system says he is guilty, that's who."

"The same system that said I was guilty."

"That's different." Chill Will leaned back.

"Sure, it is." Raymon stared at him until Chill Will lowered his eyes.

"This isn't the kind of attention we need right now," said Bigmack. "Sure, dude is a cold rapper. One of the best in the game, but he radical. He got caught up at the wrong time.

With seven Grammy nominations and all that. The boy got two platinum albums, but he a real gangster. And that's the problem. The government say he connected with some big-time hitters in the feds, serving more time than Jacob the Jeweler. They hit that boy with all kinds of charges and got them on YouTube having a shoot-out with the police."

Raymon sat up. "They got a tape?"

"Yeah! And the cops hate them."

"Where you get all this, Mack?"

"It's a new world of information dogg."

"They always trying to bring a brother down," said Raymon.

"Come on." Chill Will stood up. "You can go somewhere with that Black Lives Matter mess all you want. Your boy is a problem. A ten-million-dollar problem, and the cops want his head. What we going to do with that?"

Raymon pretended to be in deep thought. He honestly didn't know how much drama Manhood carried in, but it was too late to back out and Raymon was all in. *Just gotta finish the game,* he thought. "You think we could buy that tape?"

Bigmack rolled his eyes and Chill Will kicked an invisible ball. When Natasha returned with a clipboard in hand, Raymon said, "Just the lady I wanted to see." He jumped to his feet. "Where is Ms. Honey Drop?"

"She is in the studio recording," said Natasha.

"Yo son." Manhood walked in and sized up the doormen. He was shirtless; his upper body was covered in tattoos. "Who this fine shorty right here?"

"Excuse you." Natasha changed her stance.

"Naw baby, I didn't pass gas. I'm just the shit."

Natasha looked him over like she was his parole officer, then turned to Raymon. "Really." She walked off without saying another word with an angry look on her face.

Manhood looked around. "Nice spot."

"You see, even the ladies love them," Raymon joked.

Manhood greeted the men with hand slaps and one-armed thugs. He showed gratitude for his expensive, paid stay at the famous hotel. "Good look. Good look." And helped himself to the bar.

Bigmack watched him with a close eye. He roamed around, touched every wall, and patted the furniture. Chill Will shook his head in disbelief of what was happening right in front of him.

Natasha came back in the room and informed Raymon further about Honey's studio session.

Manhood listened and watched closely.

"She needs a break. She been going for hours," said Natasha.

"Okay, tell her to take a breather. How is the track coming?" Raymon asked.

"Mark and Play love working with her. They haven't said a word, but they haven't stopped smiling either. Personally, I think she needs a few more bridges, you know, to even out the effect of the song."

"More bridges will only take attention away from her voice," Manhood butted in.

A needle dropped, and everybody heard it. With all eyes on him, Manhood stepped forward and said, "If you want to showcase true talent, you have to give it the proper space to shine. Anybody can put perfume on trash, or dress up a duck and call it art. But a real artist only wants and needs a dry canvas to show the world, here I am."

Chill Will almost spilt his drink. Natasha appeared stuck. Bigmack nodded his head, and Raymon smiled.

"That's sound advice,' Raymon said. "And so articulate. So, what do you suggest?"

"Hey, I'm just a thug standing on a new rug," Manhood dumb down.

"Maybe we should give him the canvas." Honey stood in front of the studio doorway holding a bottle of water.

"Hold up, I don't think that's a good idea," said Chill Will.

"You right," Raymon said. "It's not a good idea, it's a great one!"

The engineer room was packed with anxious listeners. Even the security

guards found themselves unable to miss what was about to happen.

Manhood stood alone in the recording booth. He had a red bandanna

on his head and diamond earrings in his earlobes. "Mark and Play, I been

waiting on this day," he started rapping.

As the beat challenged him, he went from an in-the-pocket flow to an

unorthodox cadence. His baritone vocals bounced with the track like an

instrument part of the production. He emphasized political points with a

power brace, "Crooked coppers stop us." Then modulated his tone to set

up his clever metaphors. Even Chill Will had to acknowledge the seamlessly

effortless bars that kept every head bopping along, throughout the session.

After ten songs straight Raymon felt inspired. He harbored ill feelings

about becoming rich, only to throw it away in the face of struggling

everyday people. He looked at Manhood, listened to his words, and

thought about how the justice system wanted to take this talented man, an

artist, and put him away where no one could hear his message or feel his

pain.

In seconds Raymon had traveled to his office, opened his laptop, and

began a search for fatal accident information. He didn't know why, he just

felt compelled. He sat staring at a blank screen connected to a search engine website for more information. Then his smartphone rang. He answered with a casual greeting and listened closely.

Benjamin's shadow crept along the walls as he tried to eavesdrop in secret. He drew closer to the office door, leading with his head, and heard Raymon clearly. "The twenty third, at eight o'clock p.m. I got it."

Got what, Benjamin pondered. Before he could speculate further, he heard, "What's the name of the ship? That's dock number seven, right? Okay, that's great. I will have it picked up. 5,000 kilos correct! Nice doing business with you too."

Thump! Benjamin hit his head on the side of the doorway.

"What's up?" Raymon lowered the phone from his ear.

"I just wanted to ask you something," Benjamin lied. "But it can wait."

He watched Raymon place the phone in his pants pocket and tried to make sense of what he heard. He believed in Raymon; he tried to defend him against his own plotting father and the counsel. He didn't feel good about being involved in their ploy to see Raymon get robbed of his own inheritance. But what he had heard was undeniable. He rubbed his head with doubts and couldn't' t figure out what hurt more, the bump or the disappointment. "Busy night," said Benjamin.

"Yeah, and there's still so much to do." Raymon opened his mail. "Can you keep a secret?"

"A secret." Benjamin walked slowly.

"Yeah, a secret. See, I haven't told anyone yet, so you will be the first."

Benjamin grew anxious. "Yes, of course I can."

"We got invited to the Winter Blowout."

Benjamin nodded his head, then shook it side to side. He noticed Raymon staring at him smiling, like he was waiting for a reaction. But all Benjamin could do was shrug his shoulders and tilt his head. "What is that?"

Chapter 15

The Winter Blowout Awards show was held once a year, as one of the biggest musical celebration events. It specialized in show-casing new artists and popular songs. The event was the music industry's way of properly ending the past year of musical excellence and starting a new one-off right. Industry heavy weights, new artist and performers attended by special invitation only. A-list celebrities flocked to the show in search of one unforgettable night.

The Barclay Center was located in Brooklyn and selected to host the blowout. Groups of guests made their way along the red carpet and into the coliseum. With the sun retired for the night, bright lights and camera flashes illuminated the front of the building. Ladies in their best dresses, laced with gaudy jewelry and fancy shoes, posed for photos, while the men attempted to look sharp, clean and savvy in tuxedos and designer suits. Reporters rushed to place their microphones in front of the right lips, then asked for their tailor's names, and the night's performer's vehicles pulled up, paused at the curb, allowed passengers to exit, then rolled off down the long strip.

When a motorcade fit for a visiting president was spotted on its approach, paparazzi aimed their cameras in the proper direction. Four black Phantoms formed a square around the stretched Bentley truck. Red flags stood up like antennas, with Raymon's face printed on each one; they waved like Olympic banners with Double R written on the sides. When the truck reached the curb, all attention shifted.

Manhood stepped out first. He had on an all-white tuxedo and a pair of wraparound sunglasses; his bald head shined like a new penny. Bigmack hopped out next, followed by Chill Will; their white suits matched their shoes. They smiled brightly and waved to the crowd of fans. Natasha's white Michael Kors bodysuit made her look like a bona-fide star. Benjamin chose a more informal look; his suit and tie fit his needs.

The all-white entourage wasn't yet complete. Honey stepped out of the Bentley, wearing a diamond-covered veil over her face. Her mind-blowing gown had white fur around the bottom. She looked like a Snow Goddess Queen and the crowd loved it. They shouted her name and clapped their hands with joy. Honey was receiving a standing ovation without singing a single note. She stood frozen for a moment, not knowing how to react. Then Raymon placed his hand on her back. He was the last one to be seen, but the first one to be heard. "The Double R is in the bitch! "

He looked like a Harlem Nights Gangster in his personally made suit. He wore a white scarf around his shoulders and a matching top hat. Diamond studs hung from his ears. He was comfortable, like he had been there a hundred times before. People screamed his name, ladies held their chests, and cameras flickered. "You ready?" he whispered in Honey's ear.

News crews rushed in with questions, and request.

Honey posed for what seemed like a thousand pictures. Manhood made his presence known. "The best doing it right now is us. All these lames were scared to give a real G a chance, but the Double R kept it a stack and freed the beast. Raymon records is about real artists, real peeps doing real things. I fuck with the boy, so get down or lay down. Brooklyn where you at!"

Raymon answered random questions thrown at him from all directions. Established celebrities frowned at the amount of attention given to him and his upstart artist. "We do our own distribution, production and marketing," Raymon said. "It's a real movement on this side. Get with it!"

Bigmack was taking unapproved selfies with A-listers by positioning himself behind them and beside them, then snapping a few shots with a smile on his face.

Chill Will caught the eye of a few well-dressed ladies, put his arm over their shoulders, and headed indoors.

By the time they reached their front-row seats, drinks were being poured and the host started the show off with a few jokes of his own. "Check out my man over here." He pointed at Raymon. "He is in a class of his own. This the only black guy who got white money."

An auditorium full of smiling faces laughed and cheered. Chris Brown opened the show with an amazing performance. Then the host returned with more jokes: "This dude went from do-rags to riches, then showed up with the cast of Lord of the Rings." He pointed to Honey's faceguard. "He going broke faster than MC Hammer and he too stupid to quit."

The crowd joined in, ensuing to roast Raymon with taunts of, "Too stupid, too stupid to quit. Hey heyyy!"

Chill Will sank in his seat and placed his top hat over his face, while Raymon just laughed. He clapped his hands and showed himself to be a good sport.

Performer after performer took the stage. Awards were announced and music personalities were honored. Best female album award went to Beyonce and Nicki Minaj for their collaboration work: *Best of Both Girls, Bees and the Barbs*.

Honey felt out of place. Before she could allow her confidence to shrink any further, Raymon put his arm around her. "Next year we'll see who is really the best of all, girl," he whispered in her ear. His words made her beam inside. She tried to keep her tough-girl look going but it was to no avail. She smiled so brightly it was like someone turned on a flashlight. Raymon believed in her, and that made her believe in herself in ways she thought not possible. When she turned her head, Raymon looked her and their eyes locked.

A man wearing a black blazer walked in front of them. He had an earpiece in his ear and a clipboard under his arm. He gave Honey a silent nod and she gracefully rose to her feet. Before she could be wrenched away, Raymon locked his index finger around her pinkie. " A realist, a woman, and a fighter." He smiled.

He remembered, she thought. After she made it backstage, she sat in her own dressing room and was overwhelmed with flowers, assistance, and pampering. She changed into her performance attire and desperately tried to control her own breathing.

Raymon remained in his seat and waited for Honey's set to begin. He had to pay a lofty fee to persuade the directors to allow Honey Drop English to replace a more seasoned artist as one of the nights prime time performers. If greasing palms was what it took, he saw that as a win-win situation. He shared a laugh with a few actors seated nearby and waved at hip-hop royalty. He shook hands with music moguls, and bumped glasses with star producers. "Come on Jay, you going to make me buy Tidal off you, talking numbers like that," he shouted over a few heads.

The show came back from a televised commercial break and a soft melody multiplied. Then a well-known New York singer stepped onto the stage. "This new artist is a first-time nominee," she said. "She blows up the net with her hot single and now she has truly arrived here tonight. Ladies and gentlemen, I take pleasure in introducing New York City's own Ms. Honey Drop English."

The lights went out and applause ensued. Like a strike of thunder, Manhood's voice shot out of the sound system and silenced the crowd. "Y'all think you ready, but you have no idea, " he growled.

The stage lit up. A gigantic champagne glass full of diamonds sat in the center. A hard bass rumbled out of the speakers. Viewers leaned forward in their seats and witnesses tried not to blink. When the beat started to kick in, the flawless diamonds began to move. It looked like a crystal avalanche at first. Then Honey's head inched its way up. When her mouth was clear from the ice, her falsetto rose. "Take a sip of my love," she sang.

A crew of dancers took the stage and began gyrating their bodies to the music. Honey crept to the top of the diamonds she was previously buried under and lay on her side. She chilled atop 175-million-dollar worth of A-class jewels with a smile on her face.

The crowd went insane. They jumped out of their seats, aimed their phones, and tried to document the moment.

Honey had green pasties covering her most intimate parts. Her hair was braided to one side and held up like the B. O.'s show star of I Dream of Genie. She wore a red thong over black fishnets. And her microphone was covered in diamonds. Her body had a coconut-oil glow, while she sang her new single, "I know you thirsty, I know you want me, going to get drunk baby. Come and take a sip of my love!"

The audience was on their feet screaming and pumping their fists. Even Benjamin found it hard to hold back his cheers. He bounced on his toes like a rhythm-less fraternity boy. When Manhood swaggered onto the stage, with a microphone in his hand, paper started to fall from the sky. At first glance, audience members thought it was confetti, just another gadget a performer used to hype up the moment. But they were wrong. When the fresh bills hit heads and landed in people's palms, they knew they were experiencing something they only heard about in street tales and night clubs. It was raining money: fifty-dollar bills, five, tens, and hundreds.

Raymon stood up, and saw the auditorium flooded with cash. People went crazy. They found it hard to keep their eyes on the stage with all the real currency floating around. But Raymon's eyes were locked on Honey.

She sat up, dropped her microphone, and pressed her shirtless chest up against the cold glass. Jaws dropped and she knew she had their attentions. Her eyes found Rayrnon's, then she ran her tongue across the glass like an animal.

"Check it out," Manhood shouted. "Hot damn, girl, here we go again. Flow colder than the weather, or pool a diamond, take a swim. Keep asking about my jacket, wanna know what's up with him. It's all goody, M hoody, Honey Drop and Richie Rich," he rapped.

The dancers gavotted around him, then ran off stage.

Manhood threw up the peace sign and followed suit. Honey picked up her microphone and ended the infectious song with an acrobatic set of vocal display that left her doubters in awe and her supporters in celebration.

Raymon's eyelids felt like they were stapled open. He didn't want to move, not even for a second. Chill Will foamed at the mouth, but Raymon couldn't hear a word. Men and women scurried all over in their fancy gear, cuffing c-notes and tucking big faces. The room went dark and the cheers carried Raymon backstage into a crowded hallway. Women in their stage outfits ran left and right, changing clothes and covering up their private places. A strong scent of perfume blew past. He recognized some of the smiling faces, while trying to shuffle past them. He dipped his shoulder to squeeze in between two male dancers holding a loud conversation. With so much going on, one seemed to notice his presence as he inched his way to Honey's dressing room.

Lump! Raymon felt like he hit a brick wall. He was looking over his shoulder when he crashed. Good thing for him, he thought. If not, he would have smashed right into the chest of a 6'9" security guard named Zeus.

"What you doing back here, little man?" said Zeus looking down on Raymon and standing right in front of Honey's dressing room door.

Raymon rubbed his jaw, looked up, and searched for the right words. "That's my artist in there, Honey Drop English. I'm just trying to congratulate her, that's all."

"No visitors."

"I'm not a visitor. I told you that's my artist."

"And I told you, no visitors." Zeus stared down at him.

"Okay okay. I understand." Raymon acted like he was turning around to leave. Then he shouted," Hey Honey! Come get this roadblock."

But Zeus wasn't having that. He pushed Raymon back with one arm.

"Hold on one second," Raymon contested. "I know you just doing your job. But that's my artist in there, and all I'm trying to do is my job. My name is Raymon Platt."

"You Raymon Platt?" asked Zeus.

Raymon saw his eyes' light up and felt remedied. "Yeah, that's me. Ms. Honey Drop English is my first lady and—"

"Two racks," Zeus said.

"Two racks!"

"Two racks, fool. You heard me, and then I'll let you by."

"Oh, you want two racks." Raymon reached into his pants pocket and pulled out a roll of money. "Here you go dude."

While Zeus counted the money, Raymon slid past him and slowly turned the knob. He tiptoed into the room and quietly closed the door behind him. When he turned around, Honey was standing right in front of him shaking her head with her arms crossed. She had on a bathrobe that covered her entire body. Her hair was wet. She stood there with her eyebrows low, like she was awaiting an explanation. And Raymon didn't disappoint. He held his hands up like he was caught committing a capital crime. " I can explain. I know it looks like I was creeping, but I wasn't. I mean, I was, but not like I'm some kind of creep. Not at all. I just wanted to surprise you, I mean congratulate you on a great, no wonderful performance," he stuttered, stepped his way toward her. "You were fantastic. I knew you had it, but damn girl, you were great."

They stood face to face. The sounds of doors slamming echoed in the distance. Honey stared into the window of his soul. She could see kindness, and empathy. It made her warm. She lowered her arms and allowed her robe to open; underneath she had on nothing but her skin. Raymon's eyes slipped he felt his heart beating faster and Honey just smiled. She brushed past him and reached for the door handle. Raymon watched with exciting thoughts running through his head. *Please don't kick me out right now.*

She locked the door, looked over her shoulder, and turned around. When she came for him, no words were exchanged, just action and passion. Their lips finally met and Raymon felt like the luckiest man alive.

Honey had a determined look in her eyes that night. She knew what she wanted and it was her time to have it all.

Chapter 16

The song titled "Take a Sip of My Love" was on repeat on every Hip Hop
and R&B radio station in the city. A celebration was in order. Raymon sat at
the head of the table surrounded by his peers. His personal caterer
provided a wonderful brunch, spread out in abundance. Raymon had a
smile on his face bigger than the crescent moon. His head was spinning
with new ideas, his ears were full of gratitude, and his hands were warm
with success. He could taste victory on his tongue. He imagined himself
crossing a finish line with his hands up and a thousand cheers entrenching
him.

Honey looked at him from across the table and smiled. *Last night was a
new beginning,* Raymon thought. For the first time in his life, he felt loved.

"Last night was so litty," said Bigmack.

"It was cool." Chill Will took a drink.

"Did you see people's faces when Honey came out of them diamonds?"
Natasha said gleefully.

"Word son, she did that," Manhood said in between bites of food. "All
that money falling from the sky, that stunt damn near started a riot."

Honey sat in silence, but her face said it all. She stirred her coffee with a bashful look. She was glowing and found it hard not to look at Raymon. He didn't even try to hide his stares. He kept his eyes on her while indirect compliments filled the air.

"Ray, I would like to talk to you about your current financial state," said Benjamin.

"Let's make a toast," Raymon talked past him and lifted his glass. "To the first lady of Raymon Record and the star of the night. Salute!"

"Ray, I need to—"

"Who wants more cake?" he blocked Benjamin from reaching his point.

"Damn Ray, you not even going to listen to your accountant?" Chill Will sounded like he was bothered. "Benji trying to say something."

"It's probably nothing." Raymon waved his hand. "Benji always worried about the little things."

"This is no little thing," said Benjamin. "You have been spending a massive amount of money. And at this rate, you will be filing for a Chapter 11 by Christmas."

"Chill out, Benji. We just had a great night."

"A costly night. And if this album doesn't sell, and I mean fast, you won't have a single dime available after the holidays."

"We are not selling the album," said Raymon.

"I understand how you feel. But I was appointed to assist you with your finances, keep a record of your spending, and advise you. I'm now advising you to put the album out for sale. It's the only way."

The table grew silent. The smell of hot pancakes and fresh fruit called out. Eyes dropped to the floor, as the tension built.

"Am I the only one hearing this?" Chill Will looked around. "Okay I get it; you think I'm a fuck up. And Mack must be some hungry sidekick. But your boy over there," he pointed to Benjamin, "is college educated. He telling you some real shit, and you acting like it's nothing. We got a make some money," he yelled. "I know you sweet on this pop tart right here, but her album can't possibly cover what you been wasting, even if you sell it."

"Screw you, lame, " Honey snarled.

"I ain't the one screwing around here." Chill Will shot her a loaded stare.

"Calm down. Playboy," said Manhood. "I believe your man know what he doing. Let Richie Rich do him, and you just do what it is you do. By the way, what do you do?"

Natasha couldn't hold back her laughs.

"That's real funny," said Chill Will. "But we have come to a crossroads and we can't just piss on the blessings that have been handed to us. Damn, you were just in a cell a few weeks ago, and look where we at."

"No thanks to you," Raymon shouted over his scrambled eggs. "You keep talking about these blessing and us coming up, but there wasn't no us in that cell, was it? Naw, that was me! No visits, no letters or nothing."

"Come on Ray, you know I can't visit you in no jail" Chill Will lowered his head.

"Keep it a hundred, you just didn't give a damn. I did that time for your mess and now you want to sound like you looking out for my best interest. Save it, brah! I don't need that right now."

Benjamin couldn't believe what he was hearing. Raymon was a criminal. James was telling the truth about him having a record. An awkward moment of silence fell right on top of the group. Benjamin was lost in thought. Chill Will sank in his seat and shook his head while on mute. Honey saw Natasha lean across Manhood and snatch up some butter. Her breast rubbed against his shoulder and they shared a brief look.

Then Honey cut into her English muffin. She stopped when she noticed Raymon answering a text.

Bigmack tried to bring life back to the setting. "You need to stop drinking so damn much. That drink got you tripping."

"Who you talking to?" Chill Will sat up.

"Yo hating ass! Just play your position, that's it. You stay worrying about other people's business cause you ain't got none. Gonna call me a hungry sidekick. I'll kick yo ass, keep playing. Get a girl or something, I know what you need."

"Come on, I know playboy be getting some." Manhood smiled.

"That boy ain't had no pussy since I came out one," said Bigmack. "Just stuff your face."

Chill Will clapped back. "I ain't no hater."

"You do sound like you got a lil hater in yo blood." Manhood laughed.

"You don't know me."

"You right. But I got just the thing for you. Hey Vicky!"

"Play "Player Hater" by The Notorious B.I.G."

"Yes Daddy."

The song played throughout the suite. Natasha and Honey sang the lyrics while pointing at Chill Will. Bigmack almost choked on his turkey bacon laughing so hard. "How you do that?" he asked.

"It ain't nothing," said Manhood. Just a little program rewiring. Victoria was too white, too simple. Now my girl Vicky, she got swag."

Benjamin watched carefully, while Raymon typed in a text. Planes entered the room with his phone in hand. Raymon waved him over to the table. "Fancy Pants, you hungry? We got plenty of grub."

"No sir, no grub for me. I already ate."

"Well then, would you be so kind as to call me an Uber?" Raymon winked.

"An Uber sir. Oh yes, but of course." Planes gave him a thumbs up.

Honey put down her fork and wiped her mouth with a napkin. She could sense that Raymon was up to something, but she didn't' t know what.

Benjamin started to wonder. He wanted to raise a few questions, then he felt his phone vibrating on his waist. He reached for it and saw a text message from his father that read: Meeting Tonight. Before he could respond he saw Raymon stand.

"I would like you to take a ride with me." Raymon extended his arm.

Benjamin followed his stare and his eyes stopped on Honey. She looked around her chair like she lost something, then pointed to herself. "Me?"

Raymon laughed, then nodded his head in approval. Honey tossed her napkin and stood up. She pulled at the bottom of her turtleneck sweater dress, tugging at it to grow longer. It didn't.

They made it all the way to the front door before questions started to fly.

"Where the hell y'all going?" Bigmack turned around.

"We grown, ain't we?" said Raymon. "We be right back. Enjoy your meal."

Benjamin stood up. "We need to go over these numbers."

"Trust me." Raymon placed his blazer over Honey's shoulders. "We will later."

But Benjamin was confounded. *Trust me*, he repeated the words in his head, albeit trusting Raymon may have been, a mistake all along.

When they reached the sidewalk, Honey sucked her teeth and tilted her head. "Really," she looked at Raymon, "an Uber?"

"What?" Raymon laughed. "We needed a ride."

The all-white Rolls Royce Wraith was more than a ride. The $300,000 dollar whip was as luxurious as it was huge. Raymon opened the rear door, helped Honey inside, hopped in beside her, and closed the door. When he saw the bearded driver wearing street clothes look back at them, he said, "To Time Square my man."

Feeling protected from the outside world, Honey sat under Raymon's arm. They rolled through traffic like a king and queen in an extravagant chariot. Raymon looked at his phone for what seemed like every two minutes. The driver kept checking his rearview mirror, analyzing the couple in his back seat.

"Where you taking me?" Honey asked.

"You will see." Raymon smirked.

They played a silent game of staring and looking away from each other for a few blocks, until their noses collided and they both laughed.

"You do know that you are crazy, correct?" Honey smiled at him.

"I'm rich, that makes me eccentric."

"I knew I knew you two." the driver raised his hand. "You that from do-rags-to-riches guy."

Raymon just smiled.

"Yeah, that's you. And you that hot new chick with them bangers on the net. Y'all make a cute couple."

"What makes you think we a couple?" said Raymon.

Honey gave him a light punch to the gut. "Yes, we do sir, thank you very much."

Raymon was speechless. His mouth was still halfway open when he looked to Honey for clarity. "Yeah, this me right here." He smiled.

"I heard y'all had one hell of a performance the other night," the driver continued. "I'm mad I missed that. I'm a have to check for it on snapchat. Right now, it's all about these bills though."

Honey's eyes lit up. She leaned forward, so that the driver could hear her well. "You driving a car worth a quarter milli and you taking about paying bills."

"The car is the bill. This what I do. Everybody wanna ride in a Wraith, so I sold the crib, bought the car, and charge folks to cruise."

"You sold your home?"

"Hell yeah! I got a get this paper. The car is the house, the kitchen, and the job all rolling in one." He got a laugh out of his own pun.

"Did you really miss the whole show?" Honey asked.

"Yeah, I'm working all the time, sweetie."

"Well, how about an encore."

The driver smiled like a kid at Chucky Cheese and nodded his head wildly.

Honey pulled off her coat, tied it around her waist, then wrapped her legs around Raymon's sides, and sat on his lap.

"What are you doing?" Raymon took a deep breath.

"Sometimes all people need is a little excitement," Honey whispered in his ear. She looked over her shoulder and caught the driver staring with a shocked look on his face. "Don't just sit there, put on some music," she said.

The driver fumbled with the dashboard until he found the right button to hit.

When the beat started bumping through the sound system, Honey swayed her body in and out. She whipped her hair around like a show girl with both hands on Raymon's shoulders.
2pac's "Me Against the World" played, while Honey moved her hips in circles. "You like old school."

Her apple peach lotion aroused Raymon in more ways than one. He told himself to relax, leaned his head back, and watched the stars on the ceiling. Honey was spontaneous in a good way, and although a little awkward, Raymon enjoyed the lap dance. "And you say I'm crazy." He smiled.

Honey delivered. And as the friction increased, Raymon felt the pulsation inside his pants grow. He dropped his head, and tried to plant one right on Honeys lips, but she slipped her hand in between their faces and used her two fingers to push Raymon's head back.

"You got jokes. Oh, that's cold," the driver said, doing his best to keep his eyes forward.

After the song finished, Honey laughed and returned to her proper seat like nothing happened.

Fifteen minutes later they were motionless, and stuck in bumper-to-bumper traffic. Raymon peeked out the windshield and smiled.

"We ain't going nowhere in this for a while," Honey guesstimated. "This that city traffic. "

"That's cool, cause we already here." Raymon gave her a sly look.

Honey was silently confused. The traffic jam was like a dead ocean of cars, with not a single wave in sight. Honking horns came together like a band and played one big annoying tune. The sidewalk was full of people moving at their own pace. Raymon rolled down his window and stuck his neck out. Honey looked irritated. *What is he doing*? she thought. She crossed her arms and sank down in the large seats. "And this is where you wanted to take me?"

"Well technically, you were already here," said Raymon. "I just wanted you to see yourself."

Honey rolled her eyes. "What's that 'pose to mean?"

Then Raymon pointed toward the windshield. Honey followed his finger with her eyes, and like a floating mist, her body was pulled forward. She tilted her head and squinted her eyes. When she finally convinced herself that what she was looking at was actually real, she covered her mouth with both hands.

In the middle of Times Square, posted up next to the Jumbo Tron, high as an oak tree for all to witness, was a billboard of Honey wearing nothing but a Santa Clause jacket and some red pumps. She had one leg raised up. Under her heel was old Saint Nick himself, tied up and gaged. Above the image, written in red, were the words: Christmas Day.

Honey got out of the car to get a better look and Raymon followed. He put his arm around her and bounced his head up and down. Honey stood there feeling numb. The advertisement was the biggest billboard in the city. She felt her eyes starting to water, then she turned to Raymon and wrapped her arms around his neck. Raymon straightened his back and lifted her off her feet. They spun in circles laughing aloud.

A few hours later they returned to the Grand Dora. When the elevator reached Honey's floor, she was shining with satisfaction. Raymon kissed her on the forehead and held her waist.

"Come stay with me tonight," he said.

Honey looked at him and smiled. "You know I have to check on these kids. They are probably tearing my suite up. And my madre is letting them."

"The room is covered for insurance, no worries."

"But I am worried. I'm worried that you are spending too much on me, on the music, on everything."

"Not you too." Raymon rubbed his head.

"Seriously, Ray. Maybe you should take a second and listen. It is your money, but don't ask me not to care. Because I do."

"You care about me." Raymon pulled her closer and stopped the elevator doors from closing. "If you care so much, why you ain't staying with me tonight?"

"You know I can't. Plus, I have to get some sleep. We still got mad interviews all week. Thank you for that by the way," she said sarcastically.

"Oh, it's my fault now?"

"You the boss!"

"Well, the boss telling you to stay with him tonight."

"Then we both won't get no sleep. Stop being thirsty." Honey laughed.

"Okay! But I'm down here first thing in the morning. I want to take you and your family out for breakfast. Is that cool?"

Honey gave him a seductive wave goodbye, then the elevator doors separated them.

Raymon saw his reflection in the shiny metal surrounding him. He thought about his past. He wondered if a woman like Honey would have fallen for him if he was just some broke country boy. Then he realized what he was asking himself. They had fallen for each other in a way that felt so real. I got a girlfriend. The actualization made him smile.

When he reached his floor, the elevator doors opened, and his smile was swept away by the angry face staring back at him. "What's wrong?" he said.

"Everything is wrong," Natasha pouted with her hands on her hips. "Why you turn your phone off? I had to reschedule three meetings and two interviews because of that little stunt. Diva Decorations sent over a bill, and no one seems to know where Benjamin is."

"Did you call him?"

"He left hours ago and hasn't answered his phone, nor text."

"He probably went out to do what white boys like to do. It will be fine. Calm down, girl."

"I'm trying to calm down, but you are not making it better by telling me to calm down.

Your problems, never do they realize that they are the problem."

Raymon tried to shake her off. He could see that she was frustrated, but he wasn't so sure of the real reason.

"Oh and, your home boy keeps calling collect for hours straight looking for you. I told him you were out, but he keeps calling back."

"Who Remix?"

"That's him." Natasha held out her phone.

"You had him on hold all this time you been ranting? He only got fifteen minutes, girl." Raymon grabbed the phone.

"So! I'm sure he will call back."

"Tasha, you on one. How you even know I was in the building?"

"Si-mon told me." she stuck her tongue out and disappeared inside the suite.

"Ray! Hello! Is that you?" Remix shouted.

"Hey! What's up, brah."

"What's up. I'm a tell you what's up. You acting fake as fuck because you got a few dollars. I been waiting weeks for you to send that bond money. What type of games you playing?"

"Now hold on, homie, I ain't playing no games. I told you I got you, and that's the truth. I just have to handle a few things first."

"That's not what I'm hearing."

"What you mean by that?"

"Word is, you losing every dollar you got on dumb shit. Dudes in here laughing at you, and everything. They saying you stupid as hell."

"And you going to listen to them fools? They just hating. You remember—"

"Man look," Remix cut him off. "I didn't call you to go down memory lane. You said you was going to look out and you didn't. Matter of fact, you haven't done nothing for the homies since you got free. I never would have thought you would turn your back on the same ones that held you down. Your word is all you got in here, you remember that? Oh, that's right, you ain't in here. But you broke your word, and to me that makes you broke."

"Hold on homie," Raymon tried to explain. But the beeps indicating that there was only sixty seconds left on the call had already started.

"Just forget it," Remix shouted. "You a new man now. I hope you find some new friends that will watch your back, cause we both know, it's a cold world. Or did you forget that too?"

"I didn't forget nothing! I told you I got you. Just have a little patience, that's all I'm saying. This money ain't change me. I'm still that dude, you hear me."

Ant ant ant! The sound of a disconnected call answered him. Raymon looked at the screen and cursed out loud. He walked into the living room shaking his head. When he turned around, Manhood was standing a few feet away from him eating an apple. "Mo money mo problems."

Raymon looked startled. "Do you ever wear a shirt?"

Suddenly, Chill Will rushed into the room with Bigmack right behind him. He had a black briefcase in his hand and a strange grin on his face. "Now don't trip. We had to make a move on this. We didn't want to tell you about it just in case it went sour."

"Yeah dogg, I wanted to say something, but Chill was so certain," said Bigmack.

"Certain about what?" Raymon looked confused.

"I got with a real investment guru-type business dude," said Chill Will.

"We got with," Bigmack corrected him.

211

"Yeah, we got with this dude and made a few light investments, stock market stuff. It's all legit." Chill Will scrolled some numbers back on the briefcase. "And Bam!" The briefcase flew open and revealed stacks of money all wrapped in individual bands.

Raymon placed his hands on his head and tried to make sense of what he was seeing. His eyes shot out of his head like a cartoon character. He patted his forehead with minimum force, in disbelief. "No no no, what did you do?"

"We did ten million dollars." Chill Will slapped him on the back.

"Wow! Ten million dollars," Raymon whispered.

"We know you having a hard time with this overnight billionaire thing, so we wanted to help. Show you the way a little." Bigmack smiled.

"Ten million dollars," Ray repeated.

"Ten million big ones." Chill Will gave Bigmack a high five. "Wow!"

Raymon paced back and forth. He looked like he was going into shock. He repeated the number over and over, until he finally screamed. His outburst caused his friends to pause their celebration dance.

"What's wrong Ray?" Chill Will held out his arms. "We just did you a favor. That's ten million dollars profit right there. Come on, you got a love that. Stacks of hundreds and fifties, we did good, right? Look at this."

But Raymon was looking. He stared at the case of cash with anger in his eyes. *These fools are going to ruin everything,* he thought.

"Take it back, " he ordered.

"What?" a duet of voices sang.

"This is clean money," Chill Will tried to explain. "We can't just take it back. And why would we?"

"Come on Ray", Bigmack held his palms up. "Listen to yourself. We did this for you, for us, the team. We can't just throw it away now."

"Yes, you can," Raymon shouted. "I don't want it. I don't need it. Now get it out of here." He turned his back.

Chill Will and Bigmack looked like they were accused of cutting wind in a smelly case of who done it. Chill Will snatched his hat off his head and stared at Raymon for answers. "You done lost your mind," he said. "I know what it is, you got billionaire fever."

"What the hell is that?" asked Bigmack.

"I read about it online. He got billionaire fever. He loses money and he happy. He makes money and he acting like he robbed somebody. It's a mental sickness and he got it."

Bigmack attempted to calm Chill Will down. Manhood chuckled in the back of the room.

Raymon was trying to think fast. He had less than ten days until the results of this money game would either leave him dead broke, or well off. He had already wasted his bag of ideas, along with a fortune, just to follow the rules. He imagined the snobbish faces of Lisa, James and Michael laughing at his failure and enjoying the fact that he would be broke and out of their hair forever. He turned around and looked at the briefcase. It made his eyes itch. He could smell the fresh bills; they made his stomach tighten. Then he heard the voice of his condescending grandfather, a man he never met in person. *And sonny boy, don't spend it all in one place.* He remembered the laughs. He could taste his throat go dry. He didn't want to touch that money, but he feared he was already implicated. As Raymon panicked in all five senses, he looked up and saw Manhood rocking back and forth.

"Damn Ray, you could just put it up for a rainy day," said Bigmack.

"A rainy day." Raymon's wheels started to spin.

"Yeah, a rainy day."

"Now that makes sense. Yo, Manhood, my man. Where is the best spot for us to have a rainy day?" Raymon smiled.

"Oh, you want a have a rainy day," Manhood nodded. "Yo god, I got just the right spot. But don't let me tell you no lies, word. Just ask my girl, YO Vicky!" he shouted.

Meanwhile, Benjamin was meeting his father in Hell's Kitchen. James had cooked up a plan that would catch Raymon in violation of his inheritance rules. Steam from a nearby restaurant shot up to the sky. Benjamin stood in the alley looking up with his hands in his jacket pockets. He heard footsteps behind him, spun around, and saw two large figures coming right at him.

"Don't. look so scared," said James. "You are not being mugged."

Benjamin breathed in the cold air and the foul odor of an open dumpster made him cough uncontrollably.

"Dear God, are you all right? Pull yourself together, son." James patted him on the back.

Through watery eyes, Benjamin looked up at the pale-faced behemoth of a man standing beside his father. He looked to be about 6 feet 8 inches in height. He had a military build and the haircut to go with it. Before Benjamin could catch his breath, James introduced the muscle-bound man as Ivan.

"Now listen closely," said James. "We have a golden opportunity to catch this hoodlum red handed and regain control of the Welloff estate. He is an outsider and not worthy of the financial rewards from a company that we helped succeed. He has no one to blame but himself, so don't get weak on me, son. All we have to do is get the evidence and he is finished."

"Ray is down to about 100 million in his spending account." Benjamin lowered his head. "That is a significant amount of money for most, but at the rate he is spending, he will run through it in a few days' time. I tried to talk some sense into him, but he won't have it. I don't understand why he is in such a hurry to go broke."

A loud crash froze Benjamin's speech. Ivan pulled out a silver revolver from his coat and aimed it in the direction of the noise.

"Put that away," James ordered. "It is nothing but a city rat."

Benjamin stared at Ivan, with his mouth halfway opened. He attempted to point his finger in Ivan's direction, but James slapped his hand down. "Stop it. Boy. That's none of your concern."

"None of my concern, Father he has a gun," Benjamin said. "I can't do this."

"You can and you will. I am your father and I need you to act like a man for once in your life. Do you want me and your mother to be kicked out of our home, you out here living with the rats like some bum? Then you do as

I say."

"I don't understand. What's going on?"

"All of this was expected. Why do you think Roger froze the rest of the

inheritance? We cannot let this Raymon character get his hands on that 2.5

billion or he will make a waste of

it also," said James.

Ivan looked in every direction like a quarterback before the snap. He

had a cold look in his eyes and never said a single word.

"Look at me, son." James clapped his hands together. "You told me that

this Raymon clown has a shipment coming in on the 22nd, correct?" He

waited for Benjamin to confirm. "Good! We will intercept this shipment

and all of its illegal goods. If you are right, this is all we will need to regain

Roger's fortune and kick this outsider to the curb. Ivan here will go with

you to help you avoid any unnecessary attention."

"Father, I don't think—"

"You are right!" James interrupted. "You don't think and that is why I

will do it for you."

Benjamin was screaming inside with confusion and frustration. He

wanted to tell his father to go fish. But the sounds of puddles splashing on the sidewalk demanded more attention from James than did his own son.

Avoid attention, he thought. *This scary giant will be hard to miss.* He listened to his father explain his intentions and Ivan's involvement. He did not want to go snooping around in Raymon's business or some dirty shipping yard at all, let alone with a military-tainted chaperon. It was a mess from the start. The whole idea seemed like some over-the-top espionage activity and Benjamin felt out of place.

"You just do your part," James waved his finger at him, then motioned for Ivan to come along.

While they made their exit, Benjamin stood there with his head low, thinking about his position in it all. He seemed to have gained multiple jobs overnight: Welloff account, overseer of Raymon's spending, secret financial adviser, and now private detective. He thought back to when it all changed, and why. *Raymon Platt*, he thought. *What's really going on?*

CHAPTER 17

The liveliest adult club in New York City is called The Black Rose, and it is located on A street and Northern. Manhood and Raymon crossed the street with conviction in their eyes. Planes stayed close behind them with briefcase in hand.

Bigmack followed them and tried to reason with Raymon as they approached the club. "Think about this, Ray. It's nuts," he shouted.

Chill Will brought up the rear. He shook his head in a silent protest.

Raymon smiled while holding the door open and waving his arm wildly for his companions to enter. Chill Will muttered some words when he passed by, but Raymon wasn't trying to hear it. They traveled through a dark hallway, followed the muffled sounds of music at the end of the hall, and saw smoke escaping from the bottom of the double doors.

Before Manhood could knock, the doors crept open. A large man in a suit stood in front of them with a stone look on his face and an ear jack connected. Manhood sized him up, then gave his traditional handshake, and short hug. They shared a brief laugh, and Manhood pointed to

Raymon. Unaware of what was being said, Raymon grabbed the case from Planes, opened it, and held it in front of his chest for the large man to see.

"We don't have change here for all of that." He crossed his arms.

"Who said we needed change?" Raymon smiled, then closed the briefcase.

The bouncer stepped to the side and allowed them all to pass. A huge plexiglass thumped like a see-through drum right in front of their eyes. They could see the horseshoe-shaped bar in the middle of the club from where the stood. The bouncer bumped his way past them.

Raymon grew a little nervous. He didn't know what to expect once the glass slid back. He never saw anything like it. Half-naked women waved to him from the other side. He could see a woman in a thong on a swing high up in the air like a circus act or trapeze star. He thought once the door was open, his suit jacket might get ripped off his body from the loud music being trapped inside. He braced himself with the briefcase held tightly to his chest.

When the door slid back, a cool breeze invited them inside. "Welcome to The Black Rose." Manhood spread out his arms. "Your country boys going to learn today."

The Black Rose was lit up with black lights along the walls, a disco ball above the bar, and a moving spotlight aimed in its direction of choice. Glass booths shaped like tubes were positioned all over the club, each one containing a different woman with nothing on but pasties, shaped like flowers to cover their goodies. There were silver poles in each booth. The women put on tempting shows from behind the glass, and when a customer wanted to get up close and personal, the booth would open up and release their desired.

Bigmack had his eyes glued to one booth in particular and quickly rested his rear end in the leather love seat across from it. Chill Will tried to snatch the briefcase from Raymon's clutches but was unsuccessful. He made his way to the bar with a foul look on his face.

Women in bikini skirts carried trays covered with empty shot glasses. Cigar smoke floated around the room. Groups of men laughed, while some women enjoyed a lap dance from one of the club's stars.

Raymon rubbed his nose and smiled. Manhood ran off, found two attractive ladies, and guided them over to Raymon. Planes looked like an old terminator machine, constantly checking his surroundings.

The DJ was stationed above the main stage. When the spotlight found Raymon, he looked around like his name was being called. "Ladies! We got the dope rapper Manhood in the house tonight. So please welcome my brother home the right way," said the DJ. "That's not all! Manhood brought a special guest. It's Richie Rich himself, so I know it's about to go down. Did you hear me right? We Got Raymon Platt Jr. here at the Black Rose and the whole world knows he ain't got no problem spending a few dollars. But you know the rules, it ain't tricking if you got it. So, let's help him and his homeboys get relaxed!"

Raymon was frozen in place. Women in G-strings and thongs made their way to him in a hurry. A stripper with a light-brown complexion took him by the hand and guided him through the club like a school teacher on the first day of class. He waved at groups of men, who screamed and cheered him on. His sexy guide stopped in front of the stage, turned around, and pushed him into a black leather one seater. Raymon bounced off the soft cushions, then rested his back on the plush seat.

Manhood chuckled at the sight of Raymon being manhandled by the exotic dancers. Drinks were served and it was time to have some fun. Raymon called Planes over, opened the briefcase full of money, and filled up his own hands with cash. He didn't know if The Black Rose was ready or not, but Raymon had reckless intent. He ripped off each money band and loaded up the money guns with hundreds and fifties, ready to fire.

Chill Will refused to look. He was disgusted by what Raymon was doing. He couldn't figure out why a man would be so foolish. His thoughts transformed his feelings to anger, as the bartender refilled his glass.

Bigmack walked over with stacks of money in each hand and a money gun hanging from his shoulder. "We here now." He smiled, but Chill Will only gave him a frown in return. He didn't want any part of the stupidity he assigned to Raymon. "Another drink!" Fascinating women in all flavors surrounding them. Bigmack handed Chill Will a stack of cash and he threw it to the sky without even taking a glance. "Another drink!"

There was comfort in every corner and liquor in every glass, thanks to Raymon. Manhood snapped photos with fans. One drunken woman tried to climb his six-foot frame and he put her on her back softly.

Bigmack shot cash in the air in rapid fire with two money spitters. Planes was being used as a pole. Two workers maneuvered around him, holding his neck and pressing their bodies up against him. But he kept his cool. Dancers in fishnet stockings took turns blessing Raymon's lap with their rumps. Money fell from the sky like leaves. Hundred-dollar bills were being raked up like litter. Women performing inside their private booths broke out onto the main floor to join the action. There were breasts, money, and booze everywhere.

Manhood shouted, "Yeah!"

Bigmack screamed, " Wow!"

And Raymon just smiled.

The club was so loud with excitement, it was hard to hear the music.

Chill Will turned his back to the action. The stool he was sitting on was hot

with anger. "Fuck it, dude want a go broke, fine then," he said to himself.

Then the lights went out. The sound of a blow horn trapped everyone's

attention. The stage came alive. A spotlight lit up the shiny wood floor. The

stage had one thick gold pole in its center. The pole went up so high,

Raymon thought it might lead to the clouds. An image was blasted on the

back wall, like the Bat signal. But it was the outline of a woman. It looked

like her back was arched, while she reached over her head. It was artistic

and seductive. It demanded attention and Raymon was ready to obey.

The DJ spoke into the microphone, "Gentlemen and Ladies, on this

historic night, I now take pleasure in bringing to the stage, the girl with the

dragon tattoo, the amazing, the legendary Moliah!"

When she stepped into the light, she paused, placed one hand on her

hip, and leaned to the side like a Victoria's Secret model. She walked over

to the pole and the way her long legs crossed one over the other made

men's jaws drop and their tongues roll out like carpets. She wore a pair of black pumps. Her white fishnet stockings were pulled up over her heels. They stopped right at the top of her thick thighs. Her matching bra and panties were so clear Raymon sat up and tried to get a peek of what was hidden beneath. She rocked an all-white top hat, cocked to the side like a gun slinger, and the look in her eyes said she was ready to shoot.

Once her hands were wrapped around the cold metal, a bouncy beat took over the speakers. She moved her body with the music and all eyes followed her. She had a coco-butter shine. Her hair was wet and cut short. It hung to the back of her neck. She looked over her shoulder at the crowd and moved her waist to the beat.

Raymon was mesmerized. He watched her movements with his entire body. She was like a snake charmer, whirling and twirling her figure. Raymon stood up and pushed his way to the front of the stage. He had stacks of money in his hand and tucked all around his waist. He threw down a shot of liquor, made a nasty looking face, and tried to climb the stage. But Bigmack jumped in front of him, waving his hands and shaking his head. Raymon couldn't hear a word his pal was screaming. He had that look in his eye; it was like Moliah's body was calling him. He threw one knee up, then used his free hand to crawl onto the platform. Men in do-rags and fitted shirts cheered him on.

Moliah went for her signature move. She bent over and wrapped her ass cheeks around the pole. With her perfectly round derriere pressed against the metal and her hands on her ankles, she looked up at Raymon stumbling toward her and smiled.

When he saw her eyes up close, he couldn't believe how amazing she truly was. She rose up slowly, staring at Raymon's face, and use her finger to motion him in closer. He approached her gripping his money to his chest, like a homeless kid looking for shelter.

Moliah stuck her tongue out and licked the tip of her nose. She straightened her back, placed her hands on Raymon's shoulder, and put her hat on his head. She swayed her body against his and worked her way down. With her face at his waist, she unbuckled his belt with her teeth, then stood up and turned around. Moliah crashed her soft backside against his pelvis area, over and over, until she could feel something growing up downstairs.

Raymon refused to take his eyes off his seducer as she continued to work her magic. Suddenly, she was climbing the pole. When she reached the top, she leaned backwards and hung there upside down like a gymnast. She pulled Raymon in closer and gave him a soft kiss. Hooting and hollering ensued behind him and added to the ballyhoo. The DJ cleared his throat, men wiped sweat from their foreheads, ladies clapped, and Bigmack's eyes widened. "She's a super stripper," he said.

When her lips separated from his, she pushed Raymon backwards so hard he almost fell. Then she flipped down from the pole and landed in a perfect split. Her cheeks gyrated on the wood grain, popping and shaking with violent intentions.

Raymon shouted with joy, "Yes!" He reached in his pants and started throwing money in the air. The bills flew above the stage and landed all over Moliah's back while she worked.

"Yes, in da face," Raymon hoorayed.

He ran across the stage like he won the Superbowl, high fived strangers, and shouted. He snatched Bigmack's money gun and started spraying the crowd with bills. A pile of money covered the stage like grass in a field.

Moliah smiled. With money stacked up to her ankles, it looked like a park in autumn. She needed a broom to clean up her earnings.

While the celebrations continued, Raymon jumped off the stage without a single dollar still on him. He found Planes standing with the look of indifference on his face, reloaded his pockets with cash and, spread the love.

Chill Will's liquid consumption finally caught up to him. He lost count of shots he had taken and the room was a blur. The music felt like a second pulse keeping him alive. He lowered his eyes and struggled to identify the figure rushing in his direction.

"What's popping playboy?" Manhood landed on a stool next to him. "Your man doing it big tonight."

"You gotta be stupid. He just throwing it all away. Who does that?" Chill Will blurted out.

"I been meaning to ask, why you so butt hurt about how another man spend his money? I mean, it's his bread not yours."

"I have known that dude most my life. We grew up together. We had nothing but each other and times were hard. It don't make no sense for us to finally come up, and he acting like that," Chill Will pointed at Raymon spraying the crowd with money and laughing. "You don't get to judge me."

"I see." Manhood lit up a blunt. "You talking like it's half your stash, all that us, and we talk is for bitches. Y'all ain't married, get your own god."

Chill Will gave him an evil look, leaned forward, and felt a sharp pain in his stomach. "Let me tell you something. We don't even know you. Who the hell are you anyways? What kind of name is Manhood? Get outa here, trying to tell me something."

228

Manhood pulled out his phone, looked at the screen with a surprised reaction, and stood up. Without saying another word, he patted Chill Will on the shoulder and walked off. Chill Will continued to vent. He stared at the stool, and even though no one was there, he cursed and pointed at the leather cushion.

When Raymon found his friend, he was slumped over the bar with a shot glass in his hand. "Hey Chill," he shouted in his face. "This club is popping," He laughed.

"That's what they going to say, them dumb fools from the country," Chill Will mumbled.

"Chill, you still alive. No more drinks for this man." Raymon pointed.

Chill Will looked up with a nasty look on his face. He turned around with his fist balled up and threw a weak punch that landed on Rayrnon's chest. "I gotta beat some sense into you." He collapsed to the floor.

Raymon waved Planes over to help lift up his drunken buddy. "I guess it's time to go."

He looked around and found Bigmack slapping butt cheeks and smiling. He shouted for his assistance and Bigmack stumbled over with a confused look. It was indeed time to go. Chill Will had one arm around Planes and the other over Bigmack's shoulders. They carried him to the exit with

Raymon leading the way. Women kissed Raymon on the cheek, men shook his hand, the DJ gave up a final shoutout, and they left the fun times behind them.

When they reached the parking lot, Raymon stood there with his hands on his hips. He looked in all directions, like he was waiting for something to happen.

"This fool is heavy," said Bigmack. He looked over his shoulder at Raymon and a lightbulb came on inside his head. "Where's the mad rapper?" he asked.

Raymon put his hands on his knees and started to laugh. Planes and Bigmack stared at him with a clueless look on their faces. "What?"

Then Raymon stood up with a grin, shrugged his shoulders, and said, "He's gone."

CHAPTER 18

Dec 22nd - 23rd

James, Michael, and Lisa sat in a private room, shielded from Welloff Software workers and the rumors spreading around the office. James swiped through text messages of Benjamin's weekly reports. "This can't be right," he said. Lisa squirmed in her seat. Michael tapped on the table with his fountain pen. When James looked up at them, he wore the face of disappointment.

"My God, James, what is it?" Lisa couldn't take the suspense. "We don't have time for games. Board members are starting to panic and I can't even grab a cup of coffee without hearing the chatter from these low-level employees. So, what is it? Where do we stand?"

"Well, let's hear it." Michael tugged at his blazer.

The back of James' neck became very warm. "The status is, he is going broke. According to Benjamin's numbers, come Christmas morning, Raymon Platt will be without a single penny in his spending account."

"How could this have happened?" Michael barked. "You said that you had this under control. I knew that wimp you call a son wouldn't make a difference. He was supposed to see to it that this did not happen. Where does this leave us?" He paced back and forth.

"In the poor house." Lisa sat back in her chair. "Without the remaining balance of Roger's fortune, we will lose the company. Shareholders will drop faster than the stock value itself and we will be finished. This is a nightmare." She held her head. "How is this even possible? Who could spend that much money in so little time?"

"What about the receipts?" asked Michael. "Do we have proof of all these transactions?"

"Benjamin forwarded proof of every transaction made. I have them on record. This Raymon is spending recklessly, just as Roger required. Look at this, he spent ten million dollars at a strip club." James frowned.

"That has to be a violation of the rules." Lisa crossed her arms and stomped her foot.

"Not if the women were providing a legal service." Michael took a seat. "I do believe we underestimated this character."

Lisa buried her face in the palm of her hands. "What are we going to do?"

James turned around with a smile on his face. "We still have a chance. Benjamin has informed me that Mr. Platt has been holding secret conversations and when someone comes around him, he disconnects the calls. His action may lead to illegal activity. After all, he is a criminal, and that type of mind set does not just go away. If anything, having access to the amount of currency that we have exposed him to would only push him further into his aspirations of being a better crook."

"What are you saying, James?" asked Michael.

"I am saying we learned that he has a big shipment coming in on the 23rd at the docks downtown. And from what Benjamin has gathered, it sounds illegal."

Lisa's interest grew. "What kind of shipment?"

"Over 10,000 pounds," said James.

"And you think it could be..."

"Drugs," Michael finished Lisa's thought.

It was as if they all received a drink from the fountain of youth. Their faces came alive with ideas and new possibilities. If Raymon was caught with crates full of illegal substances, he would clearly be in violation of not only his inheritance agreement, but the laws of the land.

Michael rubbed his bare chin. Lisa placed both hands flat on the table. James nodded his head like he could see the wheels moving around in his partners' brains.

"That is brilliant," said Michael.

"You have outdone yourself." Lisa smiled. "So how will we catch this thug and his gang in the act?"

"I have already taken care of that. We won't allow the future of this company to rest in the hands of some ruffian. That is why I hired a trusted asset to accompany Benjamin on a little mission to the docks on the date of delivery."

"A company man," Lisa was excited.

"Not exactly." James tilted his head. "But he is trained in the field, a real thorough soldier only called on for times like these."

"James, you old dog," said Michael. "You had us worried and all along you had back up plan."

A knock at the door startled them. "Come in," James shouted.

A young woman wearing glasses entered in a hurry. She placed a piece of paper on the desk and rushed out of the room.

"What is that?" James watched as Lisa opened the envelope.

Michael moved in closer and attempted to look over Lisa's shoulder. "Let me see that."

It was a gold envelope with shiny writings on it.

Lisa peeled open the lid and pulled out a thick red card. Her eyes grew in size. She read the words to herself with a smirk on her face, then passed it to Michael. James looked at them with questions in his eyes. "Well, gents," Lisa sat back, "I believe we have been invited to an album release party."

Later that night the Welloff offices were as quiet as an empty church. The staff had returned to their places of rest, computers were shut down, and keyboards tucked away. A cool air crept through the executive floor hallway, coming from a crack in the stairwell door. A shadow appeared on the wall. Its owner moved like a burglar, bouncing on his toes with every step. He moved carefully down the hall, looking over his shoulder and hunchbacked. When he reached the last door on the right, he looked at the tag on the window. It read CEO James Preacher.

He slowly entered the office, closed the door behind him, and tried not to make a sound. He made it across the rug and took a seat behind the desk. When he looked up at the blank computer screen, Benjamin saw his own reflection staring back at him. He snatched off his hoody and straightened his glasses, then pulled out the keyboard from a slide built in the desk. He noticed a family picture of him and his parents. It made him pause. His father had that familiar loaded look on his face. Why was he so hard to please? Benjamin thought. His whole life, he felt like everything he did was to impress his father and make him proud. He stared at the photo for a few seconds too long. He knew his father wouldn't approve of his actions, but he had already convinced himself: this I have to do for me.

Benjamin cut on the screen and his fingers started to move like he was possessed. He flew past security codes and cliche passwords. Once he gained complete access to his father's files, he searched for answers. He knew he was being kept in the dark about many things and was fed up with being lied to. It was, by far the gutsiest of undertaking Benjamin had ever attempted, but he had to know. The veins in his neck jumped with every push of the enter key. He could feel his palms sweating as he slid the mouse around its pad. He lowered his head and tightened his eyes when he saw a file marked: Welloff Board Status Speech.

He opened the file and read his father's words with great interest. *WE HAVE BEEN IN TIGHT TIMES BEFORE, AND WELLOFF SOFTWARE HAS ALWAYS COME OUT ON TOP. WE WON'T BE DISCARDED AND REPLACED*

LIKE SOME SINKING 500 CORPORATION OF THE PAST. WELLOFF SOFTWARE WILL REMAIN THE LEADER IN A FOREVER-CHANGING MARKET. YES, THE FREEZING OF ROGER BENNET'S ESTATE HAS SLOWED DOWN BUSINESS AS USUAL. BUT I CAN ASSURE YOU THAT IT IS ONLY A TEMPORARY ISSUE. A HICCUP IF YOU WILL, IN A LONG-STANDING TRACK RECORD OF SUCCESS. ROGER LEFT HIS MAJORITY SHARES TO THE COMPANY, TO THE FAMILY, AND AS SOON AS THE PROPER PAPERWORK WE SPOKE ABOUT IS SIGNED, OUR COMPANY WILL SEE PREVIOUSLY UNREACHED HIGHS IN THE HANDS OF MYSELF AND MY COLLEAGUES.

Benjamin sat back in his father's chair and tried to decipher the underhanded doubletalk. What paperwork, and soon to be signed by whom? Roger left his fortune to Raymon, his sole heir. Only in the event that Raymon could not handle his inheritance properly was the company supposed to step in. He thought it out. Benjamin's head began to hurt. He knew his father had his eyes set on Raymon's inheritance. Without it he claimed the company wouldn't survive. What he didn't know was that seeing Raymon fail was the whole plan from the start. Yet and still, something didn't add up. He tried to read more of his father's written speech, then he heard a noise. The office was completely dark. Only the glow from the computer screen gave away his location. Benjamin used his hand to lower the screen. He was ready to write the noise off as nothing, paranoia maybe, but then he heard a woman's laugh. His body tensed. He stretched his neck and looked around like a ferret in the wild. He told his fingers to move at an alarming rate. The laugh grew closer. He could tell it was coming from down the hall. He heard a second voice and his face began to itch.

Benjamin cursed himself for trying to play Ethan Hunt for a night. He closed each file and logged off, but it was too late. The doorknob turned and he was right in the hotseat. He quickly cut off the screen and did the only thing that made sense at the time; he ducked below the desk. A hand reached into the room and flipped on the light switch by the wall. Benjamin barricaded himself in the small space and used the chair as cover. If the unexpected visitors walked around the desk, they would have found a geeky-looking slim shape cuddled underneath with a silly look on his face. Benjamin focused on remaining still. His adrenaline was pumping so hard he almost forgot to think. Who would be in his father's office this late at night? He calmed himself. He listened to the female voice and immediately recognized her cadence.

"You have been a bad boy," said Lisa.

He heard their bodies crash down on the office sofa at the same time, someone cut off the lights. He tried to shake off his obvious suspicion, but the man's voice was one he could not mistake, even if he wanted to.

"Go easy on an old man," James role played.

Benjamin fought back his urge to come out of hiding, jump over the desk, and shout: You cheating scum. But then, he would have to explain why he was sneaking around, breaking into offices and hacking into company files. So, he hugged his knees close to his chest and thought about a better move. His head was steaming with anger. He could hear the sounds of aggressive kisses being exchanged and heavy breathing increasing by the second. He couldn't just sit there while his father committed adultery. He thought about his mother. Did she know? Of course, she didn't know her husband was a lying cheat. He checked his thoughts.

When he heard the sound of his father's zipper, he had enough. Benjamin pushed himself forward, but before he could spring from his hiding place, he heard the door open.

"My God, what are you doing in here?" said James.

"Get out." Lisa held her blouse closed.

A janitor backed into the office with headphones covering his ears and music blasting. He pulled a vacuum cleaner along, while practicing his dance moves.

James and Lisa shouted, but he couldn't hear a word. He continued to dance his way onto the rug until the lights began to flicker off and on. The flashes caught his attention and he thought he was back in an old disco club. He stopped, lifted his headphones, and looked around.

James stood in front of Lisa as she corrected her outfit. He stared at the janitor with burning eyes.

"I'm sorry sir. I didn't know, I thought everyone was gone for the night," the janitor tried to explain.

"Well, you thought wrong," James barked at the man. "In fact, the only one gone is you. You're fired! Now get out."

"Please sir, it's the holidays. Don't do this."

"I don't give a damn. Leave now before I call security."

"Please sir, I have kids to feed," the janitor pleaded.

"Did you not hear what he said?" Lisa stared at him. "Or maybe your music was too loud. Leave now!"

The janitor shook his head and began to sob. When he left the room, James slammed the door behind him. "Why is it so hard to find competent assistance?"

"Competence like that which your son has." Lisa chuckled and straightened her skirt.

"Benjamin is a spoiled brat, but he will do as he is told."

"And what exactly have you told him?"

"Just enough to keep him in play. But you need not worry about that, my dear," James reached for his smartphone.

"Let's finish this conversation in the broom closet." Lisa pressed her body against his chest.

"No! I have to go."

"But you always loved the broom closet."

"My wife needs me."

"I need you, James" she pulled on his tie.

"Take it easy on an old man. I told you once already. Now let me deal with the home amongst other things. I will gladly spank you another time." James opened the door and extended his arm.

"Fine then, if you say so. But I will not play second fiddle much longer."

They exited the room together, turned off the lights, and closed the door behind them.

Benjamin waited another minute. He listened carefully for movement. When he felt the coast was clear, he rolled the chair backwards, put one hand on its cushion, and helped himself to his feet. He looked around, took a deep breath, then stepped around the desk. His mind was spinning out of control. A part of him wanted to chase his father down and give him a piece of his mind. He pulled out his phone; he wanted to call his mother and tell her about what he just witnessed. He was so angry he fumbled with the screen and dropped his phone on the desk. When he went to retrieve it, he saw a brown folder under a stack of papers. It looked familiar. Benjamin removed the stack of papers and recognized the folder as the same one he was ordered to get from Rogers Bennet's sealed office. He had never been in THE BIG OFFICE before and remembered the folder very well. It was old and torn on the sides. His father was very intense about having it on that day and Benjamin now wondered why.

Benjamin looked at his watch; he didn't know if he would get another visitor. His nerves started to jump, and without fully thinking it over, he picked up the folder and headed for the door. His father would be pissed off when he found out it was missing, but at that moment, Benjamin didn't give a damn. He swung the door open and was caught off guard by the face staring back at him. The janitor looked at Benjamin with equal dismay. Maybe he forgot the vacuum or his MP3 strapped to the side of it. Maybe he was returning to beg for his job back. Whatever the reason, a clear explanation was something Benjamin was not going to stick around for. He tightened his jaw and pushed passed the frozen janitor in a heat. He made it to the lobby and rushed out a side door, terrified and out of breath. He hid the folder inside his shirt, pressed his back against the building wall, and reached for his phone. After the call was made, he listened. for the ring.

Honey answered with, "Hey, what's up Benji."

Benjamin took a deep breath and said, "I need your help."

CHAPTER 19

Raymon sat behind his desk with a look on his face that said ALL BUSINESS. Bigmack was across from him, moving his fingers at top speed, while Raymon read off his list, "Big balloons, maybe two thousand or more. Huge champagne bottles, I want them over-sized joints. Tell the company we ain't got no time to play, we need them ASAP. I don't mind paying extra. Also, I want them gift bags, and two dozen photo booths. People like pictures. The security guards are already paid, tell them to be there early. We need them to assist with the parking arrangements. Don't forget the liquor fountains, I want two in every corner. This has to be the biggest album release party this town has ever seen," Raymon said.

"What we going to do about Chill Will?" asked Bigmack.

"Nothing! Let him rest it off. He been locked in his room for days. I will have Si-mon check on him later. That boy needs rehab. What I really need is for someone to tell me, where the hell my assistant is?"

"I don't know, Ray. I thought she would have shown up by now." Bigmack shrugged his shoulders.

"We got a few days before this album drops and she M.I.A."

"I hate to say it, but you were paying her way too much. You paying us all too much, homie. Maybe you should just..."

"You hear anything from Manhood?" Raymon jumped in and pretended to sound concerned.

"That fool probably halfway to Mexico by now. There has to be a way for us to get that ten-million-dollar appeal bond back. Let me call up some attorneys."

"No! I don't need no greasy attorney all up in my financial space right now."

"Why not? We legit, " said Bigmack.

Raymon leaned back in his chair and lifted his phone to his face. When he lowered it, Bigmack was staring right at him. "What!" They were interrupted by a knock at the door. When Bigmack turned around, he saw producers, board mixers, and engineers lined up. Raymon hopped out of his chair with a smile. "What's up?"

"We would just like to thank you for allowing us to be a part of this wonderful project," said one producer.

Raymon walked over to the door and shook hands with each and every person. Bigmack watched him receive thanks and give out hugs to his music staff. Raymon ordered everyone to pick up a bottle of wine. They popped the seals with laughter in the air. Mark and Play entered the room and Raymon waved his hands to calm down the noise. "I want to give a special thanks to our in-house producers, the legendary Planet Pluto."

"You crazy man." Mark pointed at Raymon.

"Had lots of fun," said Play.

Everyone stood there for a second with their mouths open, but no words came out. Then Bigmack stood up. "You two speak English."

"English our money language," said Play

"And Mr. Raymon speaks fluently." Mark laughed and pointed.

Raymon looked at Bigmack and the room lit up in laughter. They all planned to spend New Year's Eve with him and the crew at the album-release event. Mark and Play said they needed to get home. They carried two large bags in each hand and bowed their heads on their way to the waiting helicopter.

Benjamin hurried through the door just in time to see the celebration subside. When Raymon saw the look on his face, he stopped. "Benji where you been?"

"I need to talk to you about something," said Benjamin.

"You know what, you been acting really funny lately." Raymon took a step backwards. "You been in and out of here and nobody seems to know where you are at times. You even missed our guy's night out, which was a lot of fun might I add. Don't think I'm not hip to you. I know what you're up to."

"You do?" Benjamin stuttered.

"Oh yeah," Bigmack joined in. "You got yourself a little girlfriend."

Benjamin looked at Raymon for clarity, hesitated, and pointed his finger at Bigmack, "A girlfriend. You think I have a girlfriend?"

"Well, is it a boyfriend?" asked Raymon.

Bigmack smiled and gave Raymon a slap on the back. "We don't judge," he said.

Benjamin shook his head and started to pace on the carpet. He raised his hand to say something, but Raymon beat him to it.

"Honey is downstairs in the car waiting for me." He put on his blazer, slid his phone in his pants pocket, and headed for the door.

"But we need to talk, " Benjamin shouted.

"Benji really, you need to work on your passive aggressiveness. I'm not trying to be all up in your business. But whoever you dating, man or woman or whoever, you can't get your point across by being passive. Hit me on the hip, I'm out bitches!"

Raymon walked out of the suite, and Benjamin just lowered his head. He exhaled strongly and said, "I'm not passive aggressive."

When he turned around, Bigmack was looking right at him. "Yeah, you are dogg."

Honey sat inside the SUV wearing a Fendi jumpsuit. When Raymon opened the door, she looked at him and smiled. For Raymon, her glow seemed to light up the world. He leaned in for a kiss, but he was paused by Planes asking for a destination.

Power 105 was located in Manhattan. Successful acts had to wait in line to gain an on-air interview with their favorite disc jockeys. But Raymon had juice; he had over a dozen interviews scheduled with the most popular DJs in the Tri-State area, and some by Podcast direct.

Honey was properly prepared after days of similar questions. She handled each event like a professional: Joking, showing her humility, and exuding confidence when needed. After an hour of chopping it up about the album and her personal life, the radio host started taking calls from the streets. Fans, haters, and citizens alike called in to express their thoughts and chat with the rising star. Steven directed his question to Raymon, who was seated next to Honey the entire time.

"How could you be so foolish and waste a fortune on meaningless things?" asked Steven.

Raymon looked at the host like he was just slapped in the face with a dildo.

"Let me clarify this," said the host. "Mr. Raymon and Honey Drop English are in the building to promote a great album, not answer silly questions. Next caller please," he ended the call.

"This is Porta Bay from the south," another caller claimed. "How you going to get billions of dollars as a black man, then do nothing to help the black struggle? You selfish! Why spend big money on an album, then give it away? You stupid! I hope PETA get a hold of y'all for all that animal killing support, with your outrageous outfit. And what about the homeless? Do you give a damn? No! There's countries that ain't got clean water, they could use some help you know."

"Hold up hold up." The host cut off the call. "We trying to do an interview here, people. So, if you ain't got nothing to say about the music, please fall back," he shouted into the microphone.

Raymon twisted in his chair. He felt a hand on top of his. When he looked up, he saw Honey mouth the words, you okay. Aggressive callers continued to attack Raymon with their words. Hearing about the interview being bombarded with naysayers, money advisers, and flat-out angry folks requesting Raymon's head, the host gave Raymon a sincere apology and closed the hour out with music from Honey's album.

Raymon proceeded to confess his indifference, "I ain't tripping." But his face told another tale. The voices played over in his head. A woman claimed to have five kids, and nowhere to live. She asked him why he couldn't open a shelter, or loan her some money to feed her children. Another woman yelled at him about his night at The Black Rose. "People are starving in the streets and you throwing money in the air." He recalled her complaint. Even though Honey pretended not to be smitten, Raymon could tell it was bothering her as well.

Random rants ripped through the studio walls. Raymon tried to tell them he wasn't some self-absorbed well-heeled wallet pusher. But the black community was on his back. White America laughed. His friends questioned his sanity, and strangers looked to him for a better day. The stress weighed on his head so heavy he removed his hat in hopes of lightening the load.

Honey pressed her lips against his in the elevator. He felt reality in her kiss. What he had with her was real. He wanted to confide in her, she would understand. Then the elevator doors opened, and camera flashes

250

blinded his thoughts. He couldn't tell anyone; he was already so close. *I just have to finish the game.* So, he marched onward.

One radio station after the other brought about more of the same. Callers were more concerned about Raymon's reckless spending than the rise of Honey Drop English.

Raymon tried to reply, but his words were drowning in public opinion, and crude scrutiny.

"My demo," she said. "Walking up and down the streets, handing out CDs to strangers, trying to get people to hear me. And Raymon Platt changed my life," she testified. "He is a good man who was blessed with an unexpected gift. So, let's give him a chance."

But even Honey's smooth style, and grace couldn't save him.

"It's Christmas for Christ's sake," shouted one caller.

"You a poor excuse for a brother," yelled another.

The interview at Jamming 94.5 was cut short due to serious threats being issued by callers. Raymon ripped off his custom-made tie in frustration on their way to a secured parking lot. He took a few pills and fell asleep on a short flight to a private air strip in New York. Planes awaited in a vehicle to pick them up and drive them back to the Grand Dora.

A winter's night looked down on them. Raymon stepped out of the car feeling groggy, looked up and said, "Is you judging me too?"

Hours later, Honey's siblings played in the other room while she pranced around her luxurious bedroom in boy shorts and a tiny t-shirt. Raymon lay on her bed in deep thought.

When she looked down on him, she could tell he wasn't present. "Let the haters hate, ain't that what you told me?" she said.

"Have you heard from Natasha?" Raymon asked.

"Not in a few days. I don't know where that girl ran off to, and without saying a word. That's just weird. At first, I thought you might had sent her to China to get her feet done." Honey smiled and landed on the bed next to him.

Raymon kept a poker face. It was almost Christmas Eve and he couldn't find his assistant. He wondered if someone was trying to sabotage his mission. Two and a half billion was a lot of capital for anyone to have, let alone an orphan from West Virginia. He began to actualize the reality of what he was facing. In forty-eight hours, he could officially become a billionaire.

"Look at me." Honey pulled his face toward hers. "Hello! Where did you just run off to mentally? I know you ain't still tripping over them fools at the radio stations. They don't know you. Don't let them get into your head. You know something. When I met you, I thought you was just another fool in the streets."

"Oh, is that right," Raymon took issue.

"Yeah! I mean, you were cute in a clumsy kind of way."

"I'm the clumsy one." He grabbed her and started to roll around in the bed. He tickled her until she screamed, then kissed her on the chin lightly. Holding her in his arms, Raymon got lost in the moment.

But before he could say those three words on the tip of his tongue, Honey continued, "For real, you are a good man. I know everyone is questioning your moves, but they aren't you. And until they can wear the same shoes, they really can't judge. I mean, everybody was throwing shade when you took a chance on me. You could have signed anybody and pushed them into the light, but you chose me. Now we looking at a number-one album, and that's just the start."

"Wait what?" Raymon's face changed.

"The album went number one."

"Who told you that?" Raymon looked around with a strange feeling in his gut. "Too bad we giving it away for free," he baited her.

"There's other ways to make money," Honey batted her eyes.

"What you mean by that?"

"Okay look, but you can't get mad." She bit her nails. "You shouldn't get mad. I'm a loyal chick, and I expect the same back."

"What are you talking about?" Raymon rolled to one side.

"I was told not to tell you. Well not now anyways."

"Tell me what?" Raymon sat up.

"Seeing that I signed a 360 deal with Raymon Records, the company can make money off all my ventures, not just music," Honey said.

"This I know, but we don't have any other ventures right now. Do we?"

"Well, it just so happens that I got some movie deals and some advertisement gigs set up."

"Who set them up?"

"Benjamin." Honey smiled.

Raymon's blood started to boil. His muscles got tight. He could hear ringing in his ears. He shook his head side to side. "No, this can't be right."

"I knew I shouldn't have told you." Honey sucked her teeth.

Raymon stood up. "I don't understand. "

"He said we could expect the checks soon, Christmas morning the latest.

You could use a pick-me-up after today's fiasco. So, surprise!" Honey made a happy face.

"What else did he tell you?"

"Something about a multimillion-dollar tour advance. We already giving the album away, for free, which I thought was crazy from the start, seeing that you didn't even ask me nothing about it." Honey pouted. "But after seeing the fans reactions, the shows and social media followers, I saw your vision. It makes perfect sense. The album is the promotion, the product is the artist."

"What!" Raymon drifted off.

"He said you wouldn't understand, " Honey sat up on the bed.

But Raymon understood well. He searched his mind for a counter plan. At first, he pondered on how long Benjamin could have been involved. Then his mind rested on an answer:

Business is for family, and family is the business, he remembered. With the plot uncovered, it made perfect sense to him. Benjamin was playing both sides. The Welloff counsel had no intentions on handing over billions to him. They were playing dirty. Raymon need an ally, but he couldn't break the rules. *That's what they want,* he thought. He tried to remain calm and collect his mind. He looked at Honey playing with her phone and realized what he had to do. The only problem was it required a price he wasn't

willing to pay.

CHAPTER 20

Benjamin began to shiver the moment he stepped foot outside of his sedan. He wore a peacoat buttoned up to the collar and a pair of black gloves. Ivan parked across the street from the loading port. On a normal night, one would approach from the front, flash their import/export qualifications, and proceed to the back where large shipments were stored for pick up and transported. But it wasn't' t a normal night.

Ivan crept along the sidewalk and tried not to draw too much attention. With his back pressed against an abandoned building, he waved his arm for Benjamin to follow. He wore a black knitted hat pulled down below his blonde eyebrows, black gloves, and a black sweater - two sizes too small for his frame. When Benjamin showed up beside him, Ivan put one of his large hands on his shoulder and pointed toward the shipping docks.

Benjamin shook his head. Ivan took it as a sign of reluctance. But Benjamin was questioning his own actions. *What am I doing here*? He hadn't confronted his father about his cheating ways; he didn't know how he would break the news to his mother. At least, he could have had enough balls to tell his dad, go to hell with all your plotting and scheming over

Raymon's inheritance. But there he was, in the wrong place, thinking about the right things to say.

A full moon shined down on them. It provided a glimpse into the small alley they stood in. The smell of fresh fish was unmistakable. Benjamin threw his scarf over his nose, trying desperately to block the pollution.

Ivan looked comfortable standing in waste and unidentified feces, although he jerked his neck at the slightest noise. Men wearing hard hats and blue wind breakers walked all around the docking area, but the back gate was wide open. Ivan noticed a truck leaving and seized the moment. He hurried along the side of the building, then beelined his way to the open gate.

He moved so fast; Benjamin didn't see what happened. After the truck passed by, Benjamin saw a hand waving in the air from behind a set of crates. He could hear the beeping sounds from a crane, as he made it beyond the gate. When he got to the crates, Ivan was gone.

He looked around like he lost his dog, then heard a whistle from above him. He looked up just in time to see Ivan leap from one plate form to another. Benjamin's eyes grew larger. *Who does this guy think he is?* When he finally caught up to his acrobatic cohort, Ivan was lying on the floor behind a second set of crates using a pair of binoculars.

"What are you doing?" Benjamin tried to catch his breath.

"What is the name of the boat?" Ivan's voice was low but strong. When he spoke, it sounded like he was trying to gargle with an accent.

"The Tin Man," said Benjamin.

"And the numbers on the crates?"

"The last four digits on each crate are…" Benjamin fumbled with a piece of paper he stole from Raymon's office. "They are six. one. seven. five."

Ivan watched in silence as forklifts and cranes carried wooden boxes in different directions. A man stood in the tower right across from them; he pushed a floodlight in the direction of his choice. Ivan adjusted his scope and focused his eyes on one specific area. Benjamin tried to get a peek at what Ivan was gawking at, but when Ivan felt movement behind him, he reached back and pulled Benjamin to the wet floor.

"Hey man! What are you doing?" Benjamin said. The strength of Ivan was too much for him.

"You are taking this way too seriously. This floor is wet and cold." Benjamin held on to his peacoat. "Do you hear me?"

Ivan didn't respond. He kept his eyes glued to his binoculars. His head slightly moved from side to side, like he was on an army lookout post.

"This is nonsense. I'm just going to ask the foreman, if we can have a look inside the crates." Benjamin tried to stand up.

"Sit down." Ivan used his arm to prevent him from rising.

Water soaked through Benjamin's pants. He could feel a puddle forming around his boxers.

"Are you insane. This isn't some secret-ops mission. And you are not some Russian Jason Bourne. You ruined my slacks!"

"Let's go." Ivan jumped to his feet and ran across the deck with his back hunched over.

Benjamin thought he was watching an old Arnold Schwarzenegger film. Ivan was in full commando mode. Suddenly, Benjamin noticed the man in the tower looking in Ivan's direction,

then he reached for the floodlight. The beam was headed right for Ivan. He would surely be spotted. Benjamin panicked. A 6-foot muscle-bound man, wearing all black; he looked like a cat burglar on steroids. Benjamin had to think fast.

He kicked the crates in front of him and tried to make as much noise as his little foot could.

The man in the tower stopped short of Ivan's location and shot his beam in the opposite direction. Light illuminated the spot, but Benjamin was gone. He spun the floodlight around and focused on the containers. Not even a mouse was spotted. A few seconds passed and he gave up his suspicion, lowered his beam to the floor, and sat back in his seat.

Meanwhile, Benjamin was out of breath. He stood inside the dark container with Ivan holding the door closed. "Good job mate. Maybe you're not as useless as your father says."

Benjamin looked as if he wanted to say something back, but he was so out of breath, he gave it up. He had to sprint over to the container in record time. All of his spy-like activity was giving him a workout he was not quite ready for.

Ivan pulled a lighter from his pants pocket. Click! A flame shot up, and they saw two shelves covered with brown boxes on both sides of them. There was a small aisle running down the middle of the container. Ivan slid his feet like a basketball player on defense, moving down the aisle.

"Are you sure this is the container from the Tin Man?" Benjamin asked. He had to hold his own mouth closed, when he noticed the 6175 written on the boxes. He couldn't believe how many of them were stacked up. An odd smell snuck up into his nostril; he wrapped his scarf around his face. His eyes started to water and he felt a sick feeling build up in his tummy. As he got closer, he could clearly see the stamp on each box. it read: Vietnam. Benjamin put both hands on his head. His father was right, he thought. Raymon was importing illegal drugs into the United States. His thoughts were running away. *How stupid of me to believe in a criminal. What else could Raymon have purchase from a third world country in so much bulk?*

Click, clack click! The door was locked behind them. Before Benjamin could react, he felt the weight of Ivan push past him. Ivan used all his muscles to push open the doors. They wouldn't budge. He dropped his lighter, reached down to pick it up, but couldn't find it. He attempted to force the doors open by throwing his body into the steel, but they wouldn't move. Instead, he successfully caused a few boxes to hit the floor.

The container shook. Benjamin looked at Ivan; his face was covered in sweat. The container shook a second time. It felt like they were moving. The ground was still but the walls swayed. "Help!" Benjamin yelled.

The shelves started to vibrate and that's when Benjamin saw Ivan holding onto the steel structures. He had a hand on each one and his eyes clenched shut.

"What are we going to do?" Benjamin shouted at him.

Ivan was mumbling some words over and over. A crane lifted the container above the deck and carried it away. The elevation gave Ivan stomach pains. Benjamin tried to remain calm. He used his hands to search the floor for Ivan's lighter. He was only able to see a few inches in front of him and would have to make it count. A thump stopped them in midair. Benjamin stood up wondering what was next. The walls started to shake. He thought they would be dropped in the ocean. Then he realized, it was Ivan shaking the shelves with all his might.

"What are you doing?" Benjamin stepped back from him. "We need to get out of here."

But Ivan was like the Ultimate Warrior on the wrestling ropes. He shook the shelves and his mumbling turned into a cry mixed with an echo of screams.

The more Benjamin tried to get through to him, the more Ivan shook the shelves. They were suspended in air. The container rocked back and forth. And with Ivan's help, the boxes started to slide up against each other. Then it happened. One of the steel beams holding the container slipped.

Benjamin flew forward and slammed into Ivan's chest. Boxes busted open and their contents spilled out everywhere. Ivan's back crashed into the doors with so much force it knocked the wind out of him. Benjamin landed on top of him. He felt a wave of substance piling over his body. It was in his ears and over his eyes. It was in his mouth and down his sweater. Benjamin felt like he was being covered in dirt. His back became heavier with a strange stench.

Outside, the workers shouted orders and waved their arms around like they were having an Uber plane ride. The crane operator lowered the container to the ground. When the steel connected with the concrete, he leveled it out and placed it flat on its bottom. The foreman rush over to assess the damages. When he opened the door, he found two men covered in brown cat poop coffee. Kopi luwak is one the most expensive coffees in the world. It is sold for over $500 dollars per pound. It is made by collecting coffee beans that were eaten, then digested by an Indonesian cat-like animal called a palm civet. The price for a single cup of kopi luwak coffee runs from $65 dollar to $100.

Benjamin sat next to Ivan in the Foreman's office, trying to explain just how they ended up in the container.

Ivan was still spitting out grains, when it was explained to him what they were covered in.

The Foreman held his nose and looked at the embarrassed faces before him. After he told them the 10,000 pounds of coffee was to be delivered to Welloff Software, Benjamin made a few calls, and they were identified as Welloff Software employees. Benjamin told the Foreman they were there to inspect the shipment. His quick thinking paid off and they were let go.

As they left the docks, workers came from all directions to get a look at the night prowlers caught covered in poop. They pointed their fingers and laughed.

Benjamin lowered his head. He felt ashamed, disrespected, and above all guilty. But not for sneaking around the shipping yard, or for breaking into his father's office, and surely not for listening to his father, or allowing the PSD solder he hired to lead him on a wild-goose chase. Benjamin felt guilty for not trusting Raymon. There was more going on than he imagined, and he was determined to find out what.

Chapter 21

Manhood stood in front of the Black Rose with both hands on his smartphone, moving his fingers at a slow pace. He looked up at the silent street straight ahead with anticipation. His diamond earrings were the only sparkle of light in the gloomy neighborhood. He knew the guys would be upset with him for ditching them, but it was too late to turn back.

He tucked his phone away the moment he spotted headlights headed his way. A green sports car cruised down the street, stopped at the intersection, and flashed its lights off and on. He crossed the street with his hands inside his bomber jacket, looked both ways, reached for the door handle, then disappeared inside the car like a spook in the night.

"I thought you would never get here, Shorty." He sank down in the passenger seat.

"What, you thought, I was going to let you stand me up on our first date?" Natasha smiled.

They drove off into the night like a memory that wasn't real. Her music played at a low volume and Manhood was feeling the vibes. Natasha kept her seat close up on the wheel and her back straight up, like a cadet. Manhood reached for the middle console, reclined his chair, and peeked out the window like a private detective. He could smell her perfume exciting his every thought. When he noticed the fraternity tags hanging from the rearview mirror, he said, "The pink and green okay! I see you set tripping on me."

Natasha laughed. She had a silk scarf tied around her neck. Her short-sleeve dress shirt seemed to have been crafted in honor of her upper body. In other words, it fit so good. Manhood grabbed his winter hat from his coat pocket, pulled it down over his bald head, and gave Natasha the side eye.

"What you peeping at?" she said.

"Nothing but pure perfection." He reached for his cell phone.

He gave her directions to an exclusive Chinese restaurant in Queens. She asked him how he managed to slip away from strippers, shots of liquor, and the rest of the guys. "Them fools so drunk, all they paying attention to is the booty," he said.

They laughed about past week events and scratched their heads over Raymon's spending habits. "Why is he so reckless?" Natasha asked. "He going to mess around and go broke."

Manhood reserved a small table in the back of the dim eatery. It had a long black tablecloth and two scented candles. Natasha could tell there was more to the rapper than his tough image and legal woes. He opened doors and pulled out chairs for her. When she excused herself and headed for the restroom, he stood up and extended his hand to assist her.

"I shouldn't have to go to prison because of who I know," he shared with her. "I'm just a 26-year-old brother trying to make it to 27."

As they enjoyed each other's company, Natasha drank red wine like it was Kool-aid. She rubbed her fingers around the edge of the glass, stared into Manhood's light brown eyes, and asked him penetrating questions like: "You got kids?"

"Not yet."

"How do you know you don't have any STD's?"

" Got checked."

"What's your favorite quote?"

"If you chase two rabbits you catch none."

"Where are your people originally from?"

"Man is older than the moon, stars, and the sun."

"F.M.K, Michelle Obama, Oprah or Chris Jenner?"

"I'm fucking Chris, marring Michelle, and offing Oprah."

268

"That's cold." Natasha laughed.

"Okay, this interview is over." Manhood threw down his napkin.

He stood up, paid for their meal, then helped Natasha to her feet. She held on to his biceps and allowed him to guide her out. When they reached her car, Manhood put her safely in the passenger seat and took the wheel. He struggled to adjust the seat, then figured it out while Natasha kicked off her backless heels and put her feet up on the dashboard. It was 2:45 a.m. They drove across the highway headed to Manhattan like they owned it. Manhood rolled up his sleeves on his thermal shirt and Natasha admired his tattooed arms as he clenched the steering wheel. She was staring at the side of his face when she saw his eyes look up.

He stared into the mirror with a frozen look on his face. Natasha sat up slowly, feeling alarmed. She was just about to ask him what was up when she saw the lights. Red, blue, and white beams reflected off the black leather seats.

Manhood dropped his gaze, looked at the speedometer and realized they were traveling two miles under the speed limit.

Natasha looked behind her and saw the police cruiser hot on their bumper. She looked to Manhood; he was shaking his head and mumbling words. Then he turned his head, looked her in the eyes and said, "It's going to be all right."

He put his foot on the brakes and the car slowed down. He clicked on the turn signal and they rolled to the side of the road. When they came to a complete stop, Manhood leaned back in his seat and placed his hands in his lap.

Natasha pulled out her phone, but before she could press a button a flashlight tapped on the side glass. She turned her head to Manhood and saw that his window was already rolled down. He sat in silence with a look on his face, like he already knew the approaching outcome. Natasha rolled down her window and the bright light blinded her.

"License and registration," said the officer.

Manhood turned his head. "The wheel is on this side."

"License and registration," a second officer popped up on the driver's side. He looked to be in his twenties and mixed. His uniform didn't have a wrinkle in it. Manhood looked at him and shouted loud as he could, "I do not have any weapons or dangerous objects on me or in the vehicle. I am asking for permission to reach into my wallet and pull out my driver's license."

"We got ourselves one of them Black Lives Matter jerks," said the first officer. He was six-feet tall and when he removed the flashlight from the side of his face Natasha could see his pale skin clearly. She sighed.

"Miss, I'm a need you to put your hands on the dashboard," he said.

Natasha dropped her phone in her lap and extended her arms. She looked at Manhood with lazy eyes as he handed the second officer his license then looked at her and winked.

"Are you Trevor DuBois?" the officer asked.

His partner lowered his head and pointed his light right in Manhood's face for a closer look. "Holy shit."

In a split second he drew his pistol and aimed it at Manhood's chest. His partner looked confused, but he was taught always to back up his fellow officer. He fumbled with the ID and went for his gun. Manhood had his hands in the air before anyone could yell freeze. Natasha lowered her head and screamed.

"Get out the car," said the first officer, clearly talking to Manhood.

"Slowly," shouted the second.

Manhood reached out the window and opened the door from the other side. He moved so slow he would have lost a race with a snail even with a head start. He stepped out with his palms in the air.

271

"What did we do?" Natasha asked.

"Shut up and be quiet," said the officer.

Manhood placed his hands on the hood and the officer pulled his wrists down one at a time and handcuffed him. The first officer ordered Natasha to "step out, lay on the grass, and don't move." He put his knee on her back and started to pat her down when she shouted, "Don't touch me."

"Pick on someone your own size, pig," Manhood said with his chest pressed against the car.

"What you say!"

"I said, try that shit with a man and stop being a bitch."

The officer was so angry he rushed around the car to get in Manhood's face. "Say something else, boy." He put his gun on Manhood's cheek.

His partner gave him an odd stare and took a step back.

"This is none other than Manhood," he said. "The same piece-of-shit rapper that shot up Jimmie and Todd. You should have stayed in jail, boy."

"This is the guy?" his partner questioned.

Manhood turned his head. "Your buddies tried to kill me and you know it."

"Don't say another word or I swear to God, I will end you right here right now," the officer yelled. He paced back and forth like he was battling angels on both shoulders. His partner watched him bump his own firearm against his head and got nervous.

"Hey Bill, you wanna take them downtown?" he asked.

"For what? A ticket? This scum bag is out on a 10-million-dollar appeal bond. A stinking ticket won't even hold them for a night. We ·need to do something."

"You need to talk to your partner." Manhood lifted his head.

"You don't want to go down this road. Murder is murder no matter what you wearing."

"That's it! I'm a do it." The cop aimed his barrel.

His partner tried to push him back, but when he looked up, he froze. The first cop saw his partner's face just in time. He followed his stare over top of the car where Natasha was holding her phone up high.

"We are streaming live on the highway where two of New York's finest are about to execute the rapper known as Manhood," she said.

Overwhelmed with embarrassment, the rookie cop reached out with his hand and helped lower his partner's gun. He uncuffed Manhood and spoke loudly, "Next time, try to keep it under the speed limit sir," then dropped the I.D on the ground.

When Manhood reached to pick it up, the white cop stepped on it.

"Next time rapper," he whispered.

Manhood watched them return to their car and drive off. When he could only see their brake lights in the distance, he looked to Natasha and said, " You saved my life, shorty."

Chapter 22

December 24th

The Venue was set. Inside a rented building in upstate New York, surrounded by concrete, the album release party of the year had just begun. Raymon spared no expense on upgrading the meek building and its vacant lot. Live reindeers were lined up in a circle around the parking lot, wearing Christmas lights and red coats. Men dressed in Santa suits greeted each vehicle, took their invitations, then led the front of their reindeer chain away from the driveway.

The red carpet was rolled out. Literally! It started from the parking lot and led all the way up to the front entrance. The outside of the building was painted to resemble the fancy sled Santa Claus rode in while delivering gifts to the world. But the real wonders were inside. Twelve dozen tables carved out of ice were spread out around the ballroom. Eleven Hennessey fountains poured the dark liquor nonstop. Ten cigar rollers continued to offer fresh tobacco to guests. Nine tanks of live lobsters and eight portable bars impressed the well-dressed adults. Gift bags were handed out at the door. A peek inside found: seven gift cards, six fragrance bottles, and five golden rings. There were four selfie booths, three hookah rooms, two Persian rugs and a Partridge in a pear tree.

Raymon invited club impresarios, restaurateurs, and entrepreneurs. He had a live band on stage playing instrumentals from *Naughty or Nice*, along with their own renditions of each song. There were waiters and waitresses wearing holiday outfits and providing ·services. Smoke from a grill placed on the outside balcony rose to the sky, while cold liquor was poured into glasses.

The master of ceremonies took the stage. He stood in front of a white Christmas tree, lifted his microphone and said, "On behalf of Raymon Records, we hope that everyone is enjoying themselves. We are here tonight to propel a new artist by the handle of Honey Drop English, into the world of entertainment. And we would like to thank you all for showing your support. Feel free to take a private listen to the album in its entirety in anyone of the listening booths stationed around the room. Let us offer a cheer to Honey Drop for her hard work and future success. Number one baby." He held out his glass. "And a special salute to our host with the most, Mr. Raymon Platt Jr."

Raymon lifted his glass high up in the air and nodded his head from the back of the room.

"Salute! " A chorus of voices shouted.

The band cranked up a groovy melody and booties started moving. A bar rolled up next to Raymon and he helped himself to a drink. When he turned around, a recorder was staring him in the face.

"Don't you think this is a little too much for an album release party?" a middle-aged woman in a business suit asked.

"Haven't you media folks been paying attention?" Raymon ran his free hand over his fade. "We do everything big."

"What do you have to say about the reports claiming you are going broke?"

"You see, that's why I invited you, Amanda." Raymon laughed. "I read your blogs and you always cut right to the meat."

"So is it true," Amanda pushed.

"For example," he ignored her again, "it's like the blog you wrote about my lifestyle, saying I'm trying to keep up with the Carters."

"It has been reported that your reckless spending habits have put you and your company in the red. There are records that prove you have wasted your entire fortune on foolish, childish things like strippers and booze."

Raymon looked over her head and saw Benjamin walk into the room. He watched him carefully as he approached some familiar faces. James, Lisa, and Michael looked out of place, in tight suits and stiff shoes. He couldn't hear what was being said. But the thought alone, made him cringe.

Benjamin wasted no time. He marched into the celebration wearing a shabby blazer and walked right up to his father. "How could you!"

"Calm yourself, boy, James hushed. You look a mess."

"Don't worry about how I look. In fact, don't worry about me at all. How could you!"

"What are you whining about now?"

"Everything! The scheming, the lying, the cheating. How could you even be seen in public with this slut." He threw his finger toward Lisa.

Lisa stepped forward. "Excuse you, little boy."

"Yes! I know all about your late-night studies with your hussy," said Benjamin.

"I will not stand for this." Lisa looked to James.

"But you lay down with a married man. You two make me sick."

"What's gotten into you, boy?" James raised his voice. "I am not impressed. You had one job and you couldn't even do that correctly."

"Which job is that, Dad? Sneaking around a shipping yard for coffee, spying on another man who is just trying to live his own life, or are you talking about making sure Raymon doesn't go broke, so you greedy thieves can take what was left to him?"

"I think we need to have this conversation somewhere else," Michael mentioned.

"No, right here is fine." Benjamin reached under his shirt.

Lisa stepped behind James. He had the look of shock on his face. He watched Benjamin reach into his pants and wondered where he got the balls to talk to his own father this way. "What are you doing son?"

Benjamin pulled out the brown folder and slammed it into James's chest. "I know all about it, Father."

"Where did you get this?"

"The same place you tried to do her at."

"Those files are top secret," Michael said. "You have no right. We have details about government contracts in there. James! Put this dog on a leash or I will." He tightened his face.

Raymon took a sip from his glass and smiled. "Look at me." He was wearing a black suit, a set of diamond flooded cuff links, wrap-around shades and shiny black dress shoes. "Do I look like I'm going broke? Ninety percent of communication is nonverbal. Never believe what you hear, but always bet on what you see." Raymon excused his way past her.

"Where is the rapper, Manhood?" Amanda asked. "Did he skip town?"

Raymon stopped in his tracks, looked over his shoulder, and laughed. "Have a good night Ms. Amanda Media."

Chill Will was halfway through a bottle of wine. His Santa Claus hat was falling off his braids. "It's lit up in here," he shouted. He was leaning against the stage, slapping fifty-dollar bills in the hands of whoever passed him by. "Merry Christmas!" When he saw Raymon coming his way, he pushed his weight off the platform. "Ray, my partner! Happy holidays brah. Check it out, I'm doing like you, just giving this shit away."

Raymon glanced at his pal with disappointment in his eyes. "I thought you was through with all this drinking mess."

"Who me? What you trying to say? I got a problem or something. Naw homie, it's you that got the problem."

"I ain't got time for this." Raymon sidestepped him.

"You got the problem." Chill Will forced a laugh. "But no worries, we going to always be there for you, baby. We boys! You hear me, we boys!"

Raymon was halfway across the room, yet he couldn't stop shaking his head, thinking about the decline of his close friend. *I made associates and lost friends.* He remembered his grandfather's words. But he never thought money would cause more problems than it solved. He walked up behind Benjamin and tried to clear his mind. After all, there was still a game to be played, and won.

"Hey! What do we have here?" He rubbed his palms together. "The whole Welloff family reunited at last. Family is business you know, thanks for coming."

"It is our pleasure." James forged a smile.

"The music is a bit loud; don't you think?" said Lisa.

"Well, it is an album release party." Raymon laughed.

"Benjamin was just telling us about all the energy you put into this event," Michael lied.

"Not to mention all the money." Raymon slapped Benjamin on the back.

"Oh yes, the money." James nodded.

"That reminds me," Raymon said. "I want to thank you for loaning me your son. My man Benji, he's so sharp. His service has been, how can I put it, worth every cent."

Benjamin kept his back turned. He couldn't look Raymon in the eyes.

"You are quite welcome," said James. "I understand that you have spared no expense in making this a memorable event."

"Why yes! Money is of no concern to me. It must be the Welloff in my blood." Raymon faked a laugh and they followed his lead.

"So then, we will see you tomorrow to wish you a proper Merry Christmas," said Lisa.

"You sure will!" Raymon stared at each of them like he was trying to read their thoughts. A moment passed, then, "Well there is still so much to do. So, let me go attend to my other guests and we will be in touch. Please let me know if you need anything, something to eat, a smoke, or maybe some coffee, he searched their faces for a response. Oh no, you probably have enough that." He smiled. "All right then, have a wonderful night."

When he finally walked off, Benjamin lifted his head and exhaled in relief. "He knows something is off."

"He knows nothing," Michael waved him off.

"He is smarter than you think."

"Calm down, son. Pull yourself together."

"You asked me to see to it that he doesn't go broke, knowing that if I successfully did that, you would be able to steal what was left to him. You made me an accessory to your plot. You lied to me, sent me on missions and betrayed my trust. I believe I have earned the right to know the truth."

Lisa looked at Michael, then James lowered his head. "I suppose you have. It will all be over tomorrow anyway. Roger didn't want us to have his money, nor control of his shares, it seems. But he had no one to give it to. He left instructions in his will so that we couldn't touch it. The old fool had no one, you see. He died empty and alone."

"Good ridden," said Lisa.

"Turns out that, before he cashed his final check, so to speak, he managed to dig up this Raymon Platt, his sole heir. Please! But I know Roger. He doesn't want his money, nor his company in the hands of this clown. That is why he set up this game in the first place, to test us, to see who really deserves to come after him. He gave us a way back in, by allowing this claptrap to even start. I know how he thinks."

" But he left it all to Raymon," said Benjamin.

"It's our money! The company's money. And to make us watch some outsider just throw it away, well I always knew Roger was a sick bastard, but this takes the cake."

"It was a waste of funds," said Michael.

"And a waste of time," Lisa added.

"So, there you have it. Raymon was given 30 days to spend 500 million dollars in order to gain the remaining 2.5 billion in the frozen savings account. If he isn't broke, without a dime to his name by Christmas morning at 12 p.m., he will forfeit the inheritance and we will have beaten Roger at his own game." James clenched his fist.

"But it's his money." Benjamin stared off into space.

"Son, we have to do what's best for our family. You said you had some money you are supposed to give him tonight. And you wanted the truth, so now you have it. We need you to do the right thing, son. Withhold this advance money you speak of, just until noon tomorrow. The stipulations are our only hope of saving this company."

Benjamin was at a loss for words. He couldn't believe the position he was placed in. He watched them congratulate him in what seemed like slow motion. *Welcome to the team*; he saw Michael's mouth move. They used him as a pawn the entire time and he never knew he was on the board. Benjamin felt the room spinning. He had taken a lot of lumps the past few days. Then he realized the true source of his nausea was the fact that it was wrong. All of it. It was dirty and his hands were already filthy. The snooping around, the lies and secret meetings, the plotting, sabotage, and covert missions, all designed to rob Raymon of his rightful reign. Benjamin stuck his chest out and looked his father in the eyes. He saw that he was incapable of telling the truth. He wanted to shout, no, I won't do it, but sensed they would find another way to fulfill their evil plan. So, he switched sides and decided it was their turn to be in the blind. The night was still young, and he was ready to make things right. "I understand, Father."

Bigmack was entertaining guests. He stood in a circle surrounded by women. His green and white sweeter looked like a Christmas gift from his parents. He showed off footage from his Vegas trip and bragged about being the first one to leap out of the plane. He boasted about Moliah choosing him to spend her night with at the Black Rose. The ladies oohed and awed when they saw the former president, Baraka Obama, next to him in one picture. "That was a cool night, Barry my dude," he claimed. Out of the corner of his eye, he saw a red flash.

"Excuse me for a second, ladies." He wiggled himself free. "Hey hold up!"

"What's up, Mack?" Honey stopped.

"How you like my new grills?" Bigmack showed off his platinum and diamond teeth.

"You crazy, boy." Honey laughed. "But it's your mouth. Merry Christmas, I guess."

"Hold up, I got something here for you, too."

Honey's eyes widened when she saw Bigmack pull a small box out of his pocket.

"Now you can shine like me." Bigmack opened the box and revealed the shiny lady grills inside.

"O.M.G." Honey covered her mouth with both hands. "Thank you so much."

"It's nothing. You family now. By the way," he leaned in closer, "I'm feeling the album. Now come take some flicks. These people love you, girl."

"Maybe later." Honey smiled. "I have to give a performance. Just a short a cappella of 'Arrived'. I gotta show them the vocals is real." She hugged the box close to her chest. "Thank you again for the gift." Honey slid the jewels into her mouth. "How do I look?"

"Like a fly ass female Flavor Flav," Bigmack joked.

"You think you funny." They shared a laugh.

286

Honey put her gift back inside the box and hurried to the stage. When she reached the stairs, she felt a pull on her arm. She turned around and found Chill Will staring at her.

"Merry Christmas." He moved in for a hug.

But Honey wasn't having it. She slipped him like Money Mayweather. Chill Will tried to put some bills in her hand, but she crossed her arms and frowned. "I don't want your money."

"Why not? Something wrong with my cash? Oh but, you can spend all my home boy's bread though." Chill Will leaned back. Her red one-piece dress caressed her curves. A pair of cocaine white heels and diamond earrings shaped like Christmas trees. "Baby got back," Chill Will shouted.

"You wasted, boy. Bye." She looked over her shoulder.

"So, what! Yeah, I'm wasted, that's what I do. But I'm not the one wasting it all, you feel me?"

Honey ignored his drunken rants, grabbed the microphone, and stepped to the center of the stage. "Thank you all for coming out tonight. We put a lot of work into this project, and I hope you enjoy it as much as I have."

"We love you!" someone shouted from below.

"I really appreciate that. So many of us just want to be heard, and this right here is for you."

"Excuse me." Chill Will snatched the microphone from her hands. "!'m a let you finish, but Beyonce had the best video of all times."

Laughter mixed in with boos erupted everywhere.

Chill Will staggered back and forth with his arms spread out wide. Honey gave him a disgusted look, then stormed off the stage.

Raymon met her at the bottom of the stairs. He put his hands around her waist and asked, "What's wrong?"

"What's wrong is your drunk-ass homeboy," she spat.

"Calm down, let me take care of this."

Chill Will was still onstage cracking jokes, "Bitch think she J-Lo. But really she just ho ho ho!"

Honey had enough. She was way past ten. Before Raymon could act, she was already in full stride. Honey marched onto the stage with a hot face. She cocked her fist back and punched Chill Will in the jaw with all her might. He fell back, collapsed into the Christmas tree, and took a nap. Honey heard a roar of cheers behind her.

Then Raymon ran over and grabbed her. She shook her hand from the pain of the impact. Raymon led her down the stairs and ordered a bucket of ice. The band kicked off some upbeat tunes, while guests pointed at Chill Will and laughed.

Bigmack shook his head. "Don't that boy know she got hits?"

"He knows now." Raymon smiled.

A few moments later, Raymon stood in a corner pressing a pack of ice against Honey's hand. "Maybe we should a had you in the ring. You got a mean right hook, lady."

"He been asking for that." Honey showed no mercy. "Why you don't check your boy?"

"I think you just did that for me." Raymon laughed.

"What's so funny?"

"Nothing! I was just thinking about all that expensive pine he going to have to pluck out his ass in the morning."

"You got jokes. Oww!" Honey pulled her hand back.

"Easy baby," Raymon said. "I got you. That's what happens when you hit your hand on something dumb."

Their eyes locked, and Honey smiled.

"You see, that's not so bad."

"You changed my life," said Honey.

It came out so fast, Raymon had to look at her facial expression to feel the seriousness of her words. "What?"

"You changed my life," she repeated. "We moving out of Harlem, next week in fact."

"Is that right?"

"Me and Moms found a nice house in Long Island. A cool neighborhood, so now my hermanos can grow up in peace. You did that."

"I don't know about that," Raymon said. "You put in a lot of work. Your talent did that. All I did was put you in the booth, let the people hear you, package you up, let the world see you. But it was always you."

"I am truly grateful for you coming into my life." She put her hand on his shoulder.

"How many poor people do you think are out there?"

"What?" Honey jumped.

"How many people you think out there just need a real chance to come up?"

Honey tried to clear her head. Raymon's sudden change of gear left her stuck.

"The thing is," he said, "I don't know if I'm a good person or not,"

"Where is this coming from?"

"I want to help people. I mean, I really want to make a difference."

"You helped me," Honey said.

"You sure about that? Money changes people. Success changes lives. Look how people act when they get the bag." He pointed to the stage. "Sometimes I feel like I was better off poor. When you have everyone looking to you for everything, it makes you question who you are. Okay, you got money now. But how much does one person need?"

"Look where we are." Honey grabbed his face. "You got superstars to get on songs with regular old me. All these people, they wouldn't have a clue who I was if it wasn't for you. You did that. So yes, I'm for damn sure you helped me. I'm sure about you, and I'm sure about us." Honey pushed in closer. She put her hand on Raymon's chin and looked him square in the eyes.

He seemed worried. " I just want to help people."

But before he could utter another word, Honey wrapped her lips around his. She opened her mouth a little and tasted his tongue. They ignored the popping sounds of champagne bottles behind them.

Raymon opened his eyes and felt full. When their lips separated, he saw Benjamin struggling to keep his distance. He felt Honey's body heat against him, looked down at her pretty face and said, "I love you."

She looked at him like he was the only one in the room. Her mouth opened to say something, but Raymon's attention was pulled away by Benjamin's uncomfortable stares. *What does he want?* he thought. Then a young couple approached Honey with their phones out. She smiled and took a few selfies with the guests. Raymon blew her a kiss, then excused himself.

What's up you conniving, slithery, snaky, perpetrating weasel, Raymon thought to greet his numbers man. "You enjoying yourself?" he decided to go with instead.

"Ray, I don't know where to start," Benjamin said. "My father, Lisa, and the whole Welloff group…"

"What are you saying?"

"I'm trying to say, I know all about the will, but I just found out recently. They used me. They wanted me to help you fail, but I didn't know that. I thought I was helping you save money. Listen, they do not want you to receive your full inheritance and they are prepared to do anything they can to stop you."

Raymon looked over a crowd of heads and saw the Welloff counsel walking toward the exit. "You say you know all about the will, so you are familiar with the stipulations."

"I read it all and—"

"So, you know I can't talk to you," Raymon cut him off.

"You don't have to say a word. I'm telling you that I know all about it. it's messed up, and you need to know this."

"I need to know what exactly?" Raymon looked him in the eyes.

"They told me to withhold this advance money from you. I convinced Honey to take a few side deals, advertising deals mostly, and a few performance contracts. They are worth millions. The checks are supposed to arrive tomorrow. I have one of them right now, he pulled an envelope from his pocket. It's for six million."

"I'm not taking that." Raymon looked away.

"You don't have to. As long as Honey is your artist, Raymon Records gets a piece of any side deals she is involved in. Income, record sales, it's all profit for you."

"Why are you telling me this? Don't you want to help your sneaky dad?"

"I'm not like him. It has taken me a long time to realize that, but I'm not. Your grandfather left you his fortune. You! And it's yours's to have. You have every right to do with it as you please. And I'm not going to sit back and do nothing, while my father and his flunkies try to steal it from you. I want to see you win."

"Even if winning means your father and the whole Welloff company going belly up?"

"My father only thinks about money. There is more to life than that. I just wish he could see it."

"More to life than money." Raymon crossed his arms. Like what?"

"Like morals, principles, values and real family."

The words echoed in Raymon's ears. Real family. It was something he never truly knew. He could see sincerity on Benjamin's face and feel strength in his words. He admired his courage.

"You are a better man then I thought," said Raymon. "I knew about the side deals already. Honey told me. I tried to contact the companies, but she didn't know which ones made the deals. If you are really trying to help me, tell me how can get around this. I mean, the checks are already written and I'm running out of time."

"The money is for Honey Drop English, the artist. Her association to Raymon Records is the key. She is signed to you. If she wasn't, you nor the company would have any claims to the deals, or the money," Benjamin explained.

"You're telling me to kill her contract."

"It's the only way."

"She will never forgive me." Raymon looked around aimlessly.

"She will understand," said Benjamin.

But Raymon was already lost in his own thoughts. Once again, he would have to hurt someone he loved in order to get what he wanted. He walked around in circles, thinking of a better way. The reality of the situation hit him like a sandbag over the head. He felt dizzy. He checked his watch. It was an hour before midnight. *I can cash the check, gamble the money at a roulette table in Atlantic City, all before noon, show up at the Welloff office broke, and still collect my money*, he plotted. *But what if I win? What if the other checks show up too late?* He felt his stomach tighten up.

Every step forward felt heavier than the last. He walked through a group of guests, who patted him on his back and smiled in his face. He was lost in thought, but somehow found himself standing on the stage looking down at a hundred faces, waiting for him to speak.

"Thank you all for coming here tonight." He cleared his throat. "This whole experience has been amazing. I just want to say something," He lowered his head. "We set out to raise up a star and make her a part of the world. Our world. And in the process, somehow, we all seemed to have arrived. He spotted Honey floating through the crowd and avoided her eyes. She is a wonderful, beautiful tough little chica from Harlem and I feel lucky to know her. Truly one of a kind that girl is, and I know she will be very successful."

A round of applause started to build.

"Unfortunately," Raymon shouted. "Unfortunately, it won't be with Raymon Records."

Bigmack spun around so fast, he dropped his glass of champagne. People gasped for air, as voices scrambled all at once. Party over. Shock and confusion became the music in a chorus of what, whys, and whos.

Honey stood still, surrounded by questions. She folded her arms over her breast and waited for the punch line. He is joking. But it never came.

Raymon's face was cold and without emotion. He lowered his eyes and said, "I am officially, releasing Honey Drop English from the label." Guests threw their hands up and started to boo.

"Listen, listen! We set out to make history, take an unsigned, unknown artist, and fully back her with no help from the majors. We did a great job. You all did a great job. But the truth is, we are having some financial issues that won't allow us to go any further." Raymon tried desperately to make sense of it all.

"You broke!" someone shouted from the crowd.

Raymon could see Amanda Media whispering into her recorder as the chatter increased around her.

"Hey this doesn't mean you can't enjoy the rest of your night." Raymon waved his hands in the air. "It's all paid for. So, party on and Merry Christmas."

When Raymon rushed off the stage, the crowd focused on Honey. They pushed toward her, looking for her reaction.

Bigmack swooped in and threw his arm around her shoulders. "You knew about this?" He led her a few feet away from the mob, then she pushed him back.

"I don't need your help," she said.

She was angry and confused. She tried to make it make sense in her head. She scanned the room looking for Raymon and saw him fleeing out the back with people on his heels, yelling and pointing. She started to chase after him then stopped, shook her head, and headed in the opposite direction.

Bigmack was light on his feet. He spun past a few guests like a running back on a football field. When he pushed through the exit door, he caught

Raymon just in time. "What the hell you doing?" The warm liquor on his breath created a cloud of smoke into the cold air.

"You heard like everyone else." Raymon looked over his shoulder. "It's all gone, everything."

Bigmack put his hands on his head. "This can't be right. What happened?"

A black SUV pulled up and Raymon opened the back door.

"Naw dogg, you going to tell me something. I believed in you. I told them, naw my homie knows what he doing, and now you telling me this."

Raymon could see the hurt in his friend's eyes. "What you want me to say?"

"I just can't believe it. Everything?"

"Don't I always take care of you?" Raymon smiled. "Don't lose your trust in me, not you dogg."

Benjamin busted through the door. "You okay Ray?"

"It will all work out," he said. "And Benji, you need to get fly with your pops sometimes. Don't just let him talk that mess to you. Next time we get slick, tell them if you trying to impress me, test me! Or something like that." Raymon laughed then vanished into the backseat. The second he shut the door he was gone.

Bigmack stood there rubbing his head. He looked at Benjamin and said, "Everything!"

"Where to sir?" Planes looked in his rearview mirror.

Raymon just stared out the window. Streetlights flew past the glass, while he sank lower in his seat.

"Where to sir?"

"Do you think I'm a good person?" Raymon asked. "I mean, if given the chance, do you think I would make the right choice?"

"I just do the driving," said Planes.

"Yeah, but you are a reasonable and honorable man. Most people are not."

"I believe you would try your best, sir."

"I don't think so. It seems like every choice I make ends up being the wrong one. Maybe I should just stop making choices. What you think, Fancy Pants?"

"I was always told that choices shape a man. The question then becomes, who do you want to be, sir?"

Raymon sat in silence for a moment, separating the sabotaging thoughts sneaking into his head from the rational ones. He lifted his head and said, "You sure are easy to talk to, but you don't talk much yourself. Why is that?"

"I don't get paid to talk, sir."

"Do you get paid to drink?" asked Raymon.

"What do you mean, sir?"

"Where's the closest bar? It's time to get stuffed."

Five hours later, Raymon stumbled through the front door of his Royal suite with a brown bookbag in his hand. It was dark and quiet inside the apartment. Light from the moon shined threw the balcony. Raymon was drunk and exhausted. The news of him returning to poverty had already hit the net. He felt his way to his office and found the door was wide open. His phone died hours ago and he needed to make some calls.

But before he could plant both feet inside, his desk lamp cut on. Raymon paused like an intruder with a bag of stolen goods.

"Hey big money." Honey sat behind the desk with her legs propped up.

"I was just about to—"

"Get out of town," Honey finished his sentence. "I believed in you. I thought you believed in me too. What I can't understand is, why the games? Why the whole show? You could have told me in private. I never thought you would have embarrassed me like that."

Raymon opened his mouth to speak but couldn't find the right words. He collapsed on the couch and rubbed his forehead. "Can I explain this tomorrow?"

"I thought you was real. I thought what we had was real, but you just another... Vicky! What's another word for a donkey?"

"Asshole!"

"Yeah that' s it." Honey sat up.

"That's cold. You got Victoria in this mess." Raymon was dozing off.

"I didn't ask for none of this, and I damn sure didn't ask you to play with my heart. You just like the rest of these lames, pretending to be something you're not." Honey stood up and marched for the door.

"Hold on, hear me out." Raymon reached for her arm. "It will all make sense soon. Give me a chance. You will understand, trust me! "

"I understand perfectly." she searched his face with her eyes. "You wanted to make a nobody into a somebody. That's what you said, right! Well, here's some news for your ass, I was already somebody. I just wish I never met you."

"You got it all wrong." Raymon tried to stand up. He wanted her to know, his feelings for her were real. But his head started to hurt and he crashed back down on the cushions. He started to feel weak.

"I just came to get my stuff." Honey walked off.

"All I wanted to do was help," he said too low for anyone to hear. His vision was becoming blurry. He struggled to see Honey as she left him behind.

"I don't want nothing from you." She opened the front door. "Thanks for the ride big money."

Raymon closed his eyes, leaned his head back, and replayed the past thirty days of his life. He found love, riches, and success beyond his dreams. But it all came with a price. His closest friends lost trust in him. He became a target for hustlers, thieves, and con men. Handshakes didn't match the smiles on people's faces. Enemies posed as allies, and he was forced to live in confidential solitude. As he fell in and out of consciousness, he thought about who he was and who he wanted to be. Then he realized, all he ever wanted, he already had.

The hot climate makes his face itch. The flies over his head cause him to wonder where he is at. A small hut in front of him surrounded with children, sitting down with their backs pressed against the hay, seems to be out of place. He walks closer for a better look. Sun rays shine on the front door and he can see two figures coming out to greet him. The man is tall and lanky. His dark skin looks like it is in love with the heat. He has a woman by his side. They walk arm in arm. Raymon looks at her with joy in his heart. He has her face.

"Welcome, my son." She smiles at him.

"Where am I?" he says.

"This is a healing center in the mother land," says the man.

"Who are you?" he asks, but he already knows the answer.

"We have been waiting for you."

"Why did you leave me?"

His father laughs a powerful laugh. "We never left you, son. We are with you right now; we will always be with you."

"This isn't real." Raymon looks around at the open fields and livestock running around.

"What is real? Am I real, are you real? The purpose of life is life with a purpose. Our bodies are just vehicles that allow us to go places and connect with others."

"Connect for what? Why couldn't you just stay?"

"Listen to me, son. We love you." They reach out for him.

Raymon takes a few steps backwards and trips over something hard. He looks down to see the body of a little boy. "Help him," he screams.

His parents lean over to give him a hand. "You help him," they shout.

CHAPTER 23

Closing Account$

The sun made its entrance into the sky on Christmas morning. Suddenly the newspaper slammed into Raymon's lap and awoke him from his dreams. He looked down at the bold print: RAYMON DROPS ENGLISH. OVERNIGHT BILLIONAIRE BLOWS FORTUNE IN A MONTH'S TIME. Raymon wiped his eyes, looked up, and saw Si-mon standing over him.

"Is this true?" Si-mon asked.

"I hope so." Raymon yawned. "What time is it?"

"Unfortunately, it is time for you to check out."

"Just like that, aye." Raymon sat up.

"It is not what I wish on you. But my superiors have demanded it to be so. They are claiming that you are flat broke. They say that your account has been closed and that I should see to it that you leave. Safely of course."

"So, they want to kick me out in the cold on Christmas day. Where is everyone?"

"I have not seen anyone this morning." Si-mon shrugged his shoulders. "Ms. Honey Drop collected her family and things and left last night in an

Uber. Mr. Bigmack and Sir Chill Will have not returned. Although their coded card access numbers have been changed, so maybe..."

"I need some coffee," Raymon interrupted.

"Mr. Raymon, is it true?"

"Is what true?"

"Have you lost a large fortune and now are dead broke?"

Raymon stood up, put one hand on Si-mon' s shoulder and smiled. "I feel alive."

The front door flung open. In marched the Brothers of Bespoke, a fleet of workers and Grand Dora employees. They spread out and performed different tasks all at once. An older man wearing a Grand Dora uniform approached Raymon with a smile on his face. "Merry Christmas sir. We at the Grand Dora would like to thank you for allowing us to accommodate you."

Another worker walked over with a plastic bag in hand, with a yellow tag hanging from it. "Your property sir." He handed it to Raymon.

Raymon looked at the bag and recognized the clothes inside. They were the same clothes he walked out of jail wearing. "All pressed and clean," Raymon said. "Thank you all so very much."

Raymon changed back into his jeans and shirt, picked up his book bag, and checked his Timex watch. Still worked. He took a long look at himself in the bathroom mirror and felt good about his direction.

He reappeared in the front room after a few minutes, wearing his old get-up. He then watched workers cleaning the walls and spraying furniture like they were sterilizing the place from an outbreak of some sort. *You don't have a lot of black people up here, do you?* He saw a dozen racks full of tailored suits roll out the front door in a hurry, like they were being stolen.

The Brothers of Bespoke noticed Raymon dressed unadornedly and greeted him with their heads low. "Thank you for your business Mr. Platt. We will honor you with this closet of Raymon suits," said one Brother.

"Yes, this will forever be called the Raymon collection," said the other, as if he created the idea from thin air.

"The Raymon collection, I like that." Raymon pretended to be impressed. He extended his hand. "Merry Christmas."

The Brothers looked at the white envelope in his hand and smiled. "Thank you, sir."

While the Raymon collection made its was out the front door, Raymon shook hands with workers, and offered them all, "Merry Christmas."

He walked into his home-made studio and kissed the walls. Si-mon had a confused look on his face. Then Raymon walked up to him, with his arms stretched out. "Merry Christmas, my friend. Now go home and kiss that goat." He smiled.

Si-mon looked at the handful of money, smiled, and said, "You are very much still alive."

All of his lavish accessories were repossessed, his cell phones disconnected, yet Raymon walked the halls with a new sense of pride. When he made it to the lobby, he offered, "Merry Christmas" to everyone he could reach.

Before he could step foot outside and leave behind the place he called home for the past month, Si-mon stopped him at the door and gave him a big hug. "Thank you again, Mr. Raymon. Thank you for everything."

Raymon felt unchained. "No. Thank you," he said.

It was chilly but Raymon felt warm inside. There were no camera crews or beat writers, no reporters in sight, nor hungry entrepreneurs eager to share their ideas with him. The streets were quiet. Raymon began to laugh. It wasn't' t a loud obnoxious laugh, but a calm settle one, the kind of laugh you have with yourself when you find out what you thought was true. He rubbed his arms and stood up straight. Then he noticed a black Escalade parked by the curb. The smile on his face erased as he stared at the tinted windows. What the...

He saw the rear door open and took a step backwards. *It's a kidnapping*, he thought. Would the Welloff counsel be so ruthless, have him snatched up on Christmas morning just so he didn't make the meeting? Raymon pondered. For 2.5 billion, hell yeah, they would. He stiffened. He thought about taking off in a sprint, but then he recognized the face in front of him.

"Yo, Richie Rich, peace to the God." Manhood stepped onto the sidewalk. He had on wheat Timberlands, a peacoat, and black netted hat. He rocked too many gold chains to count, and when he smiled, a diamond blinked off the light.

"Manhood! I thought you—"

"Skipped town! Yeah, I figured you would have thought that. My bad for hitting ghost on you, but I had to handle a few things."

"Is that how you describe our union?" Natasha skipped out of the truck. " You had to handle something."

"Tasha!" Raymon's eyes widened.

"Hey Ray!"

"Where you been, girl?"

"I told you I was going out of town for a minute."

"You told me what?"

"I left you a message, didn't 't you check?"

"Well usually that's my assistant's job, but I haven't seen her in a while." He made a face.

"You can't do nothing without me." She laughed.

"I know what I'm a do with you." Manhood put his palm on her backside.

Raymon grabbed his chin and stared. "When did this happen?"

"Shorty couldn't resist me, and she so wavy, I had to wife her."

"Behave yourself, Trevon." Natasha removed his hand. "Not in public."

Raymon couldn't believe his ears. But he believed his eyes.

"I'm sorry, Ray. We should have contacted you sooner," Natasha said. I know you are a complete mess without me. I should have talked to you directly. We saw the news. We came to see if you're all right."

"I'm good." Raymon smiled.

"Naw, for reals, Richie Rich. You looked out for me in a real way. I ain't going to forget that shit. I'm a fight this appeal the right way, face it like a man, and handle my business always. So here is a little something for you, brah." He pulled out a roll of hundreds.

"Believe me when I say this, you have already helped me great deal," Raymon said. "The both of you have and Merry Christmas."

Manhood looked at him sideways, "Yo God, I don't do Christmas. That's the devil's holiday."

"Fool, please." Natasha stepped in front of him. "Thank you for everything Ray. If you need anything, don't be too shy to ask. Come on, Trevon, I'm hungry."

"This shorty right here is a mess." Manhood followed her back to the truck.

Raymon shook his head and smiled. It was already a crazy morning, and he was just getting started. When the Escalade started to pull off, he shouted, "Hold up."

"What's up? You need a ride somewhere?" Manhood stuck his head out the window.

"Naw, I'm a take a walk. But I was wondering if you had an extra coat."

Manhood smiled, pulled the coat off his back, passed it to Raymon, and said, "It's a cold world, Richie Rich. You better bundle up."

On every corner that Raymon saw homelessness, he approached the people with a giving hand. "Merry Christmas." He walked into a flower shop, then a bodega, offering a Merry Christmas to all. He checked the time on his watch, took it off, and handed it to a young boy pushing a cart full of empty soda bottles.

Ten blocks later, he was ready to face the three scrooges sitting comfortable in a building big enough to house half of Cape Verde. He wasn't nervous at all. He knew how far he had come and was ready to face his fate.

Half an hour later, he sat in a familiar office. He looked around the same gloomy room he visited a month earlier. He stared at the blank screen on the wall, wondering if it would suddenly flip on and show his grandfather's grumpy face and tell him it was all a joke. Not likely. Then the doors flew open. James marched in first with a smirk on his face, followed by Lisa and Michael. "I see you brought some flowers," said James.

"And they are so nice. Who died?" Lisa passed him by

"Nice jacket," said Michael. "I don't remember you having that on before."

"That's because I didn't," said Raymon.

312

They skipped the formal greetings, took their seats around the table, and stared into Raymon, checking him over and reading his face.

"Merry Christmas to you too." Raymon sat back in his seat.

"You played your hand very well," said James. "And you are right on time, very impressive!"

Raymon studied their faces. Their praise seemed to be more tongue-in-cheek than genuine admiration. He waited. After a few seconds passed, Michael was flipping through paperwork, Lisa swiped at her phone, James tried to win a staring competition with him, so he decided to offer, "I think I understand why the old man wanted me to spend all his money."

"Roger was very eccentric. No one knew what he was thinking most times," said Lisa.

"Maybe so, but I had a very interesting month. I learned a lot about myself, my closest friends, and others. And I had a very interesting conversation with Benjamin. I know! And you creeps tried to cheat."

Michael lifted his head. "What are you talking about?"

"I'm talking about the money you wanted Benji to withhold from me."

"That is nonsense. You knew the rules," said James.

"You knew them, too. And since I wouldn't' t break them, you went ahead and broke them yourself. Real tricky shit. Shame on you all."

"We have documents showing that you have failed to uphold your agreed upon inheritance terms," Michael barked. " According to our records, there seems to be 300,000 dollars still in your possession."

"Well according to my records," Raymon reached under the table and into his book bag. "There seems to be only a dollar in my possession. That's all I have left." He waved the bill in the air. "Me and Fancy Pants had some drinks and talked about real life shit. Good guy that one. I also gave a lot of money away to some deserving folks on my way over here. Oh, and I bought some flowers." Raymon looked at the shocked faces before him. "You see, the true value of life isn't in your bank account. It's inside of you," he said.

James leaned forward. "You broke the rules."

"I followed my rules, while you sneaky worms broke your own," Raymon said.

James sat back in his seat, Lisa frowned, and Michael crossed his arms. "What are you accusing?" James asked.

'It was written that no one should be told of our agreement. But you surely told someone."

"As say you," Lisa denied.

Meanwhile Benjamin heard the sounds of a fuss inside the boardroom. He stood out by the door debating whether to enter or run.

"I knew you would play dumb," Raymon said. "But it's cool. I don't need your confessions. I don't need your money either."

"Let's stop all this tomfoolery." James stood up. "Mr. Raymon Platt, you have been found in violation of the inheritance contract you signed, by your own admission. Nonetheless, you gave away funds without receiving any service for the investment or business ventures as specifically warranted against in the agreement. And you arrived here in an expensive coat that you did not have prior to receiving the amount given, which counts as an asset. Therefore, you have forfeited the remainder of your inheritance."

Raymon looked at his wrist for the time then remembered handing it to the young boy with the cart. He could still see the boy's smile in his head. It made him feel good. "Yeah, I violated. So, what," Raymon shrugged his shoulders. "You violated too. We all did! What makes you so much better than everyone else? Who told you that you could make the rules up in the first place? I got some rules for your ass: Never turn your back on your friends. Always keep your word. Try to be a good person. But I can see that we don't have the same rules because we don't have the same values. I had to learn that, too. We got people in the streets right outside starving, and you clowns up here playing games with billions of dollars. I mean damn! How much money do you need to live? You people got issues. I guess we all got issues, but I rather be someone trying to help others, than just helping myself while others struggle."

"You do know what this means?" Lisa picked up her pen. "You are forfeiting all your rights to your remaining inheritance. You are giving away a fortune."

Raymon looked up, straightened his head, and smiled. "Wouldn't be my first time."

"Well then, if you would just sign these forms, we can conclude this absurdity." James snatched the pen out of Lisa's hand.

He carried the folder over to Raymon and placed it down in front of him. "You are doing the right thing, son." He handed him the pen.

Raymon closed his eyes and took a deep breath. When he opens them, he looked at the forms for a second, then lifted the pen.

"Don't sign that!" Benjamin busted threw the door like a government agent. But instead of waving a badge, he had a stack of binders in his hand.

Michael stood up. "What are you doing in here?"

"This is a private meeting. You have no business here," James shouted. "Get out!

"On the contrary, Father, I was appointed to assist Mr. Raymon and maintain the records. And that's exactly what I intend to do."

"What is the meaning of this intrusion?" asked Lisa.

"Ray, you do not have to sign away your inheritance," said Benjamin.

"This is ridiculous," Michael shouted. "Call security."

"Security is a good idea. Maybe they can arrest you three crooks." Benjamin slammed the binders on the table. "Roger Welloff Bennet didn't just leave you his money. He left you his majority shares in the Welloff company."

Raymon looked at him and searched his face for meaning. "What you talking about, Benji?"

"The remainder of your inheritance is in a secured savings account. If you sign those forms, you will not only be giving away your inheritance, you will give away your rights to those shares also. Which is not stated in the contract you signed; might I add. In other words, they are playing you."

"That is enough." James stomped his foot. "Benjamin James Preacher, you are fired!"

"Don't you get it, Ray? The only way they can touch that money is by your signed permission. That's how they got access to the 500 million. No one can touch that money or the shares, without your signature."

"So, the old man didn't want me to waste his bread after all?" said Raymon.

"I didn't say that." Benjamin shook his head. "He did set the whole thing up, but they changed the contract. They took the ownership of the shares out, which makes the whole contract void, maybe even illegal." He looked at his father.

"You are a disgrace to your family," said James.

"What's wrong, Dad? Wasn't it you who told me that I should find out the truth of things? And as for the disgrace, I think you should call Mom. She has some choice words for you on that topic."

Raymon put the pen down and pushed his chair back away from the table. "So, you're saying that all this bread is mines."

"Technically yes." Benjamin smiled. "We will have to deal with the courts to straighten out a few things, but the money is yours by law."

"You little worm." Michael rushed toward Benjamin with his hands up ready to choke the life out of him.

A lightbulb cut on in Raymon's head. *They need me, they always have.* "Hold on there. I wouldn't do that. There's a new sheriff in town. This is my company and if you even think about harming my good friend, you can kiss those shares goodbye."

Lisa put her hand over her heart. James swallowed so hard he choked on his own spit. Michael froze; he looked like he was under arrest with his hands still high. The jig was up, the table was turned, and Raymon held all the cards.

"This is madness," James tried to take back control. "You knew the terms, and you failed. Now it is time to sign."

"Not so fast, Jamie. Thanks to my partner right here," he patted Benjamin on the back, "it has been made very clear to me where we now stand. So, in the words of the great Dave Chappell, I ain't signing shit!"

"This can't be happening." Lisa picked up a glass of water.

"It's happening," said Raymon. "You guys are trickier than I thought. Luckily, I have someone in my corner I can trust. Thanks for that one Jamie."

"We will sue you for breach of contract," Michael shouted.

"You sure you want to go that route? The stock market ain't looking too good for you right now. And them lawsuits take years to sort out in the courts. Ain't that right, Benji?"

"Sure do." Benjamin nodded.

They were halfway out the door when James started to foam at the mouth. He knocked the binders off the table and said, " You are a fool! Your grandfather was an old fool, and your mother was right to have had nothing to do with the both of you. You think you are smart! Let's see how smart you are when you're back in jail begging for our help. I made a living outsmarting tiny little people like yourself, and I'm just getting warmed up. You hear me boy! You are nothing!"

Raymon put his hand on Benjamin's back and allowed him to clear the doorway first then looked back at James steaming in his suit. "If you trying to impress me, jump in the air and stay there. I'll call you," he said.

They hustled to the elevator in celebration mode. "I can't believe you said that to him." Benjamin smiled.

"I can't believe you stopped me from signing them fake forms," Raymon said.

When the doors opened, they ran through the lobby like kids in a ballpark stadium. Welloff workers looked at them with odd stares. Raymon almost knock over a lady carrying a handful of folders. "Sorry ma'am." He spun around her.

They paused outside the building but maintained their excitement. "That was so crazy. I didn't know that was going to work. I mean, I thought it would work. Speaking of work, I don't have a job anymore. What am I going to do?" Benjamin rambled.

"Where did you get all that information about the will and all that?"

"My father never was good at keeping his files in order." Benjamin had a sly smile on his face.

"You the man Benji, you the man! You saved my life up there. Did you see their faces?" Raymon laughed. It was like he saw a mugging across the street or some foul actions taking place. Raymon's face changed in 1.2 seconds. Benjamin looked at him and wondered what just happened.

"What time is it?" Raymon asked.

Benjamin checked his watch. "It's 2:30."

"She must still be there." Raymon scanned the area with his eyes. "You got a ride?"

"A ride, I don't even have a job, Ray."

"We got to hail a cab or something."

"What's going on?"

"Oh shit! I got one buck on me," Raymon waved his dollar in the air. "You got some cash on you Benji?"

"I got a credit card, but that's going to be turned off soon. If I know my father, it probably already is."

Like a telepathic Uber, Planes shouted from the curb, "You gents need a lift?"

Raymon looked at Benjamin, Benjamin looked at Raymon. "Merry Christmas."

The town car cruised through the streets of New York uninterrupted, hydroplaning on rock salt and melted snow, headed to Harlem. Raymon hoped he wasn't too late. Drunk in the holiday spirit, he stuck his head out the window and hollered, "Merry Christmas to all!"

Benjamin was smiling despite the fact his life direction was altered in a flash. "Where are we headed?" he asked.

But Raymon just smiled. He couldn't seem to sit still. His body rocked back and forth while he played the drums on his legs. "Hit the music Fancy pants!"

A familiar sound came flying out the speakers. Raymon raised his eyebrow, laughed, and looked to Benjamin. "I think we going to be all right."

When they reached the corner of 142nd Street a U-haul truck was parked in front of Honey's apartment. Raymon ran from the car, cleared the front steps in one leap, and rushed for the open door like he left the stove on. He was in full stride when he saw a brown box headed right for his chest.

The impact knocked him off his feet. He hit the floor with the box landing in his lap.

"What the hell?" Honey looked down and saw Raymon wincing in pain, wearing the same shirt she met him in over a month ago. "Still clumsy I see."

"I deserved that." Raymon removed the box from his crotch.

"What do you want, Ray?"

"I just want to explain."

"There's nothing to explain! Besides, you already had your chance for that. I'm done."

"Dios Mio! Que pasa le." Honey's mother stuck her head out the apartment window.

"Nada ma! Calmete," Honey said.

Raymon stood up and looked around. "So, you just going to up and leave me like that."

"Up and leave you! You dropped me! What you expected, you were going come up here and woo me with your charms? Fool, you ain't that charming, and you haven't even said sorry."

"I'm sorry." Raymon stepped in closer. "I'm sorry for keeping you in the blind. I'm sorry for not trusting you with the truth. You said I helped you, that I changed your life. Well, you changed mines too."

"I don't know. I mean, I'm thankful for all you brought to the table, of course I am. But I never know what you are thinking or where you're headed and that's dangerous. I'm trying to do the best I can for my family. I don't know what you trying to do."

"You asked me once what it felt like to have the power to change lives. Well, it sucks! Changing lives isn't about having money, it's about having family. It's about having people you love and being able to share all that you are with them. I changed! I was powerless and broke inside, but it's different now. And I don't expect you to understand it all that overnight. It might take me a few nights just to explain." Raymon chuckled. "But I need you in my life."

Honey took a step forward. Suddenly her hands were on Raymon's chest. She opened her mouth and said, "You sound like you back to being broke."

"I wouldn't say all that." Raymon winked his eye.

"Qien es? Aww Senor Rico," Honey's mother said with glee.

Her brothers and sister squeezed into the window frame next to their mother and started making kissy noises. "Kiss her," they shouted.

"I just don't know about you," Honey looked Raymon in the eyes.

Their lips drew closer, then Raymon stopped. "Hold up. I got something for you."

Honey watched him reach into his pocket and pull out a small box. Before she could even attempt to reject another one of his expensive gifts, he opened the box and she saw the little treasure troll doll looking up at her.

"What is this?" She laughed.

"You said you like simple." Raymon smiled. "I can do simple."

He kissed her like he missed her, and she felt complete. "I love you," she let the words slip out.

"It's about damn time." Raymon smiled.

The sound of tires screeching to a halt stole their moment. Raymon pulled her closer and turned his head. Bigmack jumped out of the driver's seat of an Audi 8 and said, "Ray! There you are. We been checking for you everywhere. We ain't done, dogg. We can still fix this thing."

"What you talking about, Mack?" Raymon said.

"We got the number one album in the country." Chill Will stepped out of the passenger side.

Raymon looked at Honey still snuggled in his arms. "They late," she said before he could get the words out himself.

"It's no joke, Ray." Bigmack climb the stairs slowly with his palms out. "We ain't tripping about nothing. The past is the past. Chill agreed to go into rehab and we have a real chance here to get back right: touring, marketing, shows, and interviews all over the world. That's big money, brah."

Raymon could see Chill Will nodding his head in the background. He heard the desperation in Bigmack's voice. He felt warm with Honey's love still on his mind. And thanks to Benjamin, his future was looking bright. He knew Bigmack and Chill Will didn't know all that just yet, and he took pleasure in making them sweat. "Number one album, aye." Raymon smiled. " I think we can work with that."

CHAPTER 24

"Today we have a very special guest with us. And he has an amazing story," she said.

The studio lights illuminated the white leather couch where Raymon sat across from his favorite talk show host.

When the cameras zoomed in on his face, he told himself to relax. The live studio audience checked his every movement. He was dressed debonair in Rockstar jeans and a Ricky Owens sweater. He listened carefully as the show commenced.

"Mr. Raymon Platt, Jr. You have had a busy past six months."

"Yeah, O, it's been interesting, Raymon looked down at his Maison Margiela sneakers. Is it all right if I call you O?"

"Let me get this right. You inherit a fortune, coin the phrase From Do-Rages to Riches, then you lost it all on outrageous spending. Is that true?"

"Mostly!"

"I see you don't have on a do-rag today," She smiled.

"Naw, I don't." Raymon massages his waves. "But I still rock a fresh do-rag every now and again."

His comment got a brief laugh from the crowd.

"How did it all happen?" O asked.

"Sometimes things happen to people unexpectedly and you have to deal with it as best as you know how. At the same time, try not to lose yourself. You know what I'm saying? But I can't give you all that at this moment. There is a book coming out this summer by Natasha King, and If I was you, I would go get that joint. She's a great writer, and trust me when I say this, she has all the details."

"That was a nice plug. We will have to add that one to our book club. Now how are you feeling today?"

"I feel blessed. Although I never met my parents or my grandparents, they left me something in a weird way. I feel like I am a part of their work. Life is about more than money and for me, let's just say it's been a roller coaster ride."

"Expensive suites, fast cars, flights back and forth, switching time zones, and making it rain in any and all climates. All that from an orphan boy out of West Virginia. I bet it has been one hell of a ride." O encouraged the crowd to clap their hands, and they agreed. "You look like a new bill." She straightened her back. "So, tell us what is on your mind."

"Well, I learned a lot. I got to travel to different countries, fly in private jets, cruise on big ships, and drive nice cars. Yeah, it's all been great but…"

"But what," O leaned forward in her seat with an intrigued look on her face.

"You don't need a billion bucks to live a full life. To me it's the simple things that mean the most."

"Like what?"

"Like family and friends, helping others, and achieving unity. We all could use some unities, don't you think?"

"Well yeah." She looked at the camera and smiled. "That's why I have started a charity called A New Day Foundation. We are committed to ending poverty and putting money in the right people's hands to help other people."

"What do you mean?"

"There are hundreds of multi-billionaires right here in America, just swimming in cash like Scrooge McDuck while half the world goes hungry. And yes, some people are too lazy to get up and get it, and a lot of people just don't want it. But there is a large percentage of hardworking, forward-thinking folks that only need a chance to make a difference. Those are the ones that will push the envelope and create a bridge for the next person to cross. And after a while, we will have built a stable road of financial gain that will allow us to feed the world. Even the ones sitting on the sidelines."

"What about the billion-dollar lawsuit between you and the Welloff corporation?" she asked.

"I believe it was Robert Kiyosaki who said, the rich don't work for money, instead they work for the benefit of others, and the rewards flow back at an even greater rate. Somewhere along the lines them guys up at Welloff forgot that. But I'm a learn them."

"So once again, you are prepared to throw some money away." O lowered her eyebrows and looked to the studio audience.

"Not throw it away. Make it work for others. I started a benefit corporation so that sums of capital will go into our impoverished societies. And as we continue to generate money from our hustle, there will be more than enough to help others."

The clapping began. It created a roaring sound like a huge wave rising above... O reached for her glass of water and took a few sips. "That is amazing," she said. "Such a selfless act. I am sure there are many grateful people out there waiting to say thank you for all you are doing. In fact, here are a few of them right now."

Raymon spun his head around in every direction, looking to see who would take the stage. Then he noticed O holding a remote. She aimed at the wall, and with a click, a hidden screen lit up.

"Hello to you all." Si-mon's face popped up on the screen. "I would like to say thank you to you, Mr. Raymon, for empowering me to return to my county. Because of you, I can now be with my family and take care of our many goats."

Raymon was trying to play it cool but he was glowing inside. Before he could respond, Si-mon's face flew to the left and was replaced by another.

"Is this thing on?" Chill Will tapped the screen. "There you are. What's up, homie? Is that O sitting there with you? What's up girl! I love your show. You know what it is. Thanks for always pushing me to be a better man, brah, I really appreciate that bleep. I see you with the Hermes scarf, too. Gave them that game. Naw but for real, brah, you made a difference in our lives. Now the album is on the way! Mack and Chill baby! You know I had to plug us in real fast."

Raymon couldn't hold back his laughter and neither could the crowd. When his eyes returned to the screen, Benjamin was fixing the poncho covering his body.

"Hey Ray! We still in the Islands helping rebuild what was lost by all the flooding. Because of you, we have already relocated many families and saved lives. On behalf of us all, I would like to say thank you for everything."

Raymon wiped his eyes and nodded his head. Then the screen went blank.

The audience started up another round of applause and O stood to her feet to join them. "I must say, you have been really busy," she said then picked up her phone and read from a list, "Donations to numerous police departments in efforts to stop the violence, relief to families of victims in mass shootings, the opening of barber shops and community centers in urban neighborhoods. My God, did you keep any money for yourself?" She laughed and sat back down.

"I'm comfortable." Raymon adjusted the Patek Philip watch on his wrist.

"We haven't even talked about the groundbreaking number one album you executive produced, three number-one hit singles on the billboard charts nor the sold-out concert tickets in two countries." She sighed.

Raymon rubbed his palms together and sat back in his seat like he was just getting started.

"There is one more person who would like to say something. You have clearly touched the hearts of so many. Yet and still, while on your journey, somehow you managed to find love. And here she is, singing her smash hit song 'ARRIVED', your fiancée, the beautiful, talented, one and only, Ms. Honey Drop English."

Out of the corner of his eye, Raymon saw a panel on the wall slide back. The lights were lowered and a spotlight brought all attention to the small stage. The studio audience stood to their feet and clapped their hands like they all just won a brand-new car.

Like a gust of wind, Honey floated in holding a cordless microphone. Raymon took a deep breath, and when he inhaled, he could smell the enchanting perfume taking over the room. Honey's white dress hung down to her calf muscles. Diamonds flickered in her earlobes. When she lifted her microphone to her mouth, a monstrously sized rock on her finger almost caused the crowd eye damage.

Honey shot Raymon a look; a quick smile that said, hey bae. Her face was shining in the rays and Raymon felt so proud he poked his chest out and rose to his feet. The music began and Honey sang her assertion, "Fresh air from my mouth spreads, I've longed for now who I be."

Flawless in every way, Raymon thought. And you know what, he was right.

Remix grabbed the trash bag full of his property with one hand, picked up a pen with his other, and gave his John Hancock. The bitter face over the counter huffed at him then handed over a copy of the signed forms. As he walked through the halls, he saw a steel car parked by the wall. The aroma coming from it made his stomach growl. "Let me get one of them trays," he said.

"Keep it moving," a correctional officer ordered.

Remix laughed and waved his hand. He had almost forgotten the CO was behind him. He had better things on his mind, now that his time was up. In a few short moments he would finally be a free man.

"That's cool, I'm a get my own lunch." He kept walking. "The food in this bitch is weak any ways."

They reached a sliding steel door and the CO waved his arm. Remix swaggered his way past the corridor and into the front lobby. He saw a female receptionist giving him the eye. "Call me, girl, it's about to be lit," he said.

The CO was getting hot. "So you ever shut your mouth?"

"Fall back, I'm trying see what her mouth does."

"That's my wife! "

"Your wife! Oh, my bad. I guess you already know about that mouth, aye." Remix laughed.

The CO had to hold back from tapping Remix on the chin with his clenched fist. "All you home boys are just alike," he said. " You will be back real soon, and then I'm a fix that mouth of yours."

Remix reached for the exit, looked over his shoulder and said, "Whatever pig, stay pink!"

When he stepped into the afternoon sun, he held his hands over his eyes. It was the start of summer. He took a few steps forward before his vision started to clear up, then dropped his bag, squeezed his eyes together, and tried to find some words.

"You just going to stand there looking stupid, or you ready to ride?" Raymon stood in front of a party van with his arms spread wide, holding a bottle of champagne in each hand. The Rolls Royce parked in front of the van was missing a roof. It had four women waiting inside it. The red Bugatti parked behind the van rumbled its engine when Raymon spoke. Remix reached and picked up his bag without taking his eyes off what awaited him ahead. He couldn't. He closed his mouth and tried to act normal, like he wasn't impressed. "Ray, you a fool, boy," he said. "I told you I didn't want nothing to fancy out here."

"You think this fancy?" Raymon looked around and smiled. "Then wait until tonight!"

Remix put one arm around him, and Raymon whispered in his ear. "I told you I got you."

"There's a lot of brothers in there expecting nothing but the real from us," Remix said.

"And that's what we going to give them."

"What you got planed Ray? You always up to something. "

Raymon put his arm over Remix's shoulders, tilted his head and said: "You sure you ready for this one?"

ACKNOWLEDGEMENTS

I would like to thank my mother for her love and continued support. You never gave up on me and, look Ma no hands...lol! My father for giving me life and always reminding me to show the world who I truly am. To my sisters, Tiffy the boss, Nikki the brains, and Charnai the future, without you, I would have never known what unconditional love truly means. To Uncle Snook for showing me the importance of paying attention to details. To the entire Reid family and the Ellis family, I can't ever forget, I love you all. To my daughter, Nashanti Nada Moore-Ellis, you are the reason I will never stop pushing to be the best me, you have my heart. Special thanks to my baby cakes, your patience and love completes me. See, I do be working...lol! Last but never least, I want to thank my grandparents who may never read this book, but their love, and their spirits are all up in it.

www.ingramcontent.com/pod-product-compliance
Lightning Source LLC
Chambersburg PA
CBHW070913260626
47162CB00007B/2655